# MURDER IN THE MULTIVERSE

---

## MULTIVERSE INVESTIGATIONS MYSTERIES
## BOOK 1

### R E MCLEAN

Catawampus Press

catawampus-press.com

# JOIN THE TEAM

If you enjoy this book, you can join the Multiverse Investigators team to get new stories as they're published for FREE.

Go to multiverse-investigations.com/join for details.

*Thanks,*
*RE McLean*

1

---

## RECLUSE

San Francisco
24 March, 9:35pm

Being a recluse is a funny old business. For some people, it means refusing to use social media. For others, it means hiding out in a cave at the bottom of some rich guy's garden. For Claire Pope, it meant living in a luxury apartment in San Francisco's prestigious Pacific Heights district, and being an internet billionaire.

Claire loved the Internet. She adored it. If she could, she'd tear off its shirt and lick its nipples. For someone like Claire, the Internet was the only way to make any kind of living while refusing to deal with, you know, actual people. Let alone making the one billion, three thousand and thirty-five million eight hundred and sixty two thousand dollars and sixty three cents her accountant had told her she was worth this morning. Probably more, by now.

But Claire hated people. More specifically, right at this moment she hated the two men who were delivering her new mattress.

The mattress would be worth it, she'd been assured—finest box springs, duck feathers imported from Albania. At a cool two thousand dollars, it had better be.

But the delivery. Delivery was the very worst part. If this mattress was as relaxing as a yearlong trip to Katmandu with daily one-on-one meditation with the Dali Lama himself, it wouldn't be enough to undo the effect of watching the two men hauling the thing into her bedroom.

She hung back, keeping to the kitchen and listening to them as they grunted and groaned. She'd tried to avoid looking at them as they entered her apartment, but their large, sweaty bodies were imprinted on her retinas now.

The older one, who'd handed her a scuffed tablet on arrival and asked her to sign, had a lock of hair dangling over his forehead, slicked with sweat. It threatened to drip over the tablet. She'd refused the stylus—she had her own: clean, golden, embossed with her company logo—and he'd grunted at her.

She shuddered at the thought of that grunt. Her stomach was churning and her mouth felt as if she'd swallowed a Brazilian tree frog.

She heard the slap of mattress hitting divan and forced herself to breathe. There was muttering. *Get out*, she thought. *Leave me alone.*

The two men ambled back into her hallway. The younger one, podgy round the middle with—ugh—skin showing between the bottom of his threadbare t-shirt and the top of his jeans, flashed her a grin.

She tried to respond in kind but all she could manage was the kind of smile that would melt cheese at twenty paces.

The man snorted and followed his colleague into the corridor. She leaned against the door to fasten the locks, her skin damp. She did the same for the inner door.

She slid down to the carpet, unable to enjoy the luxury one-and-one-quarter-inch pile that—fortunately—was already in the apartment when she'd bought it two years earlier. She'd had to have it professionally cleaned (she'd hid in the kitchen, where the floor was finished with Alaskan oak boards) but at least there wasn't the horror of carpet fitters.

She glanced at the bedroom. It would smell of them. Of sweat, and day-old hot dogs, and the rank mustiness that only appeared on the rare occasion when another human being found their way into this apartment.

She tiptoed to the bedroom door. Should she open the window, to get rid of the smell? That way, she could close the door. The doors in this apartment were heavy and sealed with the highest quality rubber, but even that wasn't enough for Claire's sensitive nose.

She hadn't opened the window in thirteen months.

Could she do it?

She stood at the threshold, daring herself to sniff. She gagged. The smell was alive, an animal stench that made her wonder if she should just put the apartment on the market and move to another one.

No. That would mean removal firms, and realtors, and going outside.

She could do this.

She eased a foot over the threshold. The carpet here was as thick as in the hallway, but pale blue instead of beige. There were imprints where the men had walked.

She squeezed her eyes tight and crossed to the window.

Taking a deep breath, she fumbled for the latch. It was stiff. She tugged at it. At last it budged.

She opened her eyes. Last chance to change her mind. The drapes were still drawn, and her hand had disappeared behind them. There was a view out there, she knew.

A spectacular view of the city, and the Bay, and the Golden Gate Bridge. She'd seen it on Google Streetview. But not from here, not for two years.

That view represented at least thirty per cent of the value of this apartment. But it made her feel the way a hypochondriac would if asked to deliver the valedictory address for Harvard Medical School.

She closed her eyes again and pushed.

She felt the fabric brush her cheek as the breeze caught it, and yelped.

She fell back and clattered to the floor.

Her knee throbbed; she'd twisted it.

*No.*

She couldn't be hurt. Injury meant doctors. People touching her. And even the swankiest private hospitals had —whisper it—*other patients.*

She rubbed her knee. It wasn't swollen. She pushed out a long breath.

*OK. Retreat,* she thought. If she gave it three hours, maybe fourteen, the bedroom should be aired by then.

Maybe she should just sleep on the couch and be done with it.

No. She wasn't going to let this get the better of her. She'd paid two thousand dollars for this mattress, and she was damn well going to get use from it.

She pulled the drapes shut, trying not to look at the sky, and stepped back. She stood in the doorway, hand on the doorknob.

She pulled it shut, dipping a little with relief as she moved away from it. She padded into the living room.

Then she smelt it.

This room's scent was as familiar to her as the skin on her own hand; her subtle floral perfume mixed with the lemon cleaning mist she used every day and the oh-so-faint tang of her own body, left behind on the pillows that adorned the couch.

The men hadn't come in here. She'd made sure of that. She'd closed the door. And they smelt heavy, salty and sharp.

This was different.

She felt every hair on her skin rise up to attention, like a Mexican wave rippling down her forearms. She sniffed again, checking whether she was imagining things. No. A man had been in here. A man who wore musk aftershave, drank sweet brandy and had recently used PVA glue.

She looked back at the door to the corridor. The apartment had an inner hallway, an airlock where she insisted deliveries were left. Deliveries smaller than a two-thousand-dollar mattress.

The door was closed. She pulled it and checked the lock. She peered through the peephole to check the inner hallway. It was empty.

She took a deep breath and clicked the lock open. She eased herself into the inner hallway and put her eye to the second peephole, into the corridor.

After counting to five, she opened the eye.

The corridor was empty.

She fell back from the door and ran back through the inner door. She leaned on it and fumbled the lock closed.

Her heart was pounding in her ears. Maybe the smell was her own fear?

She took a step toward the living room, then another.

No. That wasn't her.

She looked at the window, wall-sized and with the drapes also drawn. Was he behind them? She eyed the arrangement of the fabric, looking for bulges. Nothing. Then she looked to the side of the room, the cavernous closet that housed her entertainment system.

She allowed herself the tiniest of steps toward it, relieved that the carpet absorbed her footfall. She sniffed again. She leaned toward the closet. The smell was getting stronger.

She looked back toward the kitchen. Her cellphone was on the counter. If she called the police, that would mean people in here. Large, hi-vis-clad people with chirruping radios and no respect for personal space. Would the apartment ever recover? Would *she* ever recover?

She watched the closet door, trying to remember if she'd left it open or closed. Her nostrils flared, assaulted by the rising smell of sweat coming from behind it. So he was scared, too.

She rifled through possibilities. He was probably a burglar. If she left him alone, he would slip out, hoping she wouldn't see or report him. If he took anything, she could replace it. She had nothing of value here; that was all locked up in her Swiss bank account, overlooking the lake in Zurich. Or so Streetview informed her.

She clamped her lips shut. Not breathing in a situation like this wasn't as easy as they made it look in the movies. Her chest filled with hot air, threatening to explode like a balloon at a birthday party. She opened her mouth and clasped her hand across it to muffle her dragged-out breaths.

She needed to leave him alone. He certainly hadn't come in via the front door; that had seven and a half locks and two peepholes (backup never did any harm). She'd watched it while the mattress delivery guys were here. So it had to be the window. She knew there was a balcony out there but had never ventured onto it. Too loud and smelly, full of the risk of her next-door neighbor spotting her. He was a balding businessman whom she'd seen through the spy hole, huffing his way along the corridor. He glowed with perspiration as he walked and could do with losing a few pounds. He liked to grunt and groan his way through late-night porn in the room that was directly behind her TV. There was no way he was ever clapping eyes on her.

Somehow, her intruder had unlocked the sliding doors from the outside and found a way into her apartment. She glanced at the doors again, the drapes that hung perfectly from their expensive rail. No sign of disturbance.

The smell was intensifying. If she didn't move soon, the contents of her stomach were going to turn her carpet into something Jackson Pollock might have created in kindergarten. She slid back toward the bedroom. She didn't want to watch him any more than she wanted to watch her warehouse manager directing the flow of low-quality meat through her business, or her neighbor stemming the flow of his own bodily juices after his nocturnal TV sessions.

She stood outside the bedroom, remembering what she'd left in there. She looked toward the front door again. Was it unlocked? Had one of the men stayed behind? Had there really been three of them, not two?

No. She'd taken care.

She looked at the doorknob. She took a deep breath, then regretted it.

As she reached for the knob she heard a sound. The closet door sliding open, heavy and expensive on its ball bearings. No human sounds as yet, but the stench was overwhelming, wrapping itself around her like a comfort blanket that had been used to line a litter tray. She clutched her stomach and bent over, gasping for breath.

She stood up and breathed in, her hands slipping on the doorknob. She stepped back and felt something soft behind her.

Her chest was frozen, her feet welded to the floor. She

felt the warmth of the person standing behind her, the person she'd backed into.

She could hear his breathing, deep and rasping. She didn't dare look round.

She turned the doorknob. Her gun was in there, at the top of her closet. Why hadn't she thought of that?

She felt a pain in her right side. She screamed silently, the sound more of a high-pitched moan. She twisted, raising a hand and feeling soft, warm flesh against it. She screamed again.

The pain traveled into her, sharp, intense. Like a sting from a bee the size of an elephant. She stumbled sideways and started to fall. She fell against her attacker and—finally—forced herself to turn and look.

Her eyes widened. *You*, she thought. Her vision blurred.

Behind him, flickering in her eyes, was a row of paintings. The last thing she saw as she slipped to the floor and out of consciousness was Munch's Scream mirroring her own face.

**2**

---

## KATZ

San Francisco
24 March, 9:45pm

lex Strand was working late.

This wasn't through choice. Alex wasn't the kind of woman who would tell you, if asked at a particularly irritating job interview, that she was passionate about her job. She wasn't the kind of woman who stayed in the office till midnight to impress the boss. And she wasn't the kind of woman who didn't have better things to do, although that last point was a sore one since her girlfriend of two months had dumped her in favor of a cheerleader.

A *cheerleader*. Siobhan (a cute freckled mathematician Alex was trying to expunge from her memory) could have enjoyed the attentions of Alex, a brilliant—if admittedly way too nerdy and a little too ginger—quantum physicist. But no, she preferred a six-foot-tall, ample-chested cheerleader whose understanding of physics amounted to knowing the colors of the rainbow.

Alex shook her head, trying not to think about it. It was almost ten pm and she wanted to be at home, eating donuts and watching CSI. But no, she was here in the lab.

Alex wasn't supposed to be in the lab. As a postdoc, her job was to crunch data. Dr Katz was the one who got to do all the fun stuff, while Alex and her pal Rik manipulated his data in vast spreadsheets, spewing them out the other side in the hope they might actually mean something.

So far, they'd been unsuccessful. The Cheshire Cat experiment, designed to separate quantum particles from their properties, was unreplicable, it seemed.

But tonight Alex *was* alone in the lab. A room she wasn't even supposed to be in.

She'd been working on a side project of her own after hours, composing jingles from the pulses sent out by quasars, when she remembered that she'd lent Dr Katz her coat earlier on. The lab had inexplicably turned cold—either the heating on the fritz again, or quantum freezing—and he'd poked his head into her and Rik's office to ask if he could borrow another layer.

He'd gone home hours ago, the temperature was dropping outside, and her coat was still in there. Even Alex, a Scotswoman accustomed to the cold, wasn't prepared to leave her favorite coat to the mercy of the University of Berkeley cleaners.

She pushed into the lab, peering around just in case. She resisted flicking a light on and stepped into the gloomy space.

Behind her, the door clicked shut. The room went dark. She stumbled forward and hit her foot on something hard and metallic.

"Ow!" She lifted her leg, toe throbbing. "Eejit."

Alex placed her foot down, ignoring the pain that

thrummed through it. She put her arms out to the sides. There was nothing there; exactly where in the lab was she?

She closed her eyes and pictured the lab. A row of computer monitors on benches against the opposite wall. Printouts hanging from the ceiling; one of them brushed her face, unless she was imagining it. And in the corner behind her, the object she'd stubbed her toe on: the interferometer.

The interferometer was the device that made the Cheshire Cat experiment possible. It interfered with quantum particles and separated them from their properties. At least, that was the theory. Dr Katz wasn't getting very far with it.

She scanned her mental image of the room, trying to imagine where Dr Katz might have put her coat. There were no chairs in here, nowhere he could casually sling it.

But there was a hook on the door behind her. She turned, very slowly, listening to her own breath in the darkness.

She took a step forward. If she held her arms out in front, she would find the coat before she hit the door.

She froze. Something had brushed past her leg. Something warm, and soft. Something that felt a lot like…

No.

She shook her head. "Stop it, ya twat," she told herself, and took another step forwards.

There was a yowl. Something thin and snakelike tugged its way out from under her foot and fled into the darkness.

She had no idea where the light switch was.

She took another tentative step forward. Something brushed her outstretched fingertips. It was soft, and warm, and purple, not that she could see that. But she knew.

She grabbed her coat.

It hit her in the face with an outstretched claw.

"What the—?"

She fell back and landed on the floor with a skidding thud. The benches revealed themselves to her as she flew into them, knocking a monitor onto her head.

"Ow!"

She caught the monitor before it could continue its journey to the floor, wanting to yell at her stupid coat for attacking her. But she didn't want anyone knowing she was in here.

Then she heard it. Scuffling, from the corner ahead of her, towards the door. Mice? This was an old building, but the lab was sealed. It had to be; if the quantum effects generated by the experiment leaked out to the rest of the building, the undergraduates might all turn into kittens.

The scuffling approached, whatever it was, surely not her coat. She wondered if it could see her.

"Hello?"

It stopped moving.

"Who are you? I'm armed."

Alex grabbed a pen from her shirt pocket and clicked it on. She'd read that you could kill someone with a loaded ballpoint pen, if you knew what you were doing.

Alex was a twenty-four-year-old postdoctoral student from the Scottish borders. The most damage she'd ever done with a ballpoint pen was when she'd written $E=Mc^2$ wrong on a toilet door and fifty-seven physics undergrads had failed their term paper as a result.

She leaned forwards. It had to be a mouse. Someone had unblocked one of the holes that had been meticulously filled in before Dr Katz had started working in here. He liked to talk about the amount of work that went into getting this lab ready; it made him feel important.

Alex wasn't going to let a mouse scare her. She put up

a hand to check she wasn't going to hit her head, gathered up the monitor in her lap, and stood. She fumbled the monitor back onto the worktop.

"Right. I'm getting my coat now. I don't know where you are, but watch I don't step on you."

"Meow."

"How did a cat get in here?"

"Meow."

She rubbed her eyes. In the gloom of the corner next to where her coat should be, something was glowing.

"How d'you get in here, puss?"

She shuffled towards it, careful to keep her feet steady for fear of trailing wires. Her foot hit something and she heard clattering.

"Aw, bum."

A smell engulfed the room; sharp, acrid, making her gag. She swallowed, then clamped her mouth shut.

She took a stride forward, anxious to get out of there. She'd leave her coat behind; taking it would place her at the scene of the crime.

"Meow."

"You again. Let's get you out of here."

She stumbled into the door and her face landed in her coat. It smelled of the Big Mac Rik had dropped on it earlier. She felt for the light switch and the room jumped into life.

She turned to survey her mess. The monitor she'd caught with her head sat on the workbench at a precarious angle. In the center of the floor was a growing puddle. Hovering six inches above that was the face of a tabby cat.

Only the face. The legs, tail and body were missing. The ears were nowhere to be seen.

Alex dropped to the floor and reached out to the cat. She put her hand in front of its face, waiting for it to nuzzle her. It purred and pushed its nose into her palm. Then she moved her hand downwards. She could feel the cat's chest beneath her hand, sense the vibrations as it purred under her touch.

But the cat she was stroking was invisible.

"Are you another one like Schrödinger," she said, "or are you something new?"

"Meow."

The cat licked its lips, yawned in that flip-top-head way that only cats have, and vanished. Alex's hand fell through empty space and landed in the puddle.

She stared at the spot where it had been.

"Puss?" she whispered. "Come back."

But it was gone. She stood up and wiped her wet hands on her grubby jeans.

She had to clean up. There was a box of tissues on the workbench; she righted a water bottle that had rolled under the workbench and mopped up the spillage. The smell had gone. She put it next to the monitor she'd disturbed and pushed that back into its original spot on the bench.

As she moved it, its screen flickered into life. Numbers and symbols danced on the screen, the work that Dr Katz had been doing before he'd left. It was as meaningless as the rest of the data she'd spent the last four months crunching for him at her own workstation.

She grabbed the mouse and scrolled down, heart dipping at the prospect of working through all this tomorrow. Then she stopped.

At the bottom of the screen was a sequence of numbers and letters which hadn't been completed. She started typing, working through the equations and calculating their logical conclusion.

She turned to the spot where the cat had disappeared.

Behind it was the interferometer. She'd kicked it when the door had closed on her.

She looked back at the screen. Then at the spot where the cat had been. Then back at the screen.

This was big. This was huge. This might change the way humanity viewed the universe.

Or it could be the late-night imaginings of a freckled Scottish postdoc who'd just stroked a cat with no body.

She'd check it tomorrow, when she had the data on her own machine and could work through it properly.

She grabbed the mouse and deleted her work. No one could see this.

**3**

---

## CAT

San Francisco
24 March, 11:20pm

Alex glanced both ways along the street then opened the door to her apartment block. It was a battered wooden door in a narrow doorway that clearly wasn't part of the building's original design. She took the steps two at a time, desperate to talk to someone. Schrödinger wouldn't understand a word she was about to tell him, but at least he made a good listener. That is, if he'd chosen to be alive today.

The first time Schrödinger had died was the second-worst night of Alex's life.

She'd had a tough day at work, just two months into her new job and learning how to find her way through the maze of Berkeley's faculty politics. She hadn't made any friends yet, and was sure when people looked at her they imagined not a small, geeky physicist but the girl from *Brave*. She'd heard mutters of *ach, wee lassie* follow her around the building.

She arrived home looking forward to a long, hot bath and a beer or three. The streets were dark and chilly; it was early November and Hallowe'en still hovered in the air.

"Shrew?" she'd called as she fell through the front door. "Puss, puss?"

Schrödinger—or Shrew as she had taken to calling him after realizing that his name made her look like a bit of a dork—was an old-fashioned kind of cat who would respond to all the silly, clichéd noises and mewings she could direct at him. Even in French, which she found impressive.

But that night, there was no response.

"Minou, minou," she intoned, knowing he liked the French. Then, in a more hesitant tone of voice, "Schrödinger?"

Nothing. The apartment was quiet, windows shut tight against the hum of distant traffic. There was no sound, not even a belching pipe, scratching pigeon on the windowsill (one of these days she would open the window suddenly and they'd regret it) or the refrigerator humming its disapproval of the hot dog sausages, cheap beer and Twinkies she liked to fill it with.

She hurried through the apartment, calling his name in increasingly strident tones. But he was nowhere. She tested all the window latches, peered out dreading what she might see, checked behind the couch and under her duvet.

No cat.

Finally she arrived back in the kitchen. On the table, left there from the previous night, was a gargantuan cardboard box, one Amazon had used to deliver a pencil sharpener. Schrödinger—like all cats—liked to sit in cardboard boxes, even the tiny ones that didn't even keep his generous backside warm. Maybe he'd climbed inside.

The top was closed, but not sealed. If he'd climbed in

and gone to sleep, there was a chance it had fallen shut over him.

She stilled her breathing, listening for signs of movement inside; scrabbling or sniffing, maybe the patter of him chasing his tail. But there was nothing.

Slowly, her heart thumping in her ears, she lifted the lid.

And there he was, curled up in the bottom of the box. Lifeless, motionless. Dead.

She reached a trembling hand inside to touch his fur. He was cold. She let out a high-pitched gasp and plugged her mouth with her fist. She reached out again and laid her hand gently on the top of his head. It was still.

Nausea rose up from her stomach. Overcome by tears, she rushed to the bathroom and dry-retched into the toilet.

She sat on the bathroom floor for a few minutes, recovering her breath and checking that her stomach had calmed down, then ventured back into the kitchen.

The box was still there. It was still open. And, head poking up from it, looking confused, was Schrödinger.

"Meow", he said.

She rushed to him, pulling him out of the box and spinning him around at arm's length above her head.

"Shrew, ya wee bampot," she crowed. "You had me going there."

He said nothing (he may be a quantum cat, but he was still a cat) but threw out a paw to hit her in the eye. She laughed and put him on the floor. He rubbed against her legs and trotted over to his bowl, munching noisily.

In the months after that first time, he'd only pulled the dying trick a few times, maybe once every ten times she arrived home. But over the last year it had grown more frequent, until it had reached the point where on any given day there was a fifty percent chance that he'd be dead.

Alex was tempted to tell her fellow physics postdocs —but couldn't quite bring herself to. A cat that lived in a state of quantum flux, that was both alive and dead until she actually, well, looked at him—would be a marvel, fit either for the circus or the lab.

So his strange habit of dying had become their little secret.

Tonight she was worried about him. He didn't like it when she worked late. She crossed her fingers as she climbed the stairs, muttering a physicist's prayer under her breath.

She reached the first floor. As ever, the sickly smell of marijuana from the apartment above battled the fug of frying meat from below. She heard movement behind the door to her apartment. She blew out a long, relieved breath and fell through it, ready to pick her cat up and give him a tight hug.

"Shrew?"

"Meow?" He poked his head out of his box on the kitchen table. Had he been dead until she'd called him?

She decided not to think about it and gave him a riffle behind the ears.

"Good boy." She kissed the top of his head. "Eww. Have a wash, boy."

He smelled odd. Sharp, like he'd spent the afternoon gluing his whiskers together.

"Shrew?"

She shook her head. There'd been no glue in the lab, and there was none here.

She gathered him up and switched on the TV. The news was a murder. Nothing new; this was San Francisco. Sometimes she missed her sleepy hometown.

Alex grabbed a beer and slumped onto the sofa. Schrödinger jumped out of her arms and onto the coffee table, staring at the screen. Someone called Claire Pope had been stabbed. A billionaire who'd made her fortune manufacturing pet food.

"That's your favorite, Shrew."

He continued staring at the screen. The newsreel was showing footage of the victim's apartment—something luxurious in Pacific Heights. Then it flipped to images of Claire Pope on her wedding day.

Schrödinger hissed. Alex put a palm on his back.

"Hey, boy. Shush, it's ok."

His back arched against her hand. His fur was damp, the way it got when he'd been fighting.

"You don't like that guy's specs, boy? Nor me."

She flicked to the next channel and Schrödinger calmed. He sidled into her lap and she leaned back to stare at the ceiling, musing over what she'd seen on Dr Katz's monitor last night.

## 4

## SKIRT

San Francisco
25 March, 9:15am

Alex wasn't very good at wearing black.

It wasn't that she couldn't do it. Any old idiot could open their wardrobe, pull out a black sweater and yank it over their head.

But once she'd done it, and looked at herself in the mirror, she changed.

The horror of seeing her curly red hair and pale freckled skin above a black outfit turned her into a shadow of herself. Someone who knew just how awful she looked and would rather other people didn't notice.

It's not that Alex was vain. She just didn't like wearing clothes that made people ask if she was feeling OK and tell her to go home and get some rest.

But today she had no choice.

She stood at the back of the chapel in her one and only black outfit. A fake silk shirt with two missing buttons, fastened today with a safety pin. And a skirt.

Alex hated skirts even more than she hated wearing black. This one was long, and swishy, and made her feel like the wind might blow up toward her nether regions and freeze them off at any moment.

Even in California, it could get chilly. Especially here, at the temple-like San Francisco Columbarium.

She nudged Rik Patel, her lab partner and fellow post-doc. He appeared equally out of place in a black suit that looked like he'd bought it ten years and five sizes ago.

"What's up?" he hissed.

"Nothing. Just puzzled."

"Shush." He glanced toward the front. They were in the twelfth row, just three tactful rows from the rear wall and behind all the other mourners. In fact, there were six empty rows in front of them.

"Don't you want to know why I'm puzzled?"

He frowned. "I never want to know why you're puzzled."

"OK."

She smiled sideways at him. He'd ask her as soon as this was over, she knew.

She looked around the chapel. It was minimalist, tasteful. Nothing like the imposing Scottish Presbyterian church where they'd buried her mother two years ago.

She gritted her teeth and put up a brick wall in her mind, a technique she'd learned through bitter experience. For good measure, she put a shrub in front of it. A cotoneaster, with small white flowers. Pretty. When that didn't work, she plonked a nest in the middle of it, with thirteen chirruping babies yelling at their absent mother for food.

Her stomach dipped.

The baby birds and absent mother were a bad move. She must remember not to use that one again.

She shook her head to scrub out the nest and replaced it with a balled-up scrap of paper. Then another one. She added a crisp packet, then a sweet wrapper. She felt her heart rate return to normal.

She opened her eyes and made a mental note. Litter worked.

At the front, a short, balding man who looked as if he hated wearing black even more than she did, was speaking. Simon Yang, Dean of the physics Faculty. It was a dull eulogy, peppered with clichés. *Sorely missed—celebrate her life —thoughts go out.*

She looked at Rik. If he turned, she was going to make a puking gesture with her finger. Just a quick one. No one would see.

The chapel doors swooshed open and closed behind her. She felt her body pull itself to attention, knowing she might be observed. She smoothed her skirt and concentrated on making her hair as un-ginger as possible. It never worked.

There was shuffling behind her and then the thud of butt landing on seat. She heard breathing.

She frowned and forced herself to focus. She hadn't met the woman in the coffin—had barely heard of her before yesterday—so it was difficult to summon the required grief for this occasion. Everyone in the physics department was required to attend. Some of them, those in post longer than Alex, were up at the front, dabbing their eyes. She wondered exactly who Doctor Pierce was, and when she'd last worked at Berkeley. Not for a while, that was clear.

She heard another movement behind her, and a cough. She craned her neck. A man was in the seat closest to the aisle, right at the back. He gazed at the coffin.

The man was slim, mid-thirties. He had a dark beard

with an odd hole in it, as if he'd started to shave before remembering that he had a beard. Maybe it was a skin condition. She could sympathize with that. Being a Scotswoman in California meant Alex had a permanent skin condition.

His eyes slid to meet hers and she looked down, aware that she was blushing. At least it meant she was no longer pale as a polar bear on a very cold day.

She turned back to the front. The Dean had stopped talking and was heading back to his seat. The priest patted him on the back and muttered something. Alex scanned the sparse rows of mourners in front, wondering how well they knew the deceased. Doctor Pierce had been nothing more than a photograph on the physics faculty website since Alex had joined. She'd had blonde hair pulled up in a tangled bun and wore a red and pink kaftan. She looked more like a member of the English faculty than a quantum physicist.

Alex had assumed she was on some sort of research trip that took her away for long periods. Maybe at CERN if she was lucky. Now it seemed she was just on long term sick leave.

Alex dropped her gaze to the floor. She shivered. She'd spent a year speculating about the mysterious Doctor Pierce. Envying her. Resenting her even. When she'd asked who she was or what research she was doing, she was met by awkward silences. Now she knew why.

She looked up to see that the coffin had gone, hidden by a blue curtain the color of cornflowers. Alex remembered standing by her mother's grave, flinging a handful of soil. She shuddered.

Behind her, the man had stood up. He took one last look toward the coffin, then crossed himself. He pushed the door and slipped outside. His jacket caught momentarily on the handle and Alex caught a flash of gold on his belt.

Why was there a cop here?

5
________

## LAMBORGHINI

San Francisco
25 March, 10:25am

Mike Long looked around the half-empty parking lot, admiring the cars. A Bentley, two Aston Martins. A Porsche or three, even a Lamborghini.

"Luxury apartments, luxury cars," said Monique. "None of them ever driven, probably."

"Did Claire keep a car down here?"

Monique shook her head. "No need of one, when you never go out."

Monique pressed the button for the elevator. The two of them waited in silence. It was hot down here and Lieutenant Monique Williams looked uncomfortable in her eighties-style skirt suit and raincoat, both constructed from sweaty manmade fabrics. Mike normally wore his personal uniform of crisp blue jeans and suit jacket over a plain white shirt. But today he was dressed in a dark suit.

He wondered if Monique knew where he had been.

The elevator pinged its arrival and they stepped inside. Mike pressed the button for the tenth floor.

"I want you to get the latest report from CSI," Monique told him.

"Right."

CSI had spent the last twelve hours here, scouring the apartment for anything out of place and dusting for prints. There were no prints, of course—even the dumbest intruder knew better than to take his gloves off—and so far, not so much as a molecule out of place. Claire had not only been terrified of human contact, she'd also been scared of dirt. The flat sparkled like a pin that had been waxed to within an inch of its life.

The elevator door slid open and Monique nodded for Mike to go ahead. The corridor was quiet and plush, with heavy carpet and walls that looked—and smelled— recently painted.

"You want me to start now?" Mike asked.

"Hmm?" replied Monique.

"Telling you what I see."

"Oh, that. Yes. Please."

"Right." Mike paused. "You think the murderer came in this way?"

"We're not sure. But he could have done. Let's assume he came in through the front door, yes."

Mike frowned. "So why—and sorry if I'm speaking out of turn—why isn't this corridor cordoned off? The lobby? The elevator?"

"We did," Monique replied. "Cordon was lifted early this morning. But it's a public area. Full of prints and DNA. Not much help."

"Well, no. Of course. But I guess if we found evidence that Sean had been here…"

Sean was Sean Wolf, Claire Pope's ex-husband. He had

an alibi, of course. A pretty tight one, even by Mike's grueling standards. But as a famed recluse, Claire had little or no contact with humanity. Sean was their prime suspect, alibi or no.

Monique put her hands to her neck, massaging the skin. She smiled. "Come with me." She picked up pace, heading for a smooth oak door crisscrossed with police tape.

Mike followed, feeling his breath shorten. He'd studied the photos of the crime scene but had no idea what would be there now. A pool of blood, disarrayed furniture, that mug spilling its contents across the floor? Or would it all have been cleaned up?

Monique knocked on the door. An officer clad in a white bunny suit opened it from the inside.

"You have that report for me?" Monique asked.

The bunny blushed. "Not yet. We were interrupted by—"

Monique's arched eyebrow kept the bunny from finishing her sentence. She nodded and shuffled away in search of the most senior CSI. Mike watched her stop in the kitchen and talk to a short, blonde woman in her forties, who glanced over at Mike in between answering his boss's questions. Mike couldn't make out their conversation but the woman sounded impatient, as if she was tired of being asked questions she couldn't answer.

"Go on then," Monique reminded him. "Tell me what you see."

Mike closed his eyes. "Well the first thing's the door. No sign of forced entry. And," he looked back at it, "it certainly has enough locks."

He took a step back and squinted at the door. There was a heavy black bolt at the top and another matching one at the bottom. Two deadbolts between them, each of which had a brushed nickel lock plate that looked rarely touched. Between those was a standard brass lock and a security chain. And between those and the top bolt was another, smaller bolt in brass, this one having no hole or plate to slide into. It was a waste of metal.

"Five and a half locks. Like you said."

"Look again."

Mike put a hand on the door, counting in his head. There were definitely five working locks plus that useless brass bolt. He wondered why someone as security-conscious as Claire Pope would have a lock that did nothing.

Then he thought of something, and opened the door to check its other edge.

"Two hinge bolts," he said. "Which makes seven and a half. Like you said."

"Good," said Monique. "You sure?"

Mike pulled the door fully open and examined it from the other side. He ran his hand up its edge. Fingerprint dust caught on his skin.

"Sure."

"Good. So am I. Now, tell me what else you see. I'm not going to give you any more prompts."

Mike took a deep breath. Was this some kind of test? Or was she genuinely looking for a fresh pair of eyes? He looked back at the door. The wood around the locks was pristine.

"No sign of forced entry," he said. "If the killer came in this way, he was let in."

"Mm-hmm."

"Which makes no sense."

"How so?"

Mike turned to Monique. Behind her, in the kitchen, the head of the CSI bunnies was pulling faces at them. She looked as if he wished she'd taken some other assignment this morning.

"She was a recluse. She never saw anyone," he said.

"She had a mattress delivered. Less than an hour before estimated time of death."

"A mattress?"

"It's still in its wrapper, on the bed."

"So could the killer have been one of the delivery guys?"

"That would make sense. Infiltrate the delivery company, only way to get to her. Except we have CCTV of them both leaving. No one coming back."

"No CCTV from later?"

"Nothing. The system went blank for about half an hour, right around the time we think she died."

"Hmm."

"Hmm indeed."

"She had to have seen someone. How did she get her groceries? Her Amazon deliveries?"

Mike thought of his own apartment. He had his groceries delivered every Friday evening. It was the only night he knew he wouldn't be late at work, and besides, he needed beer for the weekend. But the drivers couldn't stop for long at his flat, with it being in a restricted zone. So they would drop them at the Korean takeaway downstairs. The owner's ten-year-old son would carry them up to his flat in exchange for the gargantuan bar of chocolate he always included in the order. Most weeks they were already waiting when he got home, but sometimes he arrived as the boy was ferrying the bags up, doing it in as few trips as possible. His record was seven bags in a trip, although one of those didn't really count as it only contained a satsuma.

"Maybe she did have someone she spoke to. Someone who took in her deliveries. Groceries, all the rest of it. If I was a hermit, I'd get some neighbor's kid to do it for me. Just one person to deal with, and kids are less likely to ask questions than their parents."

"Good thought. You stay there. I'll check."

Mike watched Monique pick her way toward the white-clad senior CSI. They exchanged some words and Monique returned to Mike, shaking her head. "Next door is a single man who's away right now. Opposite is empty. And the other side is a young couple who say they've never seen anyone come or go from this apartment."

"You believe them?"

"I don't think we have any reason to suspect them, if that's what you're thinking."

Mike shook his head. "No. Nor do I. But it's difficult to believe that no one ever came here. She'd have starved."

Monique nodded. "You're right. Which is why those cameras are so important."

"Can I take a look around?"

"Go ahead."

Mike headed back into the hallway. It was spacious, which was lucky since most of it was cordoned off. A dark bloodstain bloomed on the thick carpet. The wall was splattered with dried blood, and the doorknob to the bedroom was crusted in it.

Mike stepped over the cordon, taking care where he trod. He took a pair of latex gloves from his top pocket and opened the door.

It was a large room decorated in bland shades of beige. The bed was king size, with a plastic-wrapped mattress perched on it. The pillows were stacked neatly on the floor and a quilt folded next to them.

Mike wondered what anyone examining his own room would think, if his apartment were to become a crime scene. The quilt would be scrunched into a corner, the floor covered in half-read Lee Child novels and the bedside table full of coffee mugs in varying states of decay.

He moved to the bed, his footsteps silent in the thick pile carpet. On the bedside table was a Kindle and a half-full glass of water. The glass was dusted with gray powder. For a moment he wondered why they hadn't taken it away for a DNA sample but then remembered there would be no shortage of Claire's DNA around her body.

He picked the glass up and sniffed it: just water, nothing added. He placed it back in the same spot and picked up the Kindle. He brushed the screen, and the book Claire was reading before her death flashed up, sending a shiver down Mike's spine. It was a business title, something he'd never heard of. He made a mental note of the title and resolved to download it, in case it told him something valuable about Claire's character and state of mind.

"Anything useful?"

Monique was leaning on the doorframe. Her reedy body sagged against it and she'd taken off her brown patent court shoes. Her large-toed feet, wriggling in brown hose, looked disrespectful against the cream carpet. Mike frowned but said nothing.

He put the Kindle back on the bedside table, once again leaving it exactly as he'd found it. "She was certainly the neat and tidy type."

Monique surveyed the room. "You can say that again." She walked to the window; Mike could hear the static crinkling as her legs moved together.

Monique stopped at the window and fumbled with the heavy drapes. Mike followed and grabbed the pole that controlled them. He twisted it and the drapes swished open.

"Thanks," said Monique. "Used to that kind of thing, are we?"

"Hardly. My place doesn't even have drapes."

Monique gave him an inquisitive look but said nothing. Mike shrugged.

Monique leaned her forehead against the glass and closed her eyes. "Can I tell you something?"

Mike nodded, waiting for a tidbit, something about the crime. What did this bedroom tell him, that could possibly be relevant? It was clear that Claire was a woman with total control of her life and surroundings, which made her murder all the more inexplicable.

"I'm completely stuck," Monique said. "Flummoxed. Perplexed. Mystified."

Mike looked past Monique to the kitchen where the CSIs were packing up their equipment. The senior bunny had disappeared. He had no idea what to say, so he said nothing.

Monique sighed. "Claire Pope was a recluse. She rarely met a soul in person. Her last real human contact was with her ex-husband, years ago. She doesn't seem to have had any enemies. There's no sign of anyone breaking into this flat." She turned to Mike. "Why did this bastard kill her? And, more to the point, how?"

Mike swallowed. "They stabbed her with her own letter opener."

"Oh, we know that. That's not what I mean, and you know it. The question is, how did her killer get in here, and what was his motive?"

Mike licked his lips, working through everything he'd seen. He put a hand on the glass of the sliding door in front of them. Beyond was a magnificent view of a fog-shrouded Bay, the Golden Gate Bridge a dull red off to the left.

Below them was a narrow balcony, and a six-story drop to the street.

He leaned against the window, craning his neck to look left and then right. The neighboring apartments had similar balconies, separated by a four-foot gap. No normal person would risk crossing that.

"Are you saying you want me to take this to the MIU?" he asked.

Monique nodded. She was staring out at the view and rubbing the bridge of her nose.

"Not for definite. Not yet."

"Her ex could have done it, you know. The jump."

"You think so?"

"He's a dancer."

"It's sixty feet down."

Mike looked down again. He shivered. He was scared of heights; or, more accurately he was scared of the ground at the bottom of them.

"His alibi?"

"He was on stage."

"Whoa."

"Yeah."

He turned and leaned on the glass. It was chilly.

"Boss," he said. "I'm not comfortable with this."

She shifted her weight and stood in front of him. "Why not?"

"It's just a locked room mystery. There has to be an answer."

"Maybe, maybe not."

Mike hesitated. "I don't think you should send me over there alone. Not after what happened."

# 6

## PEARL

Silicon City
24 March, 9:35pm

Claire Pope stood at the plate-glass windows that flanked one wall of her apartment, cradling a coffee. She had to check the Hong Kong markets in four hours and needed to stay awake.

She yawned and checked her watch; half past nine. She'd been up since six, responding to emails from the company that arranged shipping of her products from China to the European and US markets.

Her own home, of course, wasn't littered with the cheap, gaudy objects that had made her so wealthy. And her own earpiece was unadorned. She preferred to keep things simple, but was more than grateful that not everyone shared her aesthetic. The trinkets that she'd made her fortune from were about as tasteful as a bull in rainbow-colored Spandex and a lime green sombrero taking a stroll through a china shop.

She plugged the earpiece in and opened her personal karma room. For five minutes she floated on a sea of perfectly temperature-controlled, just ever-so-slightly salty water surrounded by purple violets that bobbed on the ripples bathing her tired skin. She closed her virtual eyes and let herself drift, doing her damnedest to clear her head. She was close to reaching the programmed relaxation level expected when she was disturbed by a large, pale brown object landing on her chest. She cried out as it pushed her down into the water, flailing with her arms and legs to keep her head above the surface.

The object barked and started licking her face. She screwed up her eyes to imagine the sea floor just beneath her and put her feet down to stand in the water, grabbing Leo's fur and pushing his soppy great face away from hers.

"Leo! How did you get in here?"

Dogs couldn't normally go into the Hive. It had been tried, of course—after all, what was a virtual paradise without man's best friend—but it turned out that they were too mobile, too clumsy, and too downright stupid to maintain the minute amounts of focus required to pass the barrier between the real and virtual worlds. Not to mention their habit of pulling out earpieces and eating them. The only way a dog could get into the Hive was via the subconscious of its owner. Or frequently, the subconscious of a neighbor who was either scared of a given dog or sick to death of its incessant yapping. Lots of dogs died that way. Virtually, at least.

Cats, by contrast, were all over the Hive. Skulking in corners, staring at you from the shadows, leaving little holes where they'd buried their poop. Sneaky little suckers, the lot of them. If Claire had control of the Hive she'd ban them. Let's face it, if Claire had control of the *real* world she'd ban them. But instead, all she could do was sue anyone who tried to adapt her product for the use of cats. A cat wearing a Pearl! Who ever heard of anything so obscene.

She blinked her eyes open to find herself standing at her window, cradling the coffee. It was still warm—the little heat pouch she'd dropped in had made sure of that. She sipped it and let herself fall back into thoughts of work, and the pile of emails sprouting in her inbox.

Claire loved email. It had a pleasingly old-fashioned feel to it, and allowed her to retain her precious privacy. Most people preferred to use the Hive to communicate, seeking each other out in chat rooms and other virtual spaces, yakking away as if they were in the same room. They'd even added modifications last year to let you share the sensation of exchanging bodily fluids. The intention was to give a boost to the porn industry, as if it needed one in a world where anyone could get jiggy with Jennifer Lawrence or Chris Hemsworth whenever they wanted to, at least in their head. But there were side effects, and the most unfortunate of these was the feel of another chat room visitor's spittle landing on the skin of your face as their conversation became animated.

Claire shuddered. Email would do for her, even if it did annoy her suppliers, along with some of her less anti-quated distribution managers. She was Claire Pope, internet billionaire, so they just had to go along with it.

But first, what she really wanted was sleep. Maybe she should lie down and go online, head for her favorite luxury hotel. Somewhere exclusive, lacking other guests or intrusive staff to disturb her solitude. She could turn on slow-down mode, enjoy a few more hours in the Hive than were passing outside. But doing that would give her a hangover, and she needed to be sharp.

She swigged the last of the coffee and flicked a switch

for a sixth cup, then passed into her bedroom. Leo wasn't in here; he would be asleep in his basket under the kitchen island at this time of day, enjoying daydreams of particularly slow-moving and easy to catch rabbits. She smiled at the thought of it.

The pale cream carpets, left behind by the previous owner, absorbed her footsteps and cradled her skin. She never wore shoes; what was the point if you never left the house? The kitchen had underfloor heating and the rest of the apartment was carpeted, so her feet were always bare.

She paused at the door to the bedroom. She sniffed the air.

Something was wrong. The normal scent of her perfume mixed with peppermint air freshener was overlaid with something sharper that she could almost taste. She licked her lips and retched, just a little bit. She could feel her skin turning clammy.

She peered into the bedroom, puzzled. No one could get into this flat. There were eight locks on the main door. The balcony door was sealed shut from the inside. She never went out there, terrified of contact with her neighbors. And the smell, the overwhelming, dirty brown smell of the outside world, even here in Silicon City with its clean energy and robotic litter pickers, made her want to puke.

The room was empty. She peered at the windows. It was getting dark now; a Hackney glided past over the street, and the Golden Gate Bridge was brightly lit against the approaching dusk. She whispered a command into the voice unit by the door and the drapes swished closed. An action she always enjoyed, that she'd repeated over and over again after moving in. Problem was, the AI that ran the in-home smart systems had become so accustomed to her doing it that every time she said the word 'close' she would hear the drapes gliding shut in the bedroom. She'd tried telling it to forget its programming, and asking it politely to stop—everything short of getting her meat tenderizer from the kitchen and punching its artificial brains out—but still it persisted.

The smell was still there. It was acrid, and heavy, and organic.

"Leo?" she called. He was in his basket, she was sure of it.

"Master Leo is currently in the bedroom," came the response from the box next to her on the wall. She scowled at it. It never called her 'Mistress Claire'. Somehow it seemed to have decided that the dog was in charge.

"Leo?" she called, louder this time. A thud came from the wardrobe. She felt her muscles release and hurried to the wall-height sliding doors, pushing them open with one finger. The AI didn't like her doing this manually; it fritzed up its memory of whether each door was open or closed at any one time and would prompt disgruntled silences for up to twenty-three minutes each time she did it.

The dog fell out of the wardrobe, panting in delight at seeing her. He was a large Labrador, the imperfection in this flat that made it perfect, like the grit that forms a pearl. Not that Leo could be described as a pearl in any way; he was a lolling, enthusiastic kind of dog who liked to lick her ears while she slept. If she shifted out of the way he would continue licking the pillow, oblivious to the change. But she loved him nonetheless.

She crouched down and wrapped her arms around him. On the wall, she heard the AI harrumph.

"Shut up, Malcolm," she told it. It whistled a short but sarcastic ditty and then went quiet.

"You gave me a scare there, boy," she told the dog, who continued licking her face and making happy little growling noises. She laughed and let him carry on, grateful that no one else would ever see her saliva-soaked face.

7

———

**FISH HOOK**

San Francisco
25 March, 12:20pm

Alex didn't feel like going into her office in LeConte Hall, the 1920s building that housed the physics department. And Rik wouldn't be there yet.

Rik was a mild-mannered, softly spoken man built like a brown bear. A brown bear that wore leather jackets, had floppy hair and liked to listen to the Michael Medved show while he worked. Alex hated it—the standard of 'debate' made her want to pull her own eardrum out with a fish hook—but it helped Rik to focus. It made him about two hundred and twenty percent less likely to decide he needed a Big Mac.

Because Rik was always hungry. Despite having a physique which made him ineligible for most rides at Disneyworld, he never stopped complaining of his stomach rumbling.

He liked to work nomadically. In the local McDonald's.

Alex slipped into the window seat next to him, grabbing the coffee he'd already bought for her and adding her habitual four sugars. It was just warm enough to drink.

Luckily the physics department had an enlightened view of digital nomads. It prided itself on embracing the twenty-first century by encouraging staff to work wherever they pleased.

Ninety-four-and-one-half percent of Alex's time was spent in front of a spreadsheet and not in a lab. Which meant that working nomadically suited her. The office she shared with Rik was a room which could only have been intended as a broom cupboard. It even had a broom. Rik used it to swipe at stray spiders but, other than that, it never saw any action.

The longer they could stay away from it, the better. And Alex had something she wanted to tell Rik; something she didn't want to discuss in the office.

"You're kidding," he said, sucking his strawberry milk-shake noisily.

"I've run the equations again. Twice. I did it at home last night and it scared my cat out of his brains. One of them is enough to deal with."

"You need to tell Katz. He'll be made up."

"He's been trying to work this out for five and a half years. I've been here eighteen months. He'll hate me."

"Who cares? You solved the Cheshire Cat conundrum. He'll want to know."

Alex eyed her partner. He didn't care about faculty politics; he saw himself crunching data and slipping out for a daily Big Mac till his plentiful kids left home and he could retire. Alex was different. She wanted to be at the cutting edge of her field, to discover something so momen-tous even her dad would know about it.

Now she had. But she'd done it while trespassing in the

lab, and using data that wasn't strictly hers. If she revealed what she'd done to Dr Katz, he'd take all the credit. If she challenged him, she could wave goodbye to her future. And besides, who'd believe what she'd seen?

"So tell me again," Rik said. "A disembodied cat's head."

"Yup." She glanced around to check no one was listening.

"You do know that the Cheshire Cat experiment isn't really about cats."

She gave him a playful but annoyed slap on his shoulder. "You don't need to tell me that."

"You sure you hadn't been hitting the Bud?"

"I don't drink Bud."

"Whisky then, or whatever you kilties wear."

"I was stone cold sober."

"Then you must have been tired."

"I saw it, Rik. It meowed at me."

He laughed. "Everything meows at you. It's that moggy of yours, it's got to your head."

"Maybe, maybe not."

She'd had enough of this. He was right, of course; their research was about subatomic particles, not sections of cats.

"Come on," she huffed. "Let's go to the broom cupboard."

He shoved the last scraps of bread into his mouth and scrunched the container into a ball, aiming it at the bin. It hit first time and he took a little bow. "Alright then. You'll regret it."

They slid in through the back doors and headed for their broom cupboard. It was almost lunchtime, but anyone seeing them would assume they'd been working out of a coffee shop somewhere. So modern. So Millennial.

Sometimes being young had its advantages; you could bamboozle older and more senior staff just by mentioning wifi hotspots.

Rik pushed open the door, trying to hide a yawn. He had five children under the age of ten at home and a programmer wife who worked long hours for a startup that had more fake grass than it did customers. Alex was amazed he even woke up in the mornings.

Alex followed and crashed into his back.

"Hey. C'mon Rik, let me pass."

"Err. Hello Professor Yang," Rik said.

"Rik. Alex. How are you? Sad business yesterday morning."

"Er, yes," replied Rik. He hadn't known the deceased but there *was* convention to be followed.

Alex shuffled in behind Rik. Simon Yang never came here. They'd only spoken to him once, at a social event ten days after her arrival eighteen months ago.

She thought about the lab, how she'd left it last night. She thought she'd tidied up, but…

"Come with me, Alex."

"Err, OK. What's this about?"

The Professor frowned. "You have a visitor."

Alex gave Rik a nervous smile. He grinned and pulled out his chair, most likely relieved it was her being picked out and not him.

She walked with Professor Yang along the pin-clean corridors, muttering her awkward thanks each time he stopped to hold a door open for her. At his office he opened the door once again and gestured for her to go through.

She gave him a nervous smile and went in.

Professor Yang's office was a disappointment. She was expecting a grand space, something that celebrated the building's nearly one-hundred-year history. Leaded windows, musty bookshelves. Maybe an experiment buzzing ominously in the corner.

But it was an office like any other. Larger than hers, but otherwise unremarkable. It was lined with shelves full of physics books, with more piled on the floor. She spotted a glass case with what looked like an early edition *Principia*.

She approached it.

"Wow. How old is this?"

"Not as old as it looks, I'm afraid. Alex, I'd like you to meet Monique Williams."

She turned to see a willowy African American woman easing herself up from a low chair. She was tall and delicate-looking, like a stiff breeze might snap her in two. She extended a hand, pale with bitten fingernails. Alex took it and the woman brushed her wrist with her other hand; a single diamond ring sparkling on its ring finger.

"Monique Williams," she said. "You must be Alex."

Alex took a step back. This woman had a voice that could puncture your eardrums at forty paces.

Alex stuck out her hand. "Alex Strand."

Professor Yang picked his way over a pile of books to sit behind his desk. He slumped into his chair, seemingly relieved to have made it.

"Monique is a Lieutenant from the SFPD."

"Oh."

She'd ridden her bicycle home on Tuesday; she didn't run a red light, she was sure. She'd recycled all her bottles and plastic this week; her landlady had warned her that recycling was the law here. She hadn't cleaned a spittoon in the street, another odd local law. But —oh no, now she had it—it was Schrödinger. It had to be. She hadn't had him neutered.

"You're expecting me to arrest you, aren't you? Monique barked.

"Er no, Lieutenant."

"Call me Monique. I don't have rank over you. Although I wish I did."

Alex looked at Professor Yang. His eyes sparkled as if he was enjoying her confusion.

"I don't understand. Has something happened? Is someone hurt?"

Monique sighed. "Apart from poor Doctor Pierce, no."

Alex wondered how she knew the dead woman. Her death hadn't been suspicious, had it?

"Alright then. How can I help you?"

"Alex, would you by any chance have a day or two to spare, to help us out with something?"

She looked at Professor Yang. He was nodding.

"I guess so," she said.

"Good. In that case, I'd like you to come with me." She stood up.

"You're not arresting me?"

Monique smiled. "Being Scottish isn't a crime."

"Of course not."

"And neither is failing to have your cat neutered, believe it or not."

"How did you—"

A laugh, more like a foghorn on a misty night at Golden Gate. "Don't worry. Come with me."

Alex stood up. She raised her eyebrows at the Dean and he gave her an encouraging nod. She turned back to the cop.

"Is this a—er—a work-related thing?'

"You could say that."

"I think it would be helpful if my lab partner came along too. Rik Patel. He's more experienced than me."

"I'm sorry. Only room for one. And you're the most suitable."

Professor Yang cleared his throat. "You've surprised us."

Alex waited for him to elaborate.

"That spillage, in Dr Katz's lab, night before last. What did it smell of?"

So he knew.

"Er, glue?"

"And can you remember what you input to Dr Katz's computer, on the same night?"

"I deleted that."

"Dr Katz undeleted it."

"How do you know it was me?"

A sigh. "CCTV."

"It was dark."

"We have infrared."

Wow. They'd thought of everything.

"So," continued the Dean. "What did you make of your calculations?"

She swallowed. "Multiple universes. It proves them."

He nodded. "Of course. Now, please go with the Lieutenant. She'll fill you in on the way."

Alex frowned. The detective gave her a lopsided smile.

Dr Yang nodded. "And be safe." He took her hand. "Won't you?"

"Er, yes. Of course." Was the lieutenant such a bad driver?

"Come on." Monique was at the door. "We'll look after you."

"I need to go via my office. Grab my bag."

"Of course."

They returned the way Alex had come. Monique said

nothing but kept pace with Alex as if she knew where they were going.

At the office, Alex coughed before opening the door. Rik was watching as she entered, his face expectant.

Monique stayed in the corridor, much to her relief.

"Everything OK?" he asked.

"There was a cop in the Dean's office. She's asked me to help her with something."

"OK." His brow creased.

"If I'm not back in a couple of days, check at the Hall of Justice, will you?"

"Have they arrested you?"

"No. But it's odd. That's all."

"Right. Good luck. I'll keep your desk warm."

*I bet you will,* she thought, as they headed outside. Rik would be back in McDonald's quicker than you could say 'quantum entanglement'. It was time for his post-lunch apple pie.

Monique was in the corridor, barking into a cellphone.

"What did you tell him?" she asked.

"Nothing."

"Good. I'm taking you to the Hall of Justice."

"You have to read me my rights."

"I already told you I'm not arresting you."

"So why the Hall of Justice?"

"You'll see."

Alex followed, still not convinced. Why *hadn't* she had Schrödinger neutered?

8

---

# BANANA

San Francisco
25 March, 1:53pm

Alex stood at the back of the room, feeling awkward. A man eating a banana stood in front of her, slowly peeling off its skin and nibbling at it.

The man turned to her as if reading her mind and gave her a supercilious smile. He leaned toward the woman next to him and whispered in her ear. She chuckled.

Alex felt heat rise up her neck and into her chin. She had no idea what she was doing here. Monique had told her to find a spot at the back, then breezed to the other end of the room with no word of explanation.

Monique cleared her throat. The room quietened.

"Alright," Monique said. "What do we have?"

Behind her was a board. The kind of thing Alex had seen on TV: map in the center, gruesome photos of the victim splattered in blood, red lines leading to various locations, leads and the like.

Except this one was different. Where normally there would be ribbons leading to the victim's regular haunts, maybe photos of her acquaintances and enemies, there was nothing.

Alex knew whose murder they were investigating. Claire Pope, internet billionaire and hermit. She thought of the way Shrew had hissed at the screen when she'd been watching the news.

Monique had stopped pacing and was leaning over a laptop. A projected rectangle of white appeared on the screen behind her, overlaying the map.

There was a squeak behind Alex as the door eased open. She turned to see a slender, holey-bearded man enter. The man from the funeral. She frowned at him and he raised a finger to his lips in return as he slid in next to her.

"So," said Monique. "This is our prime suspect. Claire's ex, and the last person with whom she had meaningful face-to-face contact. Sean Wibble, better known as Sean Wolf, the ballet dancer."

There was a snort at the front. Monique glared ahead and it stopped.

Alex squinted at the screen. He was an interesting-looking man, resembling a combination of Brad Pitt in *Thelma and Louise,* and Harry Potter. Which would be a winning combination, except that it wasn't the face of the hoarcrux-hunting, soon-to-appear-naked-on-Broadway Harry Potter, but the chesspiece-straddling, cupboard-under-the-stairs Harry. With rainbow specs.

Monique stopped pacing and looked at Alex and Holey-Beard at the back of the room. She frowned.

Alex shifted from foot to foot, hoping no one would turn around. The man with the banana had finished it now and was dangling the skin from his fingers like it was a silk handkerchief.

Monique's gaze passed on and Alex let herself relax. Beside her, Holey-Beard pushed out a sigh.

"As I was saying," Monique continued. "We need to talk to him. It needs to be handled with care, so I'm taking that on myself. The case has some—ah—unusual aspects."

Alex heard groans. Holey-Beard stiffened.

"Meanwhile, you people find out all you can about Claire Pope."

Monique hit a key and the pale face of Claire Pope appeared on the screen. She was blonde, with a sharp nose and high cheeks. She was pretty, Alex thought, stifling a memory of Siobhan, the mathematician who'd dumped her.

"We know about her career. The pet food business. *Pussy Galore* and all the rest."

*Pussy Galore* was Schrödinger's favorite. Surely this woman hadn't made billions selling *pet food*?

The man next to her laughed. "You don't believe it," he said, leaning in. "Nor did I. But it's legit. She started with cat and dog food. *One hundred and one percent*, remember that?"

Alex shook her head.

"Anyways, it had Dalmatians on the front. Funny, huh?"

She shook her head.

"No. Me either. But then she moved on to other animals. Seems there's a fortune to be made in feeding not just hamsters and budgies, but tarantulas too."

"Eww."

"Ha. Yes. Impressive, for someone who hated animals. Couldn't stand them. Or people."

"Mike, please," hollered Monique.

Holey-Beard—Mike—muttered an apology. Monique turned back to her board.

Alex leaned toward him. "If they divorced six years ago, why does she think he did it?"

"He's the only person she had contact with in all that time. She never went out."

"Never?"

"Uh-huh. She barricaded herself into that apartment like it was her own private Alcatraz. Never went out."

"How do you become a billionaire if you never go out?"

He looked at her as if she'd just asked him where babies come from. "The Internet, of course."

"But how could she run a business?"

She wondered when he would ask her what she was doing here, why she was asking questions. But Alex was naturally inquisitive and this guy, it seemed, was naturally talkative.

"Did it all remotely," he said. "Email, apparently."

"Wow."

"Mike, what did I tell you?"

Monique was advancing toward them. Alex pulled away from Mike. She tried to look innocent, never easy with a face the color of blueberry pie.

"Sorry boss," muttered Mike.

Monique was with them now. She smiled. "Good to see you two getting acquainted. Mike, this is Alex Strand. The physicist. She's going to be coming with us to interview Sean."

Mike turned to Alex. His face had lost all the casual friendliness of before. She shrank back. He looked back at Monique, his eyes sharp, and shook his head.

He leaned toward Alex as if about to speak. She leaned away, saying nothing.

"Mike, behave," said Monique.

The room was silent, the only sound the traffic passing outside.

Mike grunted and clattered out of the doors. Alex watched, puzzled.

What had she ever done to this guy? And *what* was his connection to Dr Pierce?

**9**

---

## BALLET

San Francisco
25 March, 3:21pm

They were ushered into a cramped office and asked to wait. The woman who'd brought them here was little more than a girl, waif-like with pale skin and thin, wispy hair. She wore a purple neck scarf that gave her an air of jaundice, and a loose blue blouse over a long green skirt. Alex wondered if she was a dancer, a receptionist, or maybe an aspiring rainbow.

The office was small and full of theatrical junk. In one corner a pile of cardboard boxes teetered, scrawled text on the sides listing the props they contained. A shelf held a row of ballet shoes, neatly arranged and dust-free, as if often handled. In another corner was a battered chest of drawers on which was placed an ornate silver tray with a kettle and a collection of china mugs. They were bright with mismatched floral colors. If deliberate, they would be trendy. Alex waited to see their owner before making a judgment either way.

Monique sniffed and looked around the space, picking up a few knick-knacks and then replacing them carefully. She eyed her fingers and wiped her hand on her coat.

There was a commotion behind them. Alex turned to see Mike stride through the door. The rainbow girl was behind him, looking worried.

"You can't go in there," she said, her voice cracking.

"It's all right," said Monique. "He's with me."

Mike blew a lock of hair away from his face and nodded at Monique. She looked back at him, her face blank.

"I expected you to be here first."

"Sorry," he panted, searching the room for somewhere to put his battered black leather messenger bag. He settled for the floor, bending down to place it at his feet. "I was held up. Traffic."

Monique arched an eyebrow. Then her face softened.

"How are you?"

He straightened. "I'm fine."

"You don't look it."

"I'll be fine."

Alex watched him. He was mid-height and lean, with dark brown hair that twisted around his ears. He no longer had a hole in his beard. It was full and thick, but above it was just one half of a mustache.

He caught her staring at it and put a finger to his lip. He frowned at her.

"It's rude to stare."

She felt her cheeks catch fire. "Sorry."

"Now now, Mike. Play nice."

His face darkened. "I told you I didn't need another partner."

"That's not up to you."

The door clattered open again and a large, balding

man in his mid-fifties appeared, muttering apologies. His face was flushed and there was a sheen of sweat on his forehead. He hurried into the room, offering his hand to Monique.

"Philip Gladstone. Pleased to meet you."

Monique leaned forward to shake his hand.

"Lieutenant Monique Williams. SFPD. This is Sergeant Mike Long, and—"

"I know who you are. Let's just get on with it."

Monique lowered herself to a chair. Alex shivered and remained standing behind her. Mike grunted and sat down.

Philip Gladstone plumped down behind a battered wooden desk which groaned with paperwork. On it were three framed photographs. They were of him as a younger man, performing in some ballet or other. Alex wished she was more knowledgeable.

He caught her looking at them.

"My younger and slimmer days." He pulled them toward him, regarding each in turn with a wistful look. "*Romeo and Juliet* at Covent Garden, *Manon* at the Met and finally *Candide* right here in San Francisco." He looked up at her. His eyes were small but a bright, piercing blue. "These days I'm a strictly behind-the-scenes man."

Alex nodded acknowledgement. His accent made him English, from Yorkshire. There was a trace of the years he'd spent in the US in his voice but once a Yorkshireman, always a Yorkshireman. A bit like being Scottish, she thought. But without the hair and the skin.

Monique leaned forward in her chair. "I'm sorry to bother you, Mr Gladstone. But I'm sure you'll be aware we're investigating the murder of Claire Pope. The ex-wife of Mr— of your principal male dancer."

He gave a nod designed to convey sadness. "Of course. Tragic business. Sean is distraught."

Monique raised an eyebrow. "Really?"

Gladstone frowned. "Of course. It's—" his face darkened "—it's affecting his performance. In rehearsal."

Alex swallowed. Monique gave Mike a look that said *don't believe a word of it.*

"We were hoping to ask you a few very quick questions about his performance last night," Mike said.

Gladstone blinked as if trying to understand what he was saying, then nodded. "Of course."

Alex watched Mike fumble with a notepad. He leafed through pages, finally alighting on an empty one. Monique sighed.

"Can you tell us if you were with Mr Wibble last night?" Mike asked.

"Well, yes. Of course. I was with the entire company for the whole evening."

"Were you personally with Mr Wibble?"

"Yes, I was with Mr *Wolf*." He gave him a meaningful look. "I was directing him in Swan Lake, after all."

"And was Mr— Mr Wolf on stage for the entire performance?"

"No."

Monique shifted in her seat. Alex felt her pulse rise.

Mike looked up. "No?"

"No. Sean was playing the lead but that doesn't mean he was on stage for the entire performance. I've never known a ballet where that is the case. Especially not for the male lead." He switched his gaze to Monique. "We get passed over in favor of the ballerinas, you see."

Mike opened his mouth but Gladstone interrupted him. "Tell me, son—"

"Sergeant Long," corrected Monique. Mike smiled.

"Tell me, *Sergeant*. Do you ever go to the ballet?"

Mike shook his head. Monique said nothing.

Alex raised her hand, tentatively. "I have."

Gladstone looked up at her and rolled his eyes. "Other than to see some matinee performance of the *Nutcracker*."

"I've seen that, and *Swan Lake*."

"Of course. Haven't we all. But if you or your colleagues were familiar with the ballet, you'd understand the requirements it puts on the principal dancers."

"Such as?" asked Monique.

"Well, with the performance of a ballet like *Swan Lake*, our Sean has had to train hard. He's had to rehearse for long, grueling hours. His feet are probably in permanent pain, but there's no way he'd ever admit that to me or to anyone else in the company. Ballet is an intensive discipline, Sergeant. It demands everything of a person. Everything."

Mike met his gaze. "That doesn't answer our question."

He raised an eyebrow. "No?"

"No."

Alex wondered if all ballet managers were this prickly. Compared to this guy, the Dean was a puppy.

Monique leaned in. "All we're asking, Mr Gladstone, is the times Sean was on stage. If you're not sure, I imagine we could easily ask one of the other dancers. Or it's something we could get from any member of the audience—"

"No. You don't need to do that." The theater director pulled at his collar. "I can let you have a copy of the score. That tells you most of what you need to know."

Monique smiled.

"Will it have timings on it?" asked Alex. "We need to

know at what time during the performance each scene—each dance—took place."

Monique frowned. Gladstone gave her a patronizing look. "No. Of course not. But you might be able to work it out."

"I think that would be easier with your help."

Gladstone curled his lip. "Alright then, but I don't have much time."

"Thank you, Mr Gladstone," said Monique, "We appreciate it."

"If it means you leave Sean alone, then I suppose it's worth it." He paused and looked wistfully at the photos. Alex noticed there was one of Sean too. Then he cleared his throat. "I need him here."

He walked to the doorway. "Penny!" he yelled. Alex rapped on her knee three times, then caught Monique's look and stopped. Not a *Big Bang Theory* fan then.

The rainbow woman appeared, out of breath. "Yes?"

"Where do I keep my score for *Swan Lake*?" he asked.

"Erm, in your desk."

"Right." He pulled his chair back and started rummaging through drawers. At last he slapped a document on the desk. "Thanks."

Penny gave him a frustrated look and hurried away, her feet light.

"Is she one of your dancers?" asked Mike.

Gladstone looked up from the score, which he was flicking through. "Penny? Oh, yes. Corps de ballet. Earns money to pay for shoes and the like by doing some admin work on the side. Not uncommon—we're an impoverished lot, us dancers."

Alex looked him up and down. The long nose, dark, ill-fitting jacket and straining shirt buttons made her think of

*Despicable Me* more than Rudolf Nureyev. But his clothes weren't cheap.

"Philip? What's going on?"

Alex looked round to see Sean Wolf standing in the doorway.

He did indeed resemble the boy wizard. He'd gelled his hair in an attempt to look his age, but it only succeeded in making him look like Harry Potter on his way to the school disco. His t-shirt was tight and yellow, revealing lean, muscular arms. But his glasses made her stop and stare. They looked like something Elton John might have worn in the 1970s, or maybe Dame Edna Everage on an especially flamboyant day. On anyone else they would attract attention, making him instantly recognizable to the paparazzi. But in his case, they just made him look like a lunatic who'd broken into a branch of GrandVision and started experimenting.

He stared at them, his lips pursed. "I said, what's going on?"

Monique sighed and put her hand to her face. "Mr Wolf," she said. "We were just having an informal chat with Mr Gladstone here—"

"I can see that." He looked at the director, and then back at Monique. "But why? You told me I'm not a suspect. And I don't imagine Philip here is."

His eyes flicked to Gladstone who looked down at the desk. Alex tried to imagine the group dynamics of a ballet company. Who was really in charge—the manager or the precious dancers?

"We're just establishing events on the night of Claire's death, Mr Wolf," said Mike.

He ignored Mike and stared at Monique. "You mean you're checking up on my alibi."

Monique pursed her lips. "We are double checking what you've told us."

"Why?"

Gladstone stood up and put a hand on Sean's shoulder. Sean shook it off. "Leave it, Philip. If they're checking my alibi, that means they think I killed her."

Monique stood up. "We don't think that. But we need to rule you out. I'm sure you understand that with your ex-wife never leaving her apartment it makes it very difficult for us to—"

"That has nothing to do with it. We divorced six years ago, dammit. We were only married eight months. I've been with Philip ever since." He eyed the ballet score on the desk. "You think you can use that to check when I was on stage?"

Alex watched Gladstone. He kept glancing at the door. His face was hard, and she could sense him all but holding his breath. It wouldn't be good for his company's reputation, to have their star suspected of murder.

Mike stepped forward. "We don't want any fuss. Mr Gladstone is helping us so that we don't have to involve any of your colleagues."

Sean glared at him. "Including me, it seems. I'm calling my lawyer."

"Mr Wolf," said Monique. "You haven't been charged. If we have to invoke Miranda now…"

Sean twisted his lips and looked at Gladstone, who shook his head. Sean sighed.

"Please, just show us the score," said Alex. "Tell us which parts of the ballet you were on stage for, and we can go. If we wait for your lawyer to get here then that'll take ages."

Sean glared back at her. "Who are you? You're Scottish."

She blinked. "I'm just observing."

"Well, damn well *observe* then."

Monique flashed her a look and she shrugged.

"Cops," muttered Sean. "Throwing your weight around. Intimidating people."

Alex smiled. "Look at me. I'm a five foot two, twenty-four-year-old ginger who could do with some fattening up, despite my best efforts with the chips and chocolate. You could overpower me with a flick of your big toe."

"Alex, *please*." Monique didn't sound happy. Alex thought of her broom cupboard, and the numbers she'd promised Rik she'd run this afternoon.

"Sorry."

Monique smiled at Sean. Her expression was somewhere between apologetic and patronizing. "I'm very sorry if we've given the wrong impression, sir. If you could help us get this done, then we'll be on our way." She paused. "I'm sure you want us to find whoever killed Claire as much as we do."

Sean picked up the score. For a moment Alex thought Gladstone would snatch it off him but he seemed to decide otherwise.

"OK," Sean said. "I'll walk through this with you. I'll tell you how long each piece runs and which I was onstage for. Philip will back me up."

Gladstone slumped into his chair and looked pointedly at his watch but said nothing. Sean grabbed a folding chair and held it in front of him.

"So who am I doing this with?"

Mike shuffled forwards. "Let's get this done, huh?"

Sean placed his chair next to Mike, flashing Alex a look. He licked a thumb, and opened the score.

"Right," he said. "So, Scene One is the waltz in the park. I'm in that. Philip?"

"Yes," agreed the other man. "He's in that one. Ten minutes."

Alex watched Mike flatten his notebook. Monique grabbed her elbow.

"Come with me. We need to talk."

**10**

---

## STARBUCKS

San Francisco
25 March, 4:05pm

"Let's walk," said Monique. "I need to get my steps up." She brought her wrist up to her face and shook it, checking a fitness band.

*I could do with one of those*, thought Alex. Surely steps taken to fast food restaurants and her local Chinese takeout counted? If she ran there, it would count double.

The sun had disappeared and the air felt damp, as if it had been raining while they were in the theater. Alex blinked, wondering what it was like to work in a building with no natural light. Did the bright stage lights make up for it?

Monique pulled her raincoat tighter and shivered. Alex looked up at the sky, tensing. Her thin jacket would disintegrate if it got too wet, like a wicked witch caught under a bucket of water.

"So that was helpful," said Monique, picking up pace. "Helpful?"

Monique shrugged. "Yes."

"My impression was that that was about as helpful as Dracula stopping to guide an old lady across the street."

Monique laughed. "Ruling suspects out can be just as useful as ruling them in. At least we know for sure that Sean's not our man."

Alex sighed, wondering how Monique could be so positive. "When are you going to tell me why you've brought me here?"

They were a few blocks east of the theater now, near the Civic Center. Monique stopped walking, oblivious to the young man, dressed in a suit the color of grass who'd crashed into her from behind. He muttered at her and she frowned at him as if he were an idiot.

"Did you notice anything odd about him?" Monique asked.

"Sean? Well, he did look a lot like Harry Potter."

"Not that."

"And those specs…"

"Not that kind of odd. Physics kind of odd."

"What exactly is physics kind of odd?"

"Humor me."

Alex thought of the smell in the lab, when she'd messed up Dr Katz's experiment. Schrödinger, and the way he'd hissed at Sean on the screen. The fact that her cat smelled like that too. Sometimes.

"He smelled off."

Monique didn't laugh. She didn't tell Alex she was an idiot. Instead, she nodded.

"Look," said Alex, dragging her curls behind her ears. "There was this experiment, the other night. The night Claire died. It sort of went wrong."

"Hmm-hmm. How did it go wrong?"

Alex frowned.

"It's about separating quantum particles from their properties. So if you stop a neutron from spinning, it means the spin is somewhere else. It's all about observation of properties and how it relates to whether the particle is behaving the way you think it is when you observe it. And about how things that happen in the future can affect things happening now, quantum things."

Monique was nodding.

"Did that make any sense?" asked Alex.

"Not a word."

Alex smiled. "So…?"

"This is why we want to hire you. You get this stuff, and… well, we don't."

"What stuff? It's just a locked room mystery."

Monique leaned in. "A locked room mystery with a twist."

"I'm a physicist, not a cop. Why have you got me sitting in on interrogations?"

"That wasn't an interrogation."

A cloud passed over Monique's face. People were swarming around them, parting like ants around a twig. Maybe they'd pick the two of them up in a moment, carry them somewhere.

Monique put a hand on Alex's shoulder and looked into her eyes. The Lieutenant had brown eyes flecked with hazel. Her skin was pale and blotchy, like she'd applied foundation in two different colors.

"We have this unit. You won't have heard of it."

"Try me."

Monique laughed, a high-pitched laugh that made Alex think of glass shattering.

"You don't let things get to you, do you?"

Alex frowned. "I need to get back to Berkeley."

"Don't worry about Berkeley."

"Why not?"

"Come."

Monique continued walking. She stopped at an inter-section, pausing a moment before darting across. She didn't wait for the lights. Alex followed. As she reached the other side, she felt air behind her; a bus. Its horn sounded, deep and accusatory, and she shrugged an apology.

Monique stopped walking and Alex nearly barreled into her. Monique waited for her to compose herself.

"What I'm about to tell you is confidential. You can't tell anyone at Berkeley. Not the Head of Faculty. Not your lab partner," she said.

Alex frowned. Rik was a pal. He may not be the most dynamic of guys but he was a hard worker who could be relied on for crunching data or trawling through samples. The kind of work that would make someone like Monique shudder.

Monique cocked her head. "Nor anyone else. I know you'll want to, but I need you to promise that you won't. There'll be paperwork, but for now you'll have to give me your word."

Alex sighed and nodded. Another thing to feel guilty about.

"Good." Monique carried on walking and Alex followed. Monique was a fast walker, but Alex's Vans gave her the edge over those nasty beige patent heels. "So. First up. We're stuck. On this case. It wasn't Sean, and we can't find a trace of anyone else it could be."

"Could it be one of the others? Acting on Sean's behalf maybe? Jealous?"

"They divorced six years ago. You heard what that awful theater director said. No-one else even knew Sean was married. As far as they're concerned, he's gay and always has been."

They passed the Civic Center, fighting their way through the afternoon crowds of office workers and tourists. The clouds had parted and the rough sleepers bundled up in empty alcoves were illuminated by gentle sunlight. Monique turned up a side street, stopped at a Starbucks and marched inside.

Alex followed her. "Why are we stopping?"

Monique ordered two skinny vanilla lattes. Alex would have preferred whipped cream and a bit less vanilla, but a free coffee was a free coffee.

Monique pushed to the back of the dark space and grabbed a table only just big enough to hold their drinks. She asked a neighboring couple if they were using a spare chair and then dragged it over to join the one already at their table. Alex watched all this as she sat down, placing the two mugs between them. Monique wrapped her fingers around hers, revealing chipped nail varnish on bitten fingernails. She took a tissue out of her bag, blew her nose and then stuffed it in a pocket. She looked around the coffee shop, tightening her grip on her mug. Alex stifled a yawn and drank; the late night in the lab was catching up with her. She wished she'd asked for an extra shot.

"OK," Monique muttered, leaning across the table and sending a gust of hot breath Alex's way. Alex leaned back, resisting the urge to put her hand to her nose. Her chair wobbled and she pulled herself upright, bringing her coffee up between their faces.

"You'll be wondering why I dragged you around all day."

"You might say that."

Monique looked around and lowered her voice. "Our victim hasn't come into contact with anyone for over six years, at least not face to face. She has no enemies, and the last person to see her alive was her ex-husband, who has the best goddamn alibi I ever saw."

Alex nodded.

"And Mike felt something."

"Felt something? What is he, a soothsayer?"

"He has experience which means he detects traces of something on people sometimes."

"I don't get you."

"People generally don't. Just trust me."

"You still haven't told me why I'm here."

"In cases like this, we have another string to our bow. Something we can use."

Monique leaned in further. Alex held her breath, trying not to blink.

"There's a secret unit," Monique said. She cast a quick glance about her. She needed to stop acting so suspiciously. Alex wasn't sure if she was about to be told something ground-breaking or something very, very dull.

"It's in the parking lot. Of the Hall of Justice. You won't have seen it."

"But the Hall of Justice is being cleared out. It's unsafe."

"Yes."

Alex said nothing.

"Ask me why it's being emptied. Why it isn't safe. Why the ceiling routinely leaks urine."

Alex had read the reports in the *Chronicle* but didn't know what to believe. There was a story that one time, a toilet had backed up and human excrement had leaked into the DA's office.

"OK. Why isn't it safe?"

"Quantum effects."

Alex leaned back. Another muggle thinking they understood physics. "Quantum effects? Seriously?"

"Uh-huh."

"I know all about quantum effects. It's my area. It definitely doesn't make poop leak out of the ceiling."

Monique twisted her lips. "She didn't believe us at first either."

"Who?"

"Dr Pierce. Meet me tomorrow morning. 9am sharp, at the Hall of Justice. I'll show you."

**11**

———

**PIGEON**

Berkeley
25 March, 7:15pm

"Hey, Shrew."

"Meow."

"Oh no. You definitely haven't had a weirder day than me."

"Meow."

"Two pigeons? Nice one." She gave him a ruffle behind the ears. He smelled normal.

Good. Normal was what she needed, right now.

Schrödinger jumped down off the kitchen counter and headed for the bedroom door. It was closed.

"What's up, boy? Shut yourself out of your sleeping place? That's not like you."

He hissed at the door. She froze.

There was a sound coming from somewhere. Knocking.

Schrödinger was at her feet, hissing.

"Hey, boy. C'mere."

She scooped him up and buried her face in his fur, peering over his ginger ears to look around.

Her apartment consisted of three rooms. The main living space, a tiny bedroom big enough for a family of dolls, and a shower room. More of a cubicle.

The living space was empty. She drew in a breath, readying herself to open the bedroom door.

She spat out a cat hair.

Then she spotted movement through the thin drapes next to her, a shape on her balcony. And there it was again. The knocking.

She approached the drapes, bringing Shrew up higher as if he could protect her. She felt his muscles tense.

"Shh boy, it's ok."

He leaped out of her arms and scuttled under the table. She glared at him.

"Scaredy-cat."

He licked his paw and dragged it across his face.

"Pretending to be nonchalant, are we?"

The cat ignored her. There was another knock at the window. She drew toward it, picking up a comedy bust of Albert Einstein as she passed the TV table. She pulled the fabric to one side.

The man's face was pressed against the glass. He had dark hair, and half a beard.

"You again?"

She opened the door. He was standing on her balcony, shivering. He wore a faded gray suit that looked like it needed a wash. There was a metallic smell on him, mixed with something she couldn't place. Something oddly familiar.

"Sorry. It's urgent."

She looked back to see Schrödinger emerge from his

hiding place under the table. He was advancing toward them, his nose prodding at the air.

"Hello, girl," said Mike as he slipped into the room.

"He's a boy."

"Sorry." Mike bent to Schrödinger, who arched his back to be stroked.

"I'd leave him alone if I were you. He hates people."

"I don't think so."

"Seriously. He'll bite your thumb off as soon as look at you."

"Are you sure?"

Alex frowned at Mike. He was squatting on her kitchen floor, Schrödinger perched precariously on his thigh. Shrew was purring like a pneumatic drill boring through diamond.

"Huh?"

"He likes me."

"Why?"

Mike gave the cat a gentle push. He stood up and looked at Alex. Schrödinger was looping round his legs. He shoved his nose between Mike's ankles, trying to get between his feet.

Alex stepped forwards and picked him up. He strained against her.

"Stop it," she muttered in his ear. He responded by giving her a swipe with his paw.

She was so shocked she dropped him.

"Did Monique tell you about the MIU?" asked Mike.

"The MI-what?"

"Right. Did she tell you she needed to see you again?"

"Tomorrow. What's it to you?"

He shook his head. Schrödinger was back at his feet. He rested his paws against Mike's trouser legs, meowing.

Alex frowned at him. *Stop being disloyal.*

Mike leaned down to pat the cat's head then looked at Alex. She realized he was panting.

"Forget that," he said. "I need you to come with me now. Claire Pope's life depends on it."

## 12

## MIU

San Francisco
25 March, 8:22pm

The Hall of Justice was a dark square against the night sky. Alex pulled her jacket tight as they approached the entrance.

Mike had been silent on the way in, focused on the traffic. He liked to talk to the drivers of the cars round him, berating or congratulating them on their driving. *Hey, don't pull in there, that's no space for a tank like that! Congratulations madam, an excellent use of signaling.* That kind of thing.

At the double doors, he put his hands to the glass and peered through. A security guard opened up, full of smiles.

"Hey, Sarge, how's things?"

"Good, thanks Henry." Mike placed his hand on the guard's shoulder.

"Who's your friend?" the guard asked. He looked at Alex, but not in an unfriendly way.

"New recruit."

"Ah. One of those boffins."

Mike laughed and Alex felt her flesh crawl. She resisted the urge to contradict the guard, to tell Mike to hurry.

Mike ushered her through a second set of doors.

"When are you going to tell me what's going on?"

"You'll find out very soon."

They took a corridor towards the back of the building, then he pushed through more doors and they found themselves in what looked like a service corridor. The walls were bare brick in places, plaster peeling off the surfaces. She could vaguely smell human excrement mixed with violets. She pushed her sleeve to her nose.

Mike leaned against a set of heavy iron doors and punched some numbers into a keypad. When the doors opened, Alex gagged. The smell was worse, but it was mixed with…

It was that smell again, from the lab. Heavy, and sharp, attacking her nostrils like it wanted to tear through her skin and get inside her. She held her breath.

Every vehicle in the parking lot was a squad car, except one: a VW campervan. It was a bay window pop-top, with a natty green and yellow paint job. It made Alex think of her Aunty Morag, the van she and Uncle Hamish owned when he'd been alive. They'd used it to speed around the Highlands like a couple of insane learner-drivers who believed there was nothing else on the roads. On Hamish's seventy-third birthday, he'd had a dram too many and driven it into Loch Garry, only just managing to drag his wife out before it sank in the murky water. Aunty Morag liked to embellish the story with details of the Highland songs she was singing at the time.

Mike knocked on door of the van. A crash and the sound of a man muttering *oh bum* came from inside.

After a moment, the voice called out. "Who is it?"

"Mike."

"Code word?" The voice sounded male and elderly, upper class and English. It broke on the 'd' of 'word'.

Mike sighed. "Aubergine."

The door slid open with a jolt and a head emerged. It was a young man of no more than twenty-three with sharp features, rosy cheeks and a mop of unruly hair the color of a semi-ripe banana.

"Ah. The new girl." He stumbled backwards then righted himself. "Welcome."

Alex frowned. The man was at least thirty-two years too young for that voice.

"Go on then," urged Mike.

As she entered the van, the lighting seemed to rise up from the floor to envelop her. Ahead was a large space, the kind of room you might imagine an elderly professor having as his library but much, much bigger. Immediately at her feet, between her and the man, was a puddle of coffee.

"Sorry about that." He shoved his hair back and knelt on the floor, poking at it with his sleeve. "You gave me a fright."

Alex ignored the coffee. She looked back past Mike. She thought of all those *bigger on the inside* episodes of Doctor Who and resolved not to jump out and walk around the van, just to check.

It wasn't easy.

"Nice office you have here," she said to the blond man. "Dimensional transcendence?"

"Well I'll be dingly darned." He stood and cracked a smile that betrayed dentistry that even her Scottish family would be ashamed of. "Congratulations."

She nodded. About six feet behind him, in the center of the space, was a console. It was broad and circular, with what looked like a touchscreen display all the way around it. She stepped towards it.

Mike grabbed her by the wrist. "Don't."

She shook him off. "What is all this, anyway?"

The tousle-headed man held out his hand. "Allow me to introduce myself, my dear. I am Professor Nemesis Orion, and this is the MIU."

"MIU?"

"The Multiverse Investigations Unit."

"Looks like a campervan to me."

"Not on the inside."

She leaned towards those screens again, aching to touch them.

"So can it change form?" she asked. "On the outside?"

"Of course not." He looked at her as if she'd suggested dinosaurs had never existed.

"Sorry," she said, remembering her manners. "Hello, Professor. I'm Alex."

"Pizzling coffee." He rubbed a stain on his sleeve. "And greetings to you too. Your colleague—Mike—calls me Prof."

"So what should *I* call you?"

"Nemesis, of course."

"Nemesis it is then."

He turned away and led her into the space, crashing into a desk and muttering an apology to it as he righted it. Raised platforms held a library of dusty books; some arranged on shelves, others piled haphazardly on the floor. In between the piles were small wooden desks that reminded her of school. As they passed one, she peered at it.

Nemesis caught her eye. "You're looking for the pen and ink."

She shrugged.

"We're a bit more modern than that, you'll find. The Hivers let us borrow quite a lot of their tech.

"Hivers?"

He said nothing.

They approached a circular bank of desks and the screens beyond. The screens showed the world above; the entrance to the Hall of Justice, the view from the roof. Even her lab at Berkeley.

"Are you watching us?" she asked. "Is this some kind of surveillance?"

"No. Of course not." He picked up a remote control, a big, clunky thing made of a dull silvery metal with large, yellow buttons and one big red one at the top. It slithered out of his hand and he grabbed it before it hit the desk.

"Fuzzleskut."

He hit one of the yellow buttons. More scenes of the world above sprang into life, but this time different. The offices and corridors, instead of being empty, were full of busy, serious-looking people, each sitting at a desk picked out by a well-aimed spotlight, the rooms clean and shiny.

They rounded the circular desk, which was made from what looked like cast concrete and printed in a rainbow of colors that demarcated each workstation. At the far side, sitting at a pale purple section, was a short, plump woman with the kind of smile a Disney grandma would have, before she turned out to be the wicked witch. A pair of half-moon specs hung round her neck on a silver chain. She wore a knitted jumper in a just-off tasteful shade of brown that meant it could only have come from Brooks Brothers.

"Ooh, our new recruit." She stood up, patting her thick purple curls into place. "Hello, my dear."

Alex smiled. Nemesis was a younger version of the kind of physics professor she wished Berkeley was populated by, and this woman was everybody's favorite fairytale grandparent.

"I'm Alex," she said, offering her hand. The woman offered her own hand up as if she expected it to be kissed. The hand was ruddy, with gleaming black fingernails adorned with skulls. A tattoo poked out from under the sleeve of the sweater.

"I'm Madge, my dear. Madge Ciccone."

"Madge Ciccone?"

The woman grinned. "I was born on the day Madonna had her first number one. My parents were fans."

That made this plump, matronly woman no more than thirty-five years old, forty at a push. Like everything else here, it would make sense eventually.

"Nice to meet you," Alex said. Madge gave her a little wave and sat back down at her desk.

Nemesis had his hand on her shoulder. "And here's your wingman."

Alex turned.

"Hello again. Why didn't you tell me about all this?"

Mike shrugged. He was no longer wearing a shabby suit but had changed into blue jeans and leather jacket that looked like they had come straight from an episode of *Law & Order*.

He leaned in toward Nemesis and muttered in his ear. The two of them walked slowly around the central console, deep in conversation.

"Don't mind him, dear," said Madge. "He'll soon get used to you."

"I don't get it," Alex replied. "He dragged me here, telling me it was life and death. Now I'm being given the tour."

"Things work a little differently here. Plenty of time." Madge gazed at Mike then put on a deep voice. "Detective

Sergeant Mike Long." Her eyes moistened. "He'll be showing you the ropes. Jumping with you."

"Jumping?"

"We'll be sending you to Silicon City. Didn't they tell you?"

"Silicon Valley?"

"Silicon City, dear. You're going to love it."

She watched Mike and Nemesis, deep in conversation. Mike had his hand on the gap in his beard. He traced it with his finger with an air of irritation.

"What's with his beard?"

"Don't mention it. No matter what happens to it, say nothing. It *really* annoys him."

Alex nodded. "Can I ask you a—er—a personal question?"

Madge pushed her chair back from her desk and gave Alex a look that had about as much guile as a meerkat surveying the horizon. "Of course. Fire away."

"You said you were born on the day Madonna had her first number one hit. When was that, exactly?"

Madge smiled. Her teeth were small and very, very white. "*Into the Groove*. Twenty-seventh of July 1985. Believe it or not, neither *Holiday* nor *Like A Virgin* hit the top spot. A travesty." A pause. "You thought I was older, didn't you?"

Alex blushed. "I shouldn't be so nosey."

"Everyone thinks the same thing. In Silicon City, I look my exact age. It's all the rage. Fake ageing."

"I like it," Alex said.

'Really?"

"It suits you."

"Why thank you. That's the nicest thing anyone's said to me for quite some time."

Madge glanced past Alex and licked her lips in a way that suggested nervousness mixed with anticipation.

Alex turned, expecting Nemesis and Mike to have returned. Instead, a slim, drop-dead-gorgeous young woman stood in their place, cocking her head at Alex and giving her a wry smile. She wore a purple velvet jacket and her skin seemed to shimmer in the light of the computer screens. Alex felt herself blush.

"Hello," the woman said in a midwestern drawl. "You must be Alex. I'm Sarita Jones."

# 13

## BRAW

MIU
25 March, 8:46pm

Alex struggled to gain control of her dropping jaw. "You don't look like a Jones."

Sarita raised a well-trimmed eyebrow. "Too Asian?"

Alex felt sweat sprout in her palms. "No. Too—"*Words, words*, she thought to herself. Why had she said that? "Too braw."

"Braw?"

"I don't know. Modern. Smart." *Sexy.*

Sarita laughed. It wasn't the laugh Alex was expecting; gentle, husky. Instead it reminded her of her cousin Sue's youngest son when he was watching YouTube. It was a high-pitched, infectious kind of laugh, a laugh that pushed you into a corner and smacked you in the face with its appreciation of the moment.

"You're Scottish." Sarita held her hand up and pointed to the back of it. "I'm from Michigan."

Alex decided not to ask what was wrong with her hand. "I'm Alex. Shall we start again?"

Sarita gave Alex a lopsided smile and shook her hand. "I'm in charge of Materials."

"Sounds interesting."

"It is," Sarita replied. "Very. And today it means I get to show you your kit."

"Kit?"

"Equipment. For Silicon City."

"Oh."

"You don't say much do you? Well, at least not much that makes sense."

"Get me in a bar on a Friday night and I can talk the hind legs off a donkey."

Sarita laughed again, that bizarre laugh of hers, like a hyena having a heart attack.

She turned and wove between the tiny wooden desks, in a direction that felt as if they were heading for the cab of the campervan. Alex followed. They came to a line of shelves set into a wall that seemed to be moving.

"Welcome to the funhouse," said Sarita. She winked and pulled something down off the shelves.

She held out a multicolored pile of clothes, shoving them at Alex.

"Take off your jacket."

Alex slid her jacket off and Sarita rifled inside it. Alex hoped she'd thrown away the evidence of last night's dinner; a bag of popcorn from the 7-11. Finally Sarita's fingers reached the collar. She tweaked it up to reveal the label.

"How would you describe this garment?" she asked.

"It's a leather jacket. My favorite leather jacket."

"It's plastic."

"Don't be daft."

Sarita shrugged. "Polyvinyl chloride. PVC in your language. A plastic polymer."

"Hang on a minute." Alex grabbed the jacket and brought the minuscule label up to her face. The man in the vintage clothing store had sworn blind that it was genuine leather, and she had been too polite to check.

"Believe me now?" Sarita asked.

"Yes. But what's that have to do with anything?"

"You can't jump wearing manmade fabrics."

"Why not?"

"Don't ask me. I'm not a quantum physicist, I just work with the materials. You'll need to wear natural fibers. What about that shirt?"

"I'm not taking this off."

"I'm not asking you to. Madge, d'ya mind checking the back of Alex's shirt?"

Madge reached up to put her icy fingers inside Alex's collar. "Cotton Nylon mix," she said.

"That's out too."

"But my jeans are OK. Denim, that's made of cotton."

"The dyes wreak havoc with the Spinner."

"The Spinner?"

"The machine we use to make the jump."

Alex felt her stomach shrink just a little. "That's a collo-quialism, right?"

Sarita opened her mouth to reply then noticed Alex's face, which had paled. "Yeah. Just a colloquialism."

14

___

# BAKLAVA

Silicon City
26 March, 12:18am

Claire lay back on the bed of purple violets the Hive had conjured up for her. She imagined the perfect scene—lights low, subtle music wafting in the background. Within seconds, she was surrounded by the exact scenario she'd pictured.

A low table sat in front of her, with artfully arranged plates of baklava, mini donuts and M&Ms. She reached out with an immaculately manicured hand and took a donut between her thumb and forefinger. She appraised it before swallowing it in one bite.

Perfect. It recreated the exact taste of the mini donuts served at her wedding. Piled high and smothered with molasses, they were the ideal replacement for a wedding cake.

This room—wood-clad walls, low lighting, candlelight from seemingly everywhere—had just one entrance. It was covered by a thin sheet of purple gauze. She could make out shapes beyond the fabric, hear low voices.

She'd been here many times, but no one had ever come through that entrance. If she wanted more baklava, she willed it onto the table and it appeared. If she needed a drink, she thought about a glass of her favorite Napa Valley red and it appeared in her hand.

She loved the Hive.

Tonight her heart was racing. Her real heart; here in the Hive, some bodily functions strayed from the real to the virtual.

That fabric was going to be pulled aside. Another human being was going to enter this space. Because she'd asked them to.

She closed her eyes and took a deep breath. She needed to focus, to be calm. If she panicked, the setting could disintegrate before her eyes. Even worse, it might morph into something different. A loud, student-filled bar, or a branch of McDonald's.

She shuddered. The thought of eating food recently touched by the grubby hands of a McJob filled her with horror. She only bought food that was securely packaged, and then prepared it herself.

"Time?" she asked.

"Twelve twenty p.m.," an attractive male voice returned. She nodded. Ten minutes.

She clicked her fingers; she didn't want to wait.

"Time?"

"Twelve thirty p.m."

That was better.

She saw a shadow fall on the gauze; there was someone there. She put her hand on her chest.

Was this wise?

"Is there somebody there?" she asked.

"There is," replied a familiar voice. Male. Not quite as gravelly as the voice of the AI. She wondered about the ethics of artificially enhancing another user's voice inside the Hive.

She swallowed. She brushed a stray hair away from her eye. She belched lightly into her hand—too much baklava —and waved it away.

She looked toward the shape.

"Come in," she said.

He pushed the gauze aside and stepped in. He was wearing a black suit and white shirt, with the top two buttons undone. She could see the bulge of his pecs under the jacket. He may be slim, but he still had a dancer's physique.

She looked up at him, picturing what he saw. She'd arranged herself to hide any signs of the last six years. She'd added some VR make-up and thickened her hair. She looked good, and she knew it.

"Sean," she said. "Good to see you."

# 15

# MARIO KART

MIU
26 March, 12:23am

Nemesis and Mike were waiting at the central console, with Madge wriggling in her chair and humming to herself excitedly.

"Alex," said Nemesis. "Mike is your guide for this trip. You do everything he says."

Like her, Mike was wearing garish clothes: a scarlet polo neck, mustard yellow neckerchief and sky-blue trousers that made him look like a French architect in a paint factory.

"Seriously, he's jumped before and you haven't. You do what he says," Nemesis said.

Alex tugged at her stiff cotton shirt and shook her head. "I'm not going anywhere until you tell me what this thing is going to do to me."

"It's going to send you to Hive Earth, dear," smiled Madge.

"Where is Hive Earth?"

"Well it's sort of right here, I suppose."

"In a parallel universe?" Alex asked. "I'm supposed to believe that?"

"Bingo! I knew she'd get it." Nemesis took off his specs and polished them. "Shuffling shizzmonkeys, this bit's always fun."

"But why?" asked Alex.

"Claire Pope isn't dead over there," muttered Mike.

"You mean Claire Pope exists in another universe?"

"Her equivalent."

"Do I? Exist in another universe, that is?" Alex asked.

A shrug. "No idea."

Alex wondered if he really knew the answer but wasn't telling her.

"So she tells us who killed our version of her?"

"It's not as simple as that." Mike sounded like a parent telling his two-year-old son that no, kicking that ball against the fence for the seventy-third time wasn't a good idea. "Come on."

Madge clutched her hands together and beamed at them. Mike grabbed her shoulder and looked into her eyes. She stared back at him, her cheeks flushed.

Nemesis picked up his specs, which had slid off his nose and onto Mike's shoes. "No harm in telling her," he said as he placed them back on his nose. "Your job—well, Mike's really—is to travel to another universe, find out who killed poor Claire Pope and make sure it doesn't happen again over there."

Mike frowned. "Your job isn't to solve the crime, or stop another one. Yours is to keep an eye on the physics."

"How do I do that?"

"Beats me. You're the physicist."

"I'm a postdoc. I grind numbers for a living. What sort of physics is it you want me to *keep an eye on*?"

"You'll work it out, when you get there. That's what Sally did."

She said nothing.

"Come on, now," interrupted Nemesis. "Let's get you in the Spinner while conditions are good."

Alex felt a jolt beneath her feet, Madge gave a hoot of delight and the floor started to move.

They shuffled downwards, the floor juddering with each movement. It didn't feel like the sort of mechanism Alex would trust to send her into another universe. She squeezed her eyes shut and waited for a clue that they'd jumped. A change in the air pressure, a breeze, the smell of a dropped fart dissipating.

She threw her eyes open when she felt a hand on her wrist. Who would it be, and what would they be wearing?

Madge was peering into her face, looking concerned.

"You alright, dear? You look a little queasy."

Alex blinked. "Did you jump, too?"

"Oh no, dearie. We're just going down to the jump room. Nemesis likes to do it in style."

Alex caught Mike hiding a smirk behind his hand. At last the floor stopped moving and they came to a lurching halt.

They were still standing on the same section of floor, with the circular rainbow console between them. Some sort of light within the desk was spinning continuously, reminding her of that really tricky 'rainbow road' course in *Mario Kart*. The effect was mesmerizing.

Nemesis coughed. "Welcome to the Spinner, everyone."

# 16

## COTTON CANDY

MIU
26 March, 12:25am

Nemesis must have noticed the startled look on Alex's face. "Don't worry, we're not all jumping. That's it." He pointed to a featureless curved wall beyond the console.

Madge withdrew her hands from her keypad and the console sank to the floor, creating a spinning rainbow path. Alex could feel her eyes widening but didn't care; this was seriously cool. She wished she could tell Rik.

Madge walked to the external wall and swiped a screen. A line of three virtual buttons appeared on it; red, green, and amber. They were going to be sent through an inter-dimensional portal, using *traffic lights*?

Madge placed her finger, now sporting electric blue nail varnish, on the amber button. Alex heard a swoosh behind her and bit her lip. This thing even made *Star Trek* noises.

A section of the blank gray cylinder in the center of

the space had receded and shifted to one side. Beyond it was an empty, black space. She looked at Mike, who was checking his pockets for something. Nemesis handed him a small brown object which he placed in the inside pocket of his jacket. The jacket was lime green with red lapels and turquoise sleeves.

"Here we are now," trilled Madge. "Time to get started."

Alex looked up at the ceiling, wondering what Sarita was doing. Watching them on a monitor? Designing her next tasteful outfit? Kicking back with a beer and thanking the heavens they'd gone?

Nemesis cleared his throat. "Welcome to the Spinner. This is the machine which the Hivers have provided for us to travel to their version of San Francisco."

"Didn't you build it?" asked Alex.

"I wish I had. But the Hivers are technologically advanced, as you'll learn. It was they who created this machine, they who found the portal. It was lucky that the plumber who was working on the drainage under this parking lot when they first came through was of an imaginative disposition. He immediately brought them to the University, from whence they came to me."

"How long has this been here?"

"Just a year or so."

"A year or so?" Surely the ability to travel to alternative realities was the kind of thing where you'd remember how long you'd been able to do it.

"Three hundred and seventy-two days and twenty hours. And ten seconds, if you want to pick nits."

She nodded. All this time she'd been sitting in her broom cupboard, scratching her head over data, navigating the waves of faculty politics and recording just how long you had to stand at the coffee machine before it would actually give you coffee, and this was here all along. And she was about to use it.

"So do we go in there?"

"You do. Mike, lead the way in."

Mike stepped through the door and immediately disappeared. Alex followed him, expecting to rematerialize somewhere else as soon as she walked through the door. As she reached it Madge grabbed her arm.

"Remember, don't mention his facial hair," she whispered.

Alex stepped through the door, screwing her eyes up and then quickly reopening them. She was in a dark space, Mike a dull figure just an arm's length away. She raised a hand and found a curved wall. Madge and Nemesis were outside, waving. She was still here, in a garishly painted van in the parking lot of the Hall of Justice.

The two scientists stopped waving and turned to the external wall, where they started sweeping their fingertips across controls and jabbing screens. Every now and then Madge would grab Nemesis's arm and point to a readout. He would stare at it, puzzled, then give it a thump and stand back with a smile.

Madge stopped jabbing. "It's time. We're closing the doors."

Alex felt the hairs on the back of her neck bristle. She could hear Mike's breath in the enclosed space and smell the hot dog he had eaten on the way over here. She wrinkled up her nose and clamped her mouth shut. Suddenly her bowels felt very loose.

The door slid shut with the same satisfying swish-thunk as it had opened and they were plunged into darkness. Alex stood very still, focusing on her breathing, trying to keep herself from accidentally touching Mike.

A blue light grew in the ceiling above her, falling over

them like a shower in the world's most bizarre spa. Alex shivered. Mike was standing quite still, staring down at that object in his hand, the one Nemesis had given him. She herself carried nothing; no phone, no notebook, no tricorder. It made her uneasy. But Sarita had told her that anything made of manmade materials would fall to pieces as the Spinner picked up steam.

Were they about to be spun into oblivion like some stick of quantum cotton candy? She clenched her fists and forced herself to breathe.

"Ready, people?" Nemesis's voice came from all around her.

"Ready," replied Mike.

He glanced sideways at Alex. "It feels odd the first time, but once you've brought up your dinner, you'll get used to it."

Thinking about being sick just made Alex feel sick. Like the time she had watched her brother puking over the side of a ferry and had soon joined him; then she had remembered it the next day and had to run to the hotel bathroom.

*Stop it*, she told herself. Vomiting after the jump would be acceptable, she imagined, but doing it now would just make a mess of Mike's purple leather shoes.

She took a step back and put her hands on the wall behind her. It was smooth, like the inside of a glass cylinder. Would it come with them, she wondered, or would they find themselves alone and unprotected in some alien version of the city?

And why hadn't she bothered to ask anyone what was going to happen before agreeing to this insane idea?

"Brace yourselves," came Nemesis's voice. Alex felt her throat tighten. She closed her eyes and the world went white.

17

------

# GOSLING

Silicon City
26 March, 06:30am

Claire was woken by the feel of a damp tongue working its way into her nostrils. In her dream, the tongue belonged to Ryan Gosling. It was exploring her face gently, getting to know every nook and cranny before it moved down to her neck and beyond.

She peeled herself awake, reluctant to leave the dream. She clamped her eyes shut and willed herself back into unconsciousness, ignoring the paw that had landed on her forearm.

Another paw dropped and Ryan melted into the night.

She groaned and raised an arm to clap her hand down onto Leo's head.

"Malcolm, what time is it?"

"The time is six thirty am."

The dog walker would be here in fifteen minutes.

She heaved herself out of bed and padded to the kitchen, enjoying the feel of the deep pile on her finely manicured toes. She did all her own personal grooming—as a recluse, this was something of a necessity—and had become good at it over the years. Not having a social life freed up a huge amount of time for pampering, and Claire sported what were probably the finest finger and toenails this side of the Square Mile.

In the kitchen she made herself a green bean and marshmallow smoothie and then went back to the bedroom, where she slid open the closet door. For a hermit, she had a surprisingly large and sophisticated collection of clothes. She enjoyed looking good, and would spend time each morning picking out an outfit that would be admired by no one other than her mirror.

And the AI.

Once she was dressed, she looked at it and said, "Malcolm, how do I look?"

"Mirror, mirror on the wall, you're the fairest of them all," he replied, as he always did. She allowed herself a smile. This was her favorite of the programs she'd created for Malcolm when she'd hacked his software one bored evening.

"Why thank you, Malcolm."

"My pleasure," he purred. She'd hacked his voice too; instead of the default version, expressionless and robotic, he had a voice that would be more at home on a small reptilian creature sitting in a lounge. Innuendo and everything. But it was too early for those routines.

"Time, Malcolm," she said. Sensing the urgency in her voice, he replied with a cursory, "Six forty-four."

One minute. She took Leo's lead from the kitchen drawer, ignoring his paws at her skirt. He loved Tammy, the dog walker. She was a petite girl of no more than twenty who did this to fund her way through college and looked as if she could no more control a pack of six dogs than she could bite off a man's ear. Claire had tracked her on the first day she'd had Leo, hacking into the girl's earpiece as they made their way to Golden Gate Park and checking that she was taking the planned route. Tammy had carried out her duties perfectly and Claire hadn't felt the need to spy on her again, except for the sheer joy of watching Leo play with the other dogs.

The buzzer sounded. She brought up Malcolm's visual display in the kitchen to see Tammy standing outside her front door, shifting from foot to foot. She was jogging and didn't want to break stride.

Claire slipped the lead over Leo's head and opened the inner door to the hallway. She gave him a quick pat and threw a dog biscuit into his snapping jaws—*remember who's your owner, boy*—then closed the door between them.

"Malcolm, open the outside door."

She hated those words. The outside door was the barrier between her and the world, the ring of steel that kept her safe. She only opened it for deliveries—always left for her in the hallway—and for the dog walker. As she watched it opening on Malcolm's screen, she felt her chest constrict. She had to stop watching this, it would give her a heart attack one day. But it was a compulsion, something she couldn't draw herself away from.

Tammy bent to let Leo run to her. She grabbed his collar before he could slip out into the corridor. She placed her hand in front of the screen and gave a little wave. Tammy was a sweet girl, always friendly to Leo and still waving every day a year and a half after starting this job, despite never having seen Claire's face. She wouldn't even have found her image in the Hive; Claire had made sure of that.

The door closed with Tammy, Leo and two other yapping, jumping dogs on the other side. Claire closed her eyes and let herself breathe. Only an hour till she had to open up again.

She finished her smoothie and sat down in the recliner with its corner view of the Bay and Golden Gate. On the side table next to it was her earpiece. A plain, functional model, adorned by none of the frivolous products from which she'd made her fortune. Horrible things, they were. She wouldn't allow them in her home, but she was more than happy that everyone else loved them.

She looked across to the buildings opposite: apartments just like hers. In a window, at the same level as her own, something glinted in the sunlight. She squinted and leaned toward the window to see better. There it was again; sun reflecting off glass. The windows themselves were dull, made of a glare-free glass. She put her hand to her chest. Binoculars?

*Don't be ridiculous*, she told herself. This wasn't a Humphrey Bogart movie.

She picked up the earpiece and pushed her hair behind her ear. Closing her eyes, she eased the tiny, perfectly shaped object into her ear and entered the Hive.

**18**

---

## PANCAKE

The Spinner
26 March, 06:30am

After what felt like hours but was probably about twenty-seven seconds, the light behind Alex's eyelids dimmed. She screwed her eyes up even more, not ready to open them yet.

"Open your eyes," said Mike.

She blinked them open and stared at him. He was looking at her quizzically, a deep frown creasing his brow, which had developed a rash of yellow spots. His beard was unchanged but above it, his nose bent over his mouth like a banana.

There was a flash and she became aware that the smooth gray walls had become a blur of light, spinning around them. She and Mike, however, were still. She felt her stomach do the Fosbury Flop. She closed her eyes again and took deep breaths.

"We're nearly there," he told her.

She opened her eyes. The blur was slowing, shapes and

patterns becoming distant. There was a photograph of the Taj Mahal, another of the Eiffel Tower, which seemed to advance at them as if it was growing out of the wall, and yet another of Alex's Auntie Morag laughing her carbuncles off at a Christmas party.

Then the Taj Mahal became a trolley bus, the Eiffel Tower morphed into the Sears Tower and her Aunt Morag became Schrödinger, giving her one of his *where are my biccies* stares. A ginger and white paw appeared from out of the wall and swiped at her, scratching her wrist. She looked at the skin, which was sore but not bleeding.

"Don't touch anything," Mike warned her. "Ten seconds now."

The images coalesced into patterns and shapes, like a lava lamp in a student bedroom. Bubbles fizzed up to the ceiling, popping at the top then reforming and making their way back down again before repeating the whole thing in the opposite direction. Every time they changed tack, they would change color too; from green to red to silver and then to a bright blue that was the same color as Mike's skin.

"I did warn you it would be a bit odd," he said.

"Odd?" she breathed, not sure if she'd actually said *odd* or *god*. "This is like that episode of *The Simpsons* where Homer gets high."

Mike shrugged.

She shook her head then instantly regretted it. Her stomach was doing impressions of a pancake on Shrove Tuesday.

"We're slowing," Mike said. "And now we're stopped."

She felt herself lurch forwards and then backwards. She waved her hands in front of her, desperate to hold onto something, anything, even Mike. She felt her limbs turn to blancmange and slid to the floor, finally bringing up the popcorn in a little puddle in front of her.

"Well done," he said. "Neutral colors."

She kept her eyes closed, resisting the urge to look at it, then felt a fine mist on her face. She batted at her skin, irritated.

"The Spinner cleans itself up," Mike said by way of explanation. "Your popcorn will be gone in no time."

The walls of the spinner were still now, but instead of being a pale, featureless gray, they looked as if a child had painted a rainbow on them.

The door made its familiar swoosh-thwack sound. A man was coming through, approaching Mike. The two of them shook hands, and the man turned to her.

"Good morning," he said. "And you must be Alex."

She eased herself up, taking him in. "Nemesis?"

"The one and only. Well, the one and only in this universe. Now you know why he—and I—can't jump. Too risky."

She looked him up and down. It was Nemesis alright; same beady, twinkly eyes, same wild hair. The lab coat, this time, was a pristine white.

"It would cause a rift in the space-time continuum," she suggested.

"Me and my doppelgänger being in the same room at the same time?"

She nodded.

"You and I both know there's no such thing."

"I thought there was no such thing as inter-dimensional travel until about an hour ago."

"Touché. No, me meeting my doppelgänger wouldn't cause any rifts. But it would result in one of us finding ourselves turned into a pancake on the nearest wall."

She shuddered. "So there isn't another version of me?"

"Not in this building. Not in any of the Hive universities. We've looked, quite hard. Wouldn't want to turn you into a crêpe, after all."

"So I don't exist here."

"I have no idea."

She nodded, somehow reassured that she might be here in another form somewhere, that she existed in both the known worlds. Would she seek herself out?

"Anyway," said the other Nemesis. "Enough of this idle chitchat. You're here to do some policing work. Come with me and we'll get you into your uniform."

**19**

---

## BREATHE

MOO

26 March, 05:32am

Alex expected to see a replica of the space she had just left; a circular room with screens and dials on the wall. Maybe a version of Madge waving at them. Instead, they came out onto a low rooftop. She held her breath for a moment, worried about the air in this new world.

"Breathe," said the other Nemesis. She decided it would be easier to think of him as the Prof.

She took a few gulps of air; it was sweet and pure, not like the San Francisco air she was used to. Next to her, Mike took off his multicolored jacket and slung it over his shoulder, turning his face up to the sunshine.

She looked up. One sun; that was good. And the sky was blue, not some bizarre shade of vermillion. In fact, the sky was an achingly beautiful shade of blue that would be at home at the Sistine Chapel. Gentle clouds scudded across it behind large reflective objects that glided through the air.

She stepped forwards to get a better look. Those objects were wedge-shaped, with smooth corners and what looked like advertising on the side. She couldn't read the words but could certainly make out the colors. They matched her outfit.

A woman came hurrying toward them. "Hi! So sorry I'm late. I hope your jump went smoothly."

Alex took her gaze off the sky to look at this woman. She was tall and blonde, with a perfect, slightly snubby nose and large brown eyes ringed with eyeshadow that made Alex think of a 1980's version of…

"I'm Madonna." The woman gave Alex a wide, red-lipsticked smile. She had expensive-looking teeth and smelled of violets. "You've met my counterpart, on the other side?"

Alex nodded. "Madge." The woman sighed. "I wish I could look like that."

Alex barked out a laugh and Madonna frowned. "I mean it," she said. "She's drop-dead gorgeous."

Maybe the idea of human perfection here was the cozy granny in slippers and a knitted cardigan. That wouldn't be such a bad world.

Alex breathed in again, marveling at the air. She couldn't remember what her own world smelt like; she had gotten used to the smells of the city waking her up and beating her nose to a pulp every morning. But here, the air was thick and sweet. She could smell peppermint, and chocolate, and Pop Tarts.

"Now, let's go downstairs and introduce you to the old place. Or rather the new place," chortled the Prof. Madonna bustled after him. She had the body of a woman who should have moved gracefully, like a cat crossed with an anaconda. But instead she shuffled along like a hamster trying to maintain balance in its wheel.

Alex raised her eyebrows at Mike. "Is it always like this, or does it change?"

"Stays the same," he said. "But you're not here for sightseeing. Let's get a move on."

The bald patch in his beard had gone. Instead, he had a tiny goatee that made her think of a pantomime villain. He kept stroking it absently.

They arrived at a small structure that protruded from the roof. The Prof touched its wall and a door swish-thunked open. Alex followed the others inside and into what seemed like an elevator.

They emerged into a vast, crowded space, filled with rows of desks and workstations. People dressed in vibrant colors moved around the room in silence. Every now and then two of them would come so close she thought they would collide, but then a look of recognition passed over their faces and one or the other would side-step, narrowly avoiding a tangle of human bodies.

The Prof cleared his throat. "Welcome to the Multi-verse Operations Organization."

Alex looked at all the people. Hundreds of garishly attired bodies shifting around the room. "Why is no one talking?"

"They're all plugged into the Hive. See?"

A short, stocky man in a pink balaclava and an orange jumpsuit passed, oblivious to them. The Prof pointed to the man's ear, behind which the balaclava was tucked. In his ear was a silver device that looked like a cross between a hearing aid and a bluetooth earbud.

"What's the Hive?" she asked.

"It's our version of what you call the Internet. But better. A lot better."

"How so?"

The Prof frowned for the first time. "That's not for us to discuss right now. Let's get you in your camouflage gear."

He went to a door, which opened to reveal a room full of clothes that looked as if they'd be more at home in Alex's own version of San Francisco.

Madonna passed her a dark jacket. "Here, try these on."

"But Sarita deliberately dressed us like this. To blend in."

"Sarita. Her heart's in the right place. But you need to make yourselves invisible. The more fashionable your clothes, the more attention you'll attract. Now put these on and we'll show you how to get to your destination."

# 20

## BLANCMANGE

Silicon City
26 March, 08:16am

The Prof ejected them through another swishing set of double doors, transparent from the inside, liquidly silver from outside. They stumbled onto the street, Alex's heart pounding.

Instead of being a gray, blocky lump with rats in every corner and urine seeping from the ceilings, the Silicon City version of the Hall of Justice seemed to be made entirely of mercury. The building shimmered a soft silver in the sunlight, and seemed to move internally so that the metal enveloping its structure flowed continuously. It at once had the effect of forcing you to stop and stare and making the whole thing seem to disappear into the background.

Mike fidgeted and shuffled in his camouflage clothes; a pair of black trousers and a charcoal turtleneck that, when paired with the goatee and the frown, made him look like an extra from a 'Welcome to Quebec' video.

He looked at his watch; Alex herself had a sleek black

band on her wrist. Madonna had apologized for its old-fashioned-ness but Alex was secretly hoping she could take it back with her.

"Come on then," he barked. He stepped forward and raised his arm. A wedge-shaped object adorned with video ads swooped down from above and hovered in front of them.

"This is a Hackney," Mike told her, and stepped inside. She followed.

"A Hackney?"

"Hackney, as in Hackney carriage. British slang, all the rage here. A cab." He looked at his watch again.

"How long do we have?" she asked.

"Another forty-two minutes."

"Forty-two minutes?"

"Forty-one."

"Is that all?"

She sat on the molded plastic bench that ran along the back of the vehicle, shuffling to get comfortable on the hard surface.

"Sit still," he told her.

She felt the bench beneath her shift. She held absolutely still as its shape molded to hers.

"Wow," she breathed.

Mike allowed himself a smile. "Plenty more of that," he said. "You like gadgets?"

"Can't get enough of 'em."

"Then you're gonna love it here."

To say that Alex liked gadgets was a bit of an understatement. In 2002, aged just five, she had persuaded her dad to buy her first laptop. She'd used it to learn Visual Basic and play Chuckie Egg. A year after that she'd found a Walkman in a charity shop and her love for retro tech was born. Since then she'd acquired four types of

MacBook, every PlayStation going, and even had an Apple Newton. Not that she admitted to it. She could only imagine what the toys would be like in a world where people plugged themselves into the Internet via an earpiece and taxis floated down from the sky to pick you up.

"But watch out for the NeoHivers."

"The NeoHivers?"

"Obsessives. Insane. Judging by how Claire Pope made her millions in this reality, they could be responsible for her death."

"But I thought the whole point was that she isn't dead here."

"Not yet."

Alex felt a shiver ripple down her back. They were supposed to keep Claire alive here. Just her and Mike. That was like sending Alvin and the Chipmunks after the Unabomber.

She kept quiet about her qualms as the Hackney drifted skyward. Below her, the city became a map of low, sleek buildings. Further to the North, along the shore of the Bay, the low buildings gave way to tall, sharp high-rises, like the icicles she'd get in her freezer when she didn't defrost it.

The Bay was wider here. The land ended somewhere around North Beach and where she remembered Fisherman's Wharf being was a dark island. Its only feature was a floodlit crab sculpture. She sighed; some things never changed.

After a few minutes the Hackney began its descent. The cab darkened as they sank to street level and found themselves surrounded by pink, blobby forms, buildings that seemed to sway in the breeze like blancmange. The street was deserted.

"Where are we?" she asked.

"At home this is Pacific Heights. Where Claire lived. Here it's a bit different."

Mike hopped out of the vehicle and landed smoothly on the ground. Alex followed. She stumbled in the doorway and landed flat on her face with her foot still caught on the lip of the cab's doorway.

Mike stood over her, hands on hips.

"Help me up, you numpty," she told him, wondering what Monique would say if he arrived back at SFPD with a black eye.

He reached for her hand. She pulled her foot clear of the Hackney and it rose away from them, glinting in the sunlight as it cleared the nearest buildings.

"We didn't pay," she said.

"Didn't have to. It picked up my bitbox. Well, Madonna's bitbox. It allows us to get around here, to pay for stuff, without a Hive Earth biological signature."

"Is that the thing Nemesis gave you, before we jumped?"

"Yup." He pulled it out of his pocket and tossed it from hand to hand before putting it back. "It's Hive Earth tech, so it can get through."

"You mean there's a whole planet like this?"

"There are a few far-flung places that haven't embraced the Hive yet. But yes, it's global. You like it?"

She nodded, unsure whether she did or not.

"Come on," said Mike. "We need to find Claire's apartment."

She stumbled after him, her ankle sore. The air here was just as clean as on the roof where they had landed. What had the Prof called it? The Multiverse Operations Organization.

Here, instead of flowers and peppermint, the air smelt

very slightly of the water to their north. The faint but pleasant nip of salt was overlaid with another smell she couldn't place, until she turned a corner and spotted a massive pile of fur, all curled up in a heap where the sun beat down through the gap between two buildings. The warm, heady smell of a hundred clean cats.

"Have you seen those?" she asked Mike.

"This place is full of 'em. Cats everywhere. And all of them as clean as Jimmy Osmond when he's stepped out of the shower. I think they go home when the sun comes down, when their owners unplug from the Hive."

"There are no animals in the Hive?"

"Not as far as I know. No dogs chasing toddlers on YouTube. No lolcats. They have no idea what they're missing."

Mike stopped outside a tall building. It gave out a reddish-pink glow that reminded Alex of the inside of a very shiny watermelon. Beyond it, glimmering through the gap between buildings, was the Bay, just a few streets away.

She headed toward the water.

"Where are you going?" Mike called.

"I want to see the Bay."

"Why?"

"I just do."

The Bay was Alex's favorite part of San Francisco. This was the part of the city where things opened up and she felt almost as if she was at home in Scotland. And here, in this clean, gleaming version of San Francisco, it would be something to behold.

"Wait!" he called.

She didn't stop until a jolt of electricity slammed into her and sent her hurtling to the ground.

"I told you to wait," Mike panted. He stood over her, looking irritated.

"Why didn't you warn me?"

He pulled her up.

"What was that?" she asked, rubbing her neck and checking that she did in fact feel fine. Energized even.

"It stops people from walking into the water. If a Hiver walks out here while they're plugged in, they'll just keep on walking and fall right in."

"Oh." What a waste. Maybe this place wasn't perfect after all.

"But you've done well," said Mike. "Look up there."

She followed his outstretched finger upwards. "What?"

"Claire's apartment. It's that window six stories up."

"Right. Let's get up there."

Mike gave her a look. "Up there?"

"To interview her. Find out who might have killed her, in our world."

"Don't be insane." He looked away from her, towards the Bay. "Jeez," he muttered.

"I think we should," she told him. "Who better to give us clues than the murder victim?"

"Just do as you're told."

"No." She sniffed. "Wait."

She moved towards Claire's apartment block; the smell receded. She frowned and shifted back to the center of the street.

"That's odd."

Mike was looking at the bitbox, prodding it with his forefinger. "What?"

"I thought I…" She leaned towards Claire's apartment block again. As she did, the smell receded again. "No. I must be imagining things."

"What is it? Physics stuff?"

She had a mental image of the lab; the spilled bottle of water, the cat.

"I'm not sure. I don't think so."

"You need to tell me, Alex. This is just the kind of thing you're here for."

"It's just a smell."

Mike huffed out a sigh. "You said it was odd."

She shook her head. "Everything smells off in this place. But I'd like to go inside Claire's block, see what there is."

"It's not safe."

She looked up towards the spot where she imagined Claire's window being. "Is there someone here already? Is she in danger?"

Mike followed her gaze. "She is in danger, but there's nothing we can do about it."

"Why on earth not?"

He held out the device. It was vibrating. "Because we've been recalled. Monique's orders."

**21**

---

# TEAPOT

MIU
26 March, 11:42am

Sarita leaned on the outside wall of the Spinner as they came out, grabbing Alex by the arm and supporting her as she threw up. Alex was horrified to see that yesterday's clam chowder wasn't entirely digested.

"Don't worry," said Sarita. "It affects everyone at first. It'll improve with time."

Alex gasped a thank you, took the tissue Sarita offered and wiped her face. Mike stood to one side, watching the two of them. He wore a bushy mustache that made her think of Ron Swanson from *Parks and Recreation*. He was stroking it, exposing its edges with his fingers and clearly trying to decide if it was an improvement on the goatee or not.

"Monique wants us," said Sarita. "Upstairs."

Alex followed Sarita and Mike out to the parking lot, puzzled. When they stopped at the fifth floor and Sarita breezed into Monique's office, she became even more confused. What did Sarita, materials scientist and would-be expert on the fashions of Silicon City, have to do with Monique, and the case?

"The travelers return." Monique closed her laptop. "Take a seat, you look like you need it."

Alex let herself drop into a chair and closed her eyes. The room was swaying. Beyond Monique, outside the window, San Francisco was still there. She was half expecting to return to a low three-story building that looked like a blob of mercury.

Mike sat next to Alex. Monique turned to him. "Mike," she said. "How was it?"

"Not so bad."

"Did you go to—?"

"I kept well away."

"Good. I know it's not easy, and I wouldn't have you on operational duties so soon, but we have no one who can take your place."

"I know. Thanks." Mike fidgeted in his chair and returned to stroking his mustache. Alex gave him a puzzled frown which he ignored.

"You found Claire's apartment then?"

"Kind of," said Alex. "We were six stories below it."

"Well, it was your first jump. Can't expect too much."

Sarita sat down opposite Monique, who stiffened. "What else did you find? Anything unusual?"

Alex leaned in. She could smell peppermint and coconut on Sarita's breath. "We smelt something."

Sarita licked her lips. "And?"

"It was…" she looked at the two cops. "It was the same thing I smelt at the lab. When the cat's face appeared."

"I knew it." Monique's cheeks were flushed. "Where?"

"Outside Claire's apartment."

"What was this smell?" asked Sarita.

"Let her tell us in her own time," snapped Monique, giving the room a gust of her halitosis. Alex sniffed, trying her hardest not to cough.

Sarita gave Monique a level stare.

"I'm not sure," said Alex. "It's sharp and dull, both at the same time. It whacks you round the earhole and then when you pay attention to it, it recedes, like a puff of smoke."

"Very poetic," muttered Mike.

"Have you smelt it any other times?" asked Sarita.

Alex looked at her. "Yes." She didn't add *on my cat*.

"Alex, I want you to be alert for that smell," said Monique. "And not just in Silicon City."

"Right. Why did you call us back, anyway?"

"Our suspect has gone missing."

"Damn," breathed Mike.

"Uh-huh," replied Monique. "Hasn't turned up for work. No sign of him at home. I think we can assume it's related."

Alex licked her lips. "Do you think he could have gone to Silicon City?" The smell. She lifted her sleeve and sniffed it. Was it on her?

Monique shook her head. "Only *we* have a Spinner. He's made a run for it, just like thousands before him."

"You need me to investigate?" said Mike.

"I've already got a team looking for him. And we need to protect Hive Claire. You and Alex go back."

"It's not safe," interrupted Sarita. "You know you can't—"

Monique waved an arm. "As soon as enough time's passed. I know the risks."

"Good." Sarita gave Monique a cold stare. "We'll turn you round and send you back again tomorrow morning, six am. We'll give you a couple of hours, for your second time."

"But for now," said Monique, "tell me everything you can about Claire's condo. Security, architecture, that kind of thing."

Mike cleared his throat. "The main entrance is secured by a Secured Hive Intercept Timer."

"Hive Earth sure like to have fun with their acronyms," said Alex.

"You should wait till you see their hospitals." Sarita winked at Alex.

"If I could continue?" asked Mike.

"Go on," said Sarita.

Mike licked his lips. He seemed suddenly surprised at what he found at the tip of his tongue. He gave a tiny shake of the head, a look of disgust crossing his face.

"As I said, the outside door has impenetrable security," he said. "The windows are pretty robust too. The first and second floors have Post-Ocular Overrides."

"That's all well and good," said Monique. "But not pertinent, seeing as her building here is so different from the Hive version. What we need is evidence of a suspect. Someone she has contact with, despite the reclusive tendencies. She is a recluse in Silicon City, yes?"

"Yes," said Sarita.

Alex caught movement in the corner of her eye. Beyond the glass wall that separated Monique's office from the rest of the Homicide department, Madge stood looking in at them. She was holding a china cup of steaming liquid —probably tea, but you couldn't be too sure—and stirring it with a teaspoon.

Monique's gaze had moved to Mike. Sarita flicked her eyes to Madge and frowned. Alex wondered if Madge would be invited in.

Madge mouthed something at Sarita, whose cheeks reddened. Then Madge dropped the spoon and pointed at the cup, her eyebrows raised. It seemed she was offering Sarita a cup of tea.

Sarita shook her head again. Madge shrugged and ambled away, her cardigan standing out in the dinginess of the Homicide department.

Mike had his back to the glass and hadn't noticed Sarita or Alex looking over his shoulder. "There was no sign of lights on in the apartment," he said. "We'd need to gain access to another building for that. The sixth floor of one opposite."

"It overlooks the park," Alex said.

Mike shook his head. "Not over there. The street is lined with condos."

"Oh." How had she not noticed that?

Monique raised an eyebrow at Sarita, who nodded. "We can arrange that." Outside, Madge had stopped walking and was pouring china cups full of tea from a pink and white striped teapot. She handed them round to the detectives, who accepted them as if this were nothing out of the ordinary.

Monique caught Alex staring and turned around. "What's she doing here?"

As if aware of the eyes on her, Madge turned away from the man she was speaking to and waved at them. She let her gaze rest on Monique for an instant, then mouthed a *sorry* and scurried away.

Sarita shook her head. "Typical Madge."

"I don't want her up here," said Monique.

"I'll speak to her."

"I need to maintain a semblance of normality."

"Yes, Lieutenant. Sorry." But Sarita didn't look sorry at all.

**22**

---

## SMELLY CAT

Berkeley
26 March, 6:23pm

Alex hadn't been home for nearly twenty-four hours. Schrödinger wouldn't be happy. She had no way of knowing whether he spent the intervening time alive or dead, or in a state of flux between the two. She pushed the door open slowly, calling his name quietly. She couldn't take a dead night, not tonight.

"Shrew?"

"Meow."

He stood on the table, glaring at her with a *where the hell have you been* stare. She bent to pick him up but he slipped through her fingers.

"Meow."

"I'm sorry. How was your day, Shrew?"

"Meow."

"Sorry. I'll fill your bowl now."

He glared at her again, watching intently as she reached into a high cupboard for cat biscuits and overfilled his bowl by way of apology. The sink was half-full of water; he'd turned the tap on.

"Naughty Shrew. I keep telling you not to do that."

"Meow."

"Yes, I did leave you water. It's next to your food. Still full."

He ignored her and carried on eating, then padded into the living area where he arranged himself on the arm of a chair with his back squarely towards her. Sulking again. He'd come round, soon enough.

She went into the bedroom and peeled off her shirt. It was starting to smell. She tossed it onto the overflowing laundry basket. It was wicker, a souvenir from her gap year that she'd regretted when she realized she had to lash it to her rucksack and carry it across Thailand. She pulled a clean t-shirt from a drawer. She gave it a sniff—her washing powder had struggled against her sweaty armpits lately—and decided it would do. Only Schrödinger to smell her, after all.

In the living room, she threw herself into the chair next to the cat, making the arm bounce.

"Meow."

"Yeah, yeah. Bad owner. I know. You won't believe the day I had."

He glared at her and jumped down, crossing to the couch where once again he arranged himself to face away from her. This brought his nose so close to the wall that he had to retract his head to avoid it being squashed, like the world's fluffiest and most ginger tortoise. This was one of the things she loved about him; they were both ginger, and it made both of them grumpy.

She thought over her induction into the MIU.

"I met some very odd people today, Shrew."

Silence.

"You'd have liked Madge. She seems the cat type. She'd have you sitting on her knee in no time, curled up and purring."

A muffled Meow came from over by the wall. Even sulking, Shrew liked to talk.

"Not sure what you'd make of Sarita though."

She imagined bringing Sarita back to this flat, pictured Sarita's wrinkled nose at the sight of the purple walls, the threadbare furniture, and the rug that sported a road plan designed for toy cars to zoom around on. A thrift store bargain. A far cry from the shimmering fabrics that Sarita wore.

No, Nemesis would be more at home here. She'd instantly taken to his library/lab/office, wishing she had the space for something like that and the money for all those books. Some of them, she was sure, were antiques. Would she get the chance to work her way through them, between jumps?

"Meow."

Schrödinger was back, sitting on the floor and looking up at her.

"I spent the day with a man who reminded me of you today, Shrew. Grumpy as hell, turned his back on me."

Then she remembered they'd met. She lifted the cat onto her knee and gave him a stroke. He arched his back but didn't relax.

"You liked him, didn't you?"

"Meow."

"Why, Shrew? You hate strangers. It's why you love me so much."

The cat had started to purr, vibrating beneath her hand like a small ginger drill. She leaned over and touched his ear with her nose.

Then she smelled it. That familiar cat smell she'd experienced in Silicon City. It was just like Schrödinger's scent. A scent he'd acquired around the time he'd started dying in his box.

She plunged her nose into his fur and inhaled.

She stuck her wrist in front of the cat's nose.

"Do I smell different, boy?"

He flinched and moved his face away. She wasn't going to get any answers here.

She needed to find out what that smell was. Whether it had anything to do with having made a jump into a parallel universe. Or taking on quantum properties, in Schrödinger's case.

She stared at him. When he died in his box, was he really traveling to another universe?

She laughed. *Don't be stupid.*

There was only one place she'd be able to check her suspicions. If she was right, it gave her the clue she needed to succeed at this new job. To get away from number crunching forever.

But first, she'd need to crunch some numbers.

She threw her jacket back on and grabbed her dirty shirt from the basket.

"See you later, Shrew," she called, closing the door behind her.

**23**

---

# LEO

Silicon City

26 March, 6:35pm

Claire stepped out of the shower and wriggled her feet on the bathmat. It was just as soft as her carpets but had the added benefit of sitting on top of a tiled floor warmed by underfloor heating.

If you were an internet billionaire, spending your every waking moment alone didn't have to be a hardship. Her dog made it easier. An explanation for any unusual noises around the apartment, a warm body to curl into at night, and someone to talk to.

Normally he came into her bedroom and settled on the bed while she was in the bathroom, ready for a post-shower fuss. He liked to stand on his hind legs next to her glass-topped dressing table and stroke her face adoringly. It was lucky no-one ever saw that her skin was covered in scratches.

But today he wasn't waiting for her. Maybe he was still asleep in his soft bed under the kitchen island; he did this sometimes after a trip to the dog groomer's. Claire had no clue why this was necessary, but Tammy insisted on offering it as part of her service and so, every other Tuesday after taking him to the park, she would walk him and the rest of her brood to a groomer's somewhere in the Haight and have all of them titivated to within an inch of their doggy lives.

When Leo had returned home, Claire told him a pile of barefaced lies. "Hello, handsome," she exclaimed, opening the door to the outer hall after Tammy had safely closed the one on the other side and retreated to the elevator.

But Leo didn't look handsome. His normally soft, pale brown Labrador fur was curled and colored so he looked like he'd had a blue rinse followed by a shampoo and set. And the smell! He smelt of patchouli oil mixed with cigarette butts. Straight into the shower, he had gone. It took a while to clean the blue dye from the shower tray but an hour or so later he had been clean and dry, curling up on the couch in front of *Lassie*.

Yes, Leo was probably sleeping it off.

She dropped the wet towel into the laundry basket and shrugged on her robe. Only Leo would see her moving around the apartment—that was, if the lazy mutt had woken up yet—but still she felt the need to be modest. The robe was made of silk, hand-spun by virgins from some remote Indian village. Or so she'd been told. It probably came from a Chinese factory, much like the product her own company manufactured, the ubiquitous Pearl.

The Pearl had been a brainwave. When the Hive took off, and reached the point where it was impossible to participate in society without an earpiece, she had considered ways to piggyback on this and make some cash, enough to pay for an apartment where she wouldn't have to listen to the neighbors shouting at each other all night.

She'd considered going into business manufacturing a rival to the earpieces themselves. After all, the software may be locked down to the Hive Corporation, but anyone could use their API to manufacture an access device. But earpieces weren't changing hands quickly enough. If she designed one with obsolescence built in, she would rightly gain a reputation as just another hack leeching off of the Hivers. And if she didn't, the money would soon dry up. So she came up with the Pearl, an ornament designed to enhance the earpiece visually, make it unique to the wearer and help people remember which one was theirs when they put it down in a bar.

Pearls took off. And even better, people wanted to replace them every time fashions shifted. And in Silicon City, as in New York, LA and Paris, fashions were like the sands of time. Right now the fashion was for brightly colored, plumed pearls that made their wearers look like a tiny parrot was trying to burrow into their brain.

She slipped a silk shirt over her head and pulled on black jeans. *Even a recluse has standards*, she thought, smiling to herself. A woman worth one billion, six hundred and forty million dollars and five cents had to keep up standards.

She was hungry. Time for a smoothie. She padded into the kitchen where Leo was rousing from his nap.

"Hey boy," she purred, bending to him. She ruffled his fur between her hands. He was animal, and warm, and smelly. Everything she should hate. But she loved him.

His collar was on the floor next to his bed, where she had dropped it before shepherding him to the bathroom earlier. She frowned at it; this vestige of the outside world disgusted her, but she knew he couldn't be walked without it.

She held the red collar at arm's length, preparing to return it to the hallway where Tammy could pick it up next time. Then she spotted the tag.

Leo wore a tag on his collar—name, Tammy's contact details. Certainly not her own.

But Leo's collar was a silvery metal, and this one was bronze.

She held it gingerly between her thumb and forefinger. She would need to disinfect herself after this.

She brought the tag to her face. It was engraved in the same font as the original one.

Maybe he'd lost his tag and Tammy had replaced it? She admired the girl's initiative, but wished she could find something more tasteful.

She squinted to read it. Instead of the dog's name and a cell number, it had five words inscribed on it.

*Claire. You are in danger.*

**24**

___

## ALCATRAZ

Berkeley
26 March, 7:05pm

The streets leading to the campus were full of students. Alex always felt out of place when she passed through them. She wasn't old enough to obviously be a member of staff, but neither was she young enough to disappear amongst them.

And as a postdoc, she didn't come into contact with many of them. Despite being an undergraduate herself not so long ago, she felt like an alien species now, threading her way through the groups that travelled towards Berkeley's bars and clubs.

As she reached the edge of campus, her phone buzzed. She grabbed it, knowing who it would be.

It wasn't.

"Hey, Dad."

"Hey," he replied, mocking the Americanism. "Howya doin'?"

"Stop it."

He laughed. "Sorry, lass. I can't resist."

"I know. Shall we start again? Hello, Father."

"Aw, bum. Don't go all English on me. Stick with the yank lingo."

"How's things?"

"Oh, alright. Alright."

She frowned, knowing they weren't. He didn't know that she'd been speaking to her Aunty Morag, her mom's sister. Morag was worried about him, about his ability to cope on his own.

"What time is it there?" she asked.

"Three in the morning. Just home from work."

"Right."

Dad worked as a hospital porter, and often took the night shift. It made it easier for them to communicate across the time zones.

"Tough day?" she asked, thinking of her own.

"Ah, not so bad. The usual, you know. You?"

"Usual for me too. Data crunching."

"Away with you, the fancy scientist. I'm sure it's more fun than that."

"It isn't, Dad. It really isn't."

"It'll get better."

"Anyway, I'm just on my way to meet a friend. Is there a specific reason you phoned, or can I call you back later?"

"I'm coming to see you."

She stopped walking.

"What?"

"You heard me. I've booked a ticket and I'm coming out in five days."

"You can't afford it."

"I saved up. Besides, I won't need to pay for accommodation when I get there, will I?"

She swallowed. Her condo had strict rules about

overnight guests, and how long they stayed for. More than a few nights would be considered subletting, and could get her evicted.

But he was her dad.

"Of course. But isn't it easier for me to come home for a visit?"

"Alex lass, when was the last time you came home?"

"Um."

"Exactly."

She bit her lip. It was almost a year since she'd last gone home to Gretna, on the Scottish border with England. She loved her hometown, her home country. But she'd come here to escape and doing so just made the memories loom larger when she had gone back.

"I'm sorry, Dad."

"It's alright, hen. I understand. I miss her too."

"I know."

This was the closest she'd come to confiding in him since Mom had died. She knew he was drinking, and that he was in danger of losing his job. But she'd never found the courage to ask about it.

She hated herself for it.

She took a deep breath.

"That's great news, Dad. I'll show you the sights."

"Really? Alcatraz?"

"Yes. And everything else."

"Sounds grand. Call me when you're done with your pal and we'll sort it all out, aye?"

"Yes, Dad. Sounds good."

She put her phone in her pocket. She was outside LeConte Hall now, home of the physics department. The building looked empty, and there was no sign of Rik.

She shuffled between her feet. The air was chilly already and the sun was dipping below the neighboring buildings. She wondered if this was such a good idea. What if Professor Yang was still there?

She checked her watch. Seven thirty.

"Hey."

She looked up. Rik ambled towards her, crumpling an apple pie wrapper into his pocket.

"Hey. Thanks for coming."

"No problem. Dana's expecting me back by nine. We need to be quick. What's up? And where have you been?"

"I need your help with something. Let's go in, and I'll tell you what I need."

THE BUILDING WAS DIMLY LIT, security lighting washing down the walls. Alex looked at Rik. How much could she tell him?

She cleared her throat. "Rik, do you know much about that work Hank Prout is doing on parallel world theory?"

"A bit. Not really our area."

"Well…"

He stopped and turned to her. "Is that it? Are you switching teams? They're insane, over there. It's not proper science, and you know it."

"Maybe it's really…"

He slammed a fist into his palm and she jumped.

"Hell, Alex. I'll miss you."

She held up her palms. "I'm not going anywhere. They just need me in the city for something."

"What kind of something?"

They arrived at the broom cupboard. Rik had a key; he'd been here longer than her and was seemingly more trustworthy.

She waited while he unlocked the door and switched

on the lights. The tiny space flickered to life. It was just as she'd left it two nights ago, her desk strewn with printouts.

She felt her body sag.

"OK," she said. "There's something I need to look for. In the data."

"Can't this wait till the morning?"

She turned to him. "I won't be here tomorrow. Sorry."

"Still out on your secret project?"

"It's not a secret project. They just needed a— an expert witness."

"What kinda court case requires a witness who's an expert in the Cheshire Cat phenomenon?"

Alex shook her head. The name of this study was what had attracted her to it; it sounded fun, and quirky. For post-docs like her and Rik, it was anything but. It wasn't even new research; they were just trying to apply an effect that had already been created in an Israeli university, in different circumstances.

"I can't tell you. Please, don't push it."

"Okey doke. So—tell me if I'm wrong. You have some data you need to check, and you need it for this court case tomorrow."

"Something like that, yes."

"Let's get on with it, then."

**25**

———

## BUCKET

San Francisco
26 March, 7:25pm

**M**ike leaned on the bar and cradled his beer. He was tired from the effort of working with a new partner. Keeping her from getting herself killed, making him look stupid in front of the MOO team, or causing the multiverse to implode.

He wanted to get home to his quiet studio apartment. He would kick back with a bucket of ribs and watch a game. Shave his beard. It always grew back by morning, in the same random shape the Spinner had imprinted on it. But still he tried.

"Hey."

She pulled out the stool beside him and motioned to the bartender.

"Hey," he replied.

"How was today?" she asked.

"Don't ask."

"I have to. It's my job."

Mike had never warmed to Sarita. A materials scientist claiming to be from the University of the Back of Beyond in Michigan, something about her didn't quite add up. She knew too much about Silicon City for a start. Except when it came to picking out clothes for them. Which was supposed to be her job.

He took a swig. "Go on then. What d'you need to know this time?"

"Tell me what she did. How she reacted to being over there."

"What d'you expect?"

"Mike. Just tell me. Please."

He put his bottle down with more force than was strictly necessary and eyed her. "Alright. She smelt something off, you know about that. Then, on the way back, she kept asking questions. Wanted to know if she could look herself up. I explained how it was."

"Did she accept that?"

"I think so."

"Anything else?"

"No. She was like a kid at Disneyworld. Just like I was with Sally, first time around."

"How you getting on?"

He shrugged. "I miss her. She knew what she was doing."

"She'll mellow. Give her a chance."

"I damn well hope so. I don't have the energy."

"Yeah, well. You stick with it. Keep an eye on her for me, huh?"

"If you say."

"Good. Let me know if she does anything out of the ordinary."

# 26

## BROOMSTICKS

San Francisco
27 March, 6:00am

The next morning was cold and damp, like a freshly caught kipper bathing in a tub of Jell-O. Alex arrived at the Hall at 6am sharp, feeling energized like she hadn't in months.

Nemesis had given her a code for the service doors. She punched it in, feeling like a kid on her way to Narnia. The doors shuddered under her weight as she pushed them open. Revealing the same anonymous parking lot as yesterday.

Today, she knew the routine. She walked past the squad cars, keeping her distance from the handful of officers standing around them talking, and headed around a back fence towards the van. Today it was red and yellow, with a Peace symbol on the side. Hiding in plain sight.

She mounted the metal steps and knocked on the door. "It's open!"

Nemesis sat at a purple-topped section of the central

console. He glanced up and leaned towards her as she approached, toppling off of his chair and spilling coffee all over the parquet floor.

"Morning," she said. This job was like all her birthdays at once. Even her twenty-third, when Schrödinger had brought her a mouse and laid it on her forehead while she slept.

She just had to prove her worth. Rik was working on that now, despite not knowing what he was looking for.

"A very good morning to you too," he replied, pulling himself back onto the chair. "Get a good night's sleep?"

"Yes," she lied.

Schrödinger had chosen to sleep next to her on the pillow. When a normal cat does this it's a pleasant, cozy experience. But for Alex, it meant waking up to find her cat dead next to her at least three times in the night. She'd close her eyes again and open them to find him yawning and stretching, or simply sleeping quietly, his body rising and falling with each breath. In the moment between sleeping and waking, even the most jaded physicist gets a bit of a shock at seeing their quantum cat dead.

"Excellent," he said. "I trust you kept away from the chowder?"

"Absolutely.    Cauliflower    and    bread.    Plain. Monochrome."

He raised an eyebrow. "I hear that potatoes can be good."

"Oh. OK."

"But don't worry. You'll get used to it. Maybe no puke today, eh?"

She nodded. Her stomach, which was currently attempting to win the Olympic medal for the butterfly stroke, didn't agree. She swallowed and tried not to think about the taste of boiled cauliflower.

"What's the score today?" she asked. "Same as yesterday?"

"Yes," he replied. "You need to get kitted out first. Sarita's waiting for you."

Alex surveyed the room to get her bearings, trying to remember exactly which of the sets of doors had led to Sarita's space. She headed for the one that looked the most familiar and pushed it open.

Sarita was in her office, busying herself with supplies and clothing, pulling things from shelves, tutting at them and putting them back. Alex allowed herself a few moments to watch. Sarita moved like the kind of cat she sometimes wished Schrödinger was, all sinews and grace. If Sarita found herself walking along a mantelpiece full of ornaments and photo frames, Alex would be happy to bet she'd make it to the other end without knocking anything off. Unlike her poor Shrew, who found that kind of experience so stressful he would sometimes drop dead and fall to the floor halfway along.

After a few moments, she started to feel like a peeping Tom. She cleared her throat and Sarita looked up.

"How long you been there?" Sarita's accent was sharper today, with a crunchiness to it.

"Not long."

"Good. Let's get you ready."

# CHAPLIN

MIU
27 March, 9:05am

Alex headed for the Spinner. She was disappointed Sarita didn't come with her this time.

Nemesis was still alone at the console, watching YouTube on the largest of the screens. He sat sideways in a chair, draped over the arms like a languorous teenager.

Alex cleared her throat and he jumped up. The chair clattered over and bumped towards her, coming to rest at her feet.

She looked down at her outfit. "Maybe we should wear different clothes."

"Why? The outfits we give you are the height of Hiver fashion. And they're made of natural fibers. If you indulged yourself in some nice snug nylon underwear, you'd find yourself landing in Silicon City as naked as the day you were born. We found out the hard way the first time we sent someone through."

"Who was that? Mike?"

"No."

Alex wondered if it had been the mysterious Sally.

Nemesis pressed a button on the console. The YouTube screen, which had been showing pictures of a young man falling out of a window into a pile of dirty snow, switched to a wall of indecipherable equations.

"Hello."

Alex looked round to see Mike and Madge enter together. They didn't have the air of two colleagues in the world's strangest police department. Instead there was an easy, quiet familiarity between them.

Madge wore a green woolen pompom hat that looked like she'd knitted it herself using broom handles. Below that was a sensible coat made of some nasty waterproof material, the kind designed for hiking but more commonly seen walking around golf courses. She bustled to her work-station, hanging her hat and coat on an ornate hat stand.

"Good morning my dear, and may I say what a wonderful morning it is. Like all my *Holiday*s at once."

Alex grinned back at her. "Are we all set?"

Madge stared into her face like a proud grandmother sending a child off to school for the first time. "If you don't mind me saying, this is a very special day for you. Your first proper trip to Hive Earth. *Like a Virgin*, you might say." She snorted and put her hand to her mouth. "I'm sorry. I won't do that again. Promise."

Alex smiled, indulging her. Madge looked like the most incongruous Madonna fan she'd ever seen, like Rosanna Arquette had spent the opening scenes of *Desperately Seeking Susan* shopping at Goodwill.

Alex looked at Mike. He wore a frown and a slightly less bushy mustache. She wondered how many types of facial hair trimmer he owned.

"Will we be watching Claire's apartment?" Alex asked. He nodded. "Surveillance."

"Can't we just leave a camera? Surely the Hive has the sort of tech we can access remotely."

"You'd be surprised not," said Nemesis. "When you're lucky enough to have a virtual world at your fingertips, or indeed in your ear, you don't really bother with boring things like surveillance cameras."

"What about the police in Silicon City? Why aren't they watching Claire?"

Mike shook his head. "It doesn't work like that."

Alex sighed. "Tell me how it does work then."

Mike raised an eyebrow. "You're not a cop. You don't understand the chain of command, working at the appropriate level for your rank. This is like that. You just have to put up with it."

She gritted her teeth. She was just beginning to think they might get along. But he didn't want her here. Then she remembered the reference to Sally, and the look on his face in Monique's office.

"I'll do as I'm told," she said.

"It's for your own safety."

"Come on, then. Let's get you in the Spinner," said Madge.

Three minutes later, they were below the central hub of Nemesis's library again, looking at the smooth gray wall that concealed the Spinner.

Madge and Nemesis were already at the outer wall, sweeping their hands across its surface and jabbing randomly at what she supposed must be buttons.

"In you go, my lovelies," said Madge. Mike gave her a sad smile.

Alex followed Mike in. She reached out for the wall to steady herself.

"Don't touch the walls," said Mike. "Stand still, in the middle."

She swallowed and pulled her hand in to her side. It was worse this time, knowing what was coming. Her stomach was already yelling at her. She folded her arms across her chest and shifted her feet, widening her stance in the same way she did when forced to stand in a moving carriage on the BART.

Mike snorted. "You don't need to do all that," he said. "Just relax. Lean into it. You'll enjoy it more that way."

She closed her eyes and focused on her breathing.

When she opened them again, the walls were spinning and Mike's head had turned into a giant tomato. She clapped her hand over her mouth, then realized her fingers were now cocktail sausages. She threw them away from her, and they metamorphosed into tiny cucumbers.

At last the spinning stopped and her fingers turned from dark green to the color of grass, then the color of limes and finally to her own fleshy digits. She tugged at them, checking everything was in working order.

She looked back at Mike, expecting his head to be working its way back through shades of pink. His head was that of a man in his thirties, as it should be. But the mustache had changed.

"Oh no," she said, pointing at it.

He fingered it and sighed. "I'm Charlie Chaplin again, aren't I?"

She opened her mouth to correct him but then thought better of it. "Yes. Charlie Chaplin."

The doors opened and the Prof entered, extending his hands to them. He did a brief double take at the sight of Mike's mustache but said nothing.

Out on the roof, Madonna stood next to a pink wedge-shaped object that resembled a smaller version of the

Hackney. Alex was looking forward to the feel of that seat against her nether regions.

"Is this our cab?" she asked.

"Better," replied Madonna. Her hair wasn't blonde today but brown and wavy, nearly as unkempt as Alex's.

"Nice hair," Alex said. "Looks just like her in the *Like a Prayer* video."

"Like who?" Madonna looked puzzled.

"No one." So this world had Hitler but no Madonna. That was just wrong.

"Yours looks pretty good too."

Alex put her hand to her hair to discover that it was sleek and lustrous, so slippery that her hands kept sliding off it. She did a little dance inside, and wondered how Madonna would react if she did some *Vogue* moves.

"That's our squad car," said Mike.

The object changed from a uniform pink to black and white, the SFPD seven-pointed star on the side. Alex peered at it to see that the initials were different: SCPD. She smiled. "I like it."

"Turn it off," said Nemesis. He closed his eyes for a moment and the vehicle turned pink again.

"Are you telepathic?" Alex exclaimed.

He frowned. "No. I used the Hive."

"Ah." She looked at his earpiece. It looked different today, adorned with a row of jet black feathers. "Do we get one?"

"Sorry," said Madonna. Her own earpiece had gold and neon jewels dangling from it, like an earring had eaten its own weight in bling. "They don't work on Old Earthers. Mess with your metabolism."

Alex realized she hadn't puked this time. Cauliflower and bread every night from now on. "I didn't throw up after the jump."

Madonna gave her a relaxed smile. "Sorry, my dear. Have you sailed on the Vallejo ferry?"

So they had Vallejo here too. "Just once."

"Did you throw up?"

"I felt a bit wobbly, but I looked at the shore and I was fine."

"And have you been to Disneyworld?"

Alex nodded.

"Imagine the most vomit-inducing ride you went on. Now think of that ferry."

"OK."

"The Spinner is the ferry. The Hive is the theme park ride."

"Oh."

"We can't let you do it. Sorry, darling."

Getting access to the Hive was the only way she'd be able to trace her own doppelgänger. But maybe this was for the best. She was supposed to be focusing on the case, after all. Her place in the MIU depended on it.

She shrugged. "OK. Shall we get going then?"

# 28

## SHAG PILE

Silicon City
27 March, 10:07am

The car was smaller inside than the Hackney, but just as comfortable. Alex settled herself into the seat and waited for controls to appear.

Mike climbed in after her and took his jacket off. A coat hook slid out from the wall. He settled into the seat opposite her, closing his eyes in pleasure as it molded to him.

"I hope you're driving," Alex said. "I don't have a US license."

Mike raised an eyebrow and sat back.

"Map reference thirty-seven point seven nine by one twenty-two point four three," he said.

The vehicle started to drift upwards, turned towards the location of Claire's home, and glided above the city.

"Wow."

Mike shuffled in his seat. "It's not always so bad here."

"Seems pretty good to me. Self-driving cars, air that's

cleaner than my Auntie Morag's kitchen counter, and districts that actually make sense. Not to mention that Hive we're not allowed into."

"It's not all good. Think about the Hive. How did it get there?"

"What do you mean, get there?" She looked out of the window, more like a translucent section of the wall, and down towards the rooftops. As her gaze dropped, so did the transparent section of wall, following her eyes downwards. She dared herself to look straight down and felt a lurch in her chest as the plastic seat beneath her disappeared, being replaced by the view of the city moving past below. She swallowed then looked up again, the view shifting with her.

"Well it's like the Internet, isn't it?" she said. "Tim Berners-Lee, world wide web, and all that. The Internet didn't really get there, did it? It just grew."

Mike shook his head. "It's different here. Imagine Facebook is the whole Internet. The only way you can get online—in fact the only way you can interact with the world in any meaningful way—is via the News Feed."

Alex shuddered. "Adverts for floor cleaners and funny cat videos all day. No thanks."

"I didn't mean that bit. I mean the privacy bit. The Hive is owned by a conglomerate. Called the Hive, appropriately enough. It's a private company, set up by some woman called Betsy Woznik. She's a recluse like our Claire. No-one ever sees her. It's all fronted by her partner, Mr Jobs."

"Steve Jobs? Seriously?"

"No. Montague Jobs. No relation. Apple was never a thing here."

"Oh." No bad thing, thought Alex. She was more of

an Android woman herself. "So is that why we can't go into the Hive? We don't have an account?"

"I don't think so. It's more about our biological signature. Our DNA is off. Just by a tiny bit. Not enough for you to see it, but enough for the algorithms."

"Shame."

"Yup. To get in, you need to be a bona fide biological Hiver. With good credit. Which leaves out the poor, and anyone with a disability that affects their genetic code. Here we are."

The car gilded to a halt and the side door slid open with that pleasing swish-thunk sound.

They were hovering six inches off the ground. Alex was ready for it this time and clambered out with the grace of an It girl having her butt photographed by paparazzi.

Once they were both out, Mike muttered "Vehicle up." The vehicle obligingly lifted itself upwards, coming to a rest about two stories up.

"Couldn't we use that to watch Claire?" asked Alex. "Will it go up to six stories?"

"There are laws about that sort of thing. The police would be onto us in no time."

"But we are police."

"Did you see me bring my badge with me?"

"No."

"Exactly. And even if I did, it would mean nothing here. It's all biodigital. So we keep a low profile. Don't attract attention."

"Right."

The street next to Claire's building was busier today, with brightly colored people moving around in that strange dance she'd seen in the MOO offices. Whenever two people came close to each other, one would step to the side, allowing the other to pass. Alex wondered if they could see each other virtually, inside the Hive. And how it was they decided who should step aside.

"What are those things on their ears?" she whispered.

"The earpieces?"

"No. The things attached to them."

Almost all of the people around them had objects clipped to their earpieces. On most, these were brightly colored, in designs that clashed with their clothes. Pink and green feathers, yellow glitter, and something that looked suspiciously like tinsel. Alex could only imagine what Christmas would look like here. If indeed Christmas wasn't entirely virtual.

A few of the older adults had earpieces that were more muted, verging on tasteful. Pearls and black jet dangled from their ears, sometimes accompanied by what must be fake rubies and emeralds. And the children had brightly colored rubber or plastic appendages. A small boy passed Alex and pulled a big chunk of a rubbery substance off his earpiece, molding it with his fingers and breathing on it. It changed from a muddy brown to bright sunshine yellow. He licked it and fixed it back in place.

"Is that Play-Doh?" she asked.

"No idea," said Mike. "But those things on their earpieces are Pearls. They're how Claire Pope made her fortune in this world. She manufactures them, designs them."

"She's not a recluse? Or a pet food magnate?"

"Yes. And no. She's a recluse sure enough—I wish she wasn't—but she's not a pet food magnate. And she has a pet, living up there in that flat."

"How d'you know all this stuff?"

"Madonna sends information across. And Sarita knows a fair bit."

"Sarita?"

"Come on, we're on the clock. Let's get upstairs."

He walked to the building across the street from Claire's and held the door open for Alex. The building was identical to Claire's, its smooth pink softness a mirror image. In the foyer, a large man with faintly orange skin and a purple three-piece suit sat at a desk. He cocked his head at them as they entered.

Mike held out the device he'd been cradling on their jump yesterday. The bitbox. The man nodded and waved them through.

"What is that thing?" whispered Alex, as they walked into the elevator.

"Bitbox. It's a kind of quantum transmitter, whatever that means. It's how Madonna communicates with us. How Madge can send me messages when I'm here. You saw me use it yesterday, to pay for the cab."

"Messages? Let me see."

"She only uses it for emergencies. It uses quantum morse code, takes ages to say anything."

Alex tried to imagine Madge in her bulky cardigan and her blue rinse, using something called a bitbox. She remembered Madge's hands moving across the convex wall that had held the controls for the Spinner. "How does it work?"

"Keep quiet, now. Don't attract attention."

Mike poked his head through the elevator doors and looked left and then right. He motioned for Alex to pass him and she slid into the deserted corridor.

As they walked, the walls changed, turning from a dull gray into a pastoral scene, filled with a poppy field above which flitted brightly colored butterflies.

"Motion sensors," she breathed.

"Nothing we couldn't do at home, if we had the

money," Mike said. Alex nodded. She wanted one of these for her place.

They came to a door. The image flickered, pushing vine tendrils around its frame. Alex could smell the poppies and feel a soft breeze on her face. That wasn't something she could recreate in her apartment, only the smell of week-old pizza when she opened the refrigerator.

Mike put his palm on a panel next to the door and it slid open. He stepped inside and Alex followed, shielding her eyes. This was probably the most garish room she had ever stood in. Worse even than what Aunty Morag had done to her back bedroom to celebrate the millennium—silver wallpaper with orange and purple swirls. *Sci-fi*, she'd called it. Above it had hung a glitter ball, onto which she projected images of cartoon characters gamboling across the celling. All this was offset by a green shag pile carpet (*like grass*, Auntie Morag had said) and a music system that pumped out loud rap music at the flick of a switch (*I'm getting down with the kids*, Morag had said).

This, believe it or not, was worse. Mainly because it was three-dimensional. In fact, if Alex screwed her eyes up in just the right way and tipped her head sideways, it seemed to be five-dimensional.

Fractals skidded across the walls, crashing into each other in violently colored explosions. The ceiling was a deep, lustrous black which seemed to have a mind of its own and which she worried would swallow her whole given half the chance. It was either covered in velvet, or it was the skin of a living, breathing creature.

The furniture was cast in odd, gravity-defying shapes, like something Dr Seuss might invent when he had a particularly bad head cold. Something which may or may not have been a couch sprouted from the floor, wobbling and leaning precariously. Beside it was a kind of coffee table, which looked more like a large dog turd covered in purple glitter. Wine glasses sat drunkenly on its top, leaning between its swirling folds and making Alex gag.

"What on earth is this place?" she asked.

"Rental. The Hive equivalent of Airbnb," Mike replied. "Madonna found it for us. Don't look around too much if you value your sanity."

Alex passed between the furniture, heading for the window opposite. It felt like her eyeballs had been twanged out of their sockets, twisted a few times and then put back in. Upside down. She leaned against the full-length window, panting.

"I need air."

Mike was staring out of the window. "Look over there." He pointed to the building opposite.

"Claire's condo?"

"The one and only."

"Nice one. So we watch from here." There was no sign of movement in the apartment. The bedroom drapes were closed and the living room was empty. From what she could make out, it looked like the kind of space you'd see in an interiors magazine in her old world. Simple and tasteful. Alex longed to jump over there and sit in that room instead of this.

Mike sat on the floor next to her, making himself as comfortable as you can on a pink and yellow spotted carpet. "You smelt anything yet?" he asked.

She wrinkled up her nose. "Plenty, but not what I was hoping for."

It was frustrating; she'd hoped that the smell would slap her in the face when she'd entered the building. But all she'd caught was the sharp tang of the water mixed with the metallic scent of Silicon City outside, followed by a faint floral smell in the corridor, then the wet stink of Play-Doh in here. It seemed to chime with the décor.

"Tell me if you smell it again, huh?"

"Yeah."

She sat next to him and peered out of the window. There was no movement apart from a Hackney passing overhead.

"You think whoever killed her is going to try it here?" she asked.

"That's the theory."

"Why? If she's a different Claire Pope, one who made her billions from the Pearl and not from budgie food, who's to say she has the same enemies?"

"It's not the first time it's happened. We were already worried, and then when you told us about your suspicions…"

Whoah. Were they basing this entire investigation on something she thought she'd smelled?

"I could be wrong. I don't exactly have experience with inter-dimensional crime."

"Madonna says we're right to be suspicious. She's been tracking Claire's Hive footprint."

"Is that easy?"

"No. Not with someone as paranoid as Claire, anyway. But if anyone can get close, it's Madonna."

"What did she find?"

"Claire's been meeting someone. In virtual space. Someone who doesn't exist."

"Surely no one really exists, in the Hive?"

"Everyone has a bio signature, that corresponds with their digital one. It's all encrypted, so no one can match them up. But you can't enter the Hive without both."

"And this guy has…?"

"This guy has no biosig. We have no idea how he's got into the Hive."

"You think Claire knows he's dodgy?"

"No idea. But our only option is to wait, and watch. If he's going to hurt her, he'll have to get close to her in meatspace."

"Can't Madonna trace him somehow? Watch him when he's with Claire? In the Hive?"

Mike shook his head. "Claire wraps eleven layers of encryption around all her activity in there. No idea if she's almost as brilliant as Madonna, or if she's hired a security botfarm."

"A botfarm?"

"Hive term. All the wealthy have them. The equivalent of a ten-foot fence and video surveillance, with an invisibility cloak thrown in."

She said nothing, but gazed at the stillness opposite. If Claire was in danger, it felt wrong that they were over here, just waiting.

"Get comfortable," he said. "We have one-and-one-half hours till we need to go back."

⁂

An hour later, there was still no sign of movement opposite. For the twenty-third time, Mike hauled himself up and paced the room.

"She's normally up and about at this time of day," he said. "I'm worried."

"Maybe something's happened to her."

"I hope not."

"Would we know, if it had?"

"If there was an emergency call, Madonna would tell us. Or the Prof."

"So is sitting here watching an empty window going to get us anywhere?"

"It's not empty."

"Looks it to me."

Mike shook his head. "She's a hermit. Never goes out. She's in there."

"Maybe we've got it wrong. Maybe in this world, she's a social butterfly."

"I trust my sources."

Alex sighed. She had pins and needles in her big toe and was desperate for some air.

"I'm going out," she said.

"What?"

She stood up. "I'll get us some coffee. I need caffeine, don't you?"

"I don't think that's wise."

"Do they have coffee shops here?"

"Alex, it's a highly advanced civilization. The population wear the most garish clothes I ever saw and they communicate via an immersive form of virtual reality."

"Do they have coffee shops?"

"Of course they do. There's one on the first floor of every building."

"Right. That's where I'm going." She hesitated. "How do I pay?"

He eyed her. She yawned and he followed suit. "Oh, OK then," he said. "I need something to keep me awake."

He took the bitbox out of his pocket and poked at it. Then he held it out.

"I suppose I'll need to test you with this thing at some point," he said. "You may even get your own, next time."

Alex surveyed the bitbox. "How do I use it?"

"I put it into shopping mode. There's credit for two skinny mochas with whipped cream."

"How do you know what I drink?"

"Just go, alright. But be quick about it. We have twenty-eight minutes before we have to leave."

"Right." She put the device in the pocket of her purple jeans (she secretly longed to keep them after the jump, they matched her bedroom at home) and headed for the door.

"I'll be right back," she lied.

**29**

---

## CHOPIN

Silicon City
27 March, 11:27am

The elevator played tunes from *Evita* as she descended. She listened to the familiar, enervating tones. She longed for a bit of Chopin, and his Piano Concerto No 2 boomed out of the invisible speakers. She stared at the blank walls around her, suddenly uncomfortable. Maybe this was the price you paid for a technologically advanced world. And she hadn't even set foot inside the Hive.

The elevator slid to a halt so smoothly she wasn't aware she'd arrived at the lobby until the door swished open. Perhaps the doors made a unique sound for each person who walked through them. If you liked *Star Wars*, elevator doors would sound like the swoop of a lightsaber.

She gave the receptionist a shy wave and sped to the doors. She didn't have long and had no idea how she was going to do this. But the bitbox might help.

The coffee shop was right next to the front doors.

Another one faced it across the street, in Claire's building. She doubled back on herself and went inside, preferring to keep Claire's building in sight.

The place was called the Bumble Bee. Everything was yellow, except for the chairs, the canisters of coffee on the shelves behind the barista, and the window frames. Which were all black. The barista himself was dressed in a striped black and yellow onesie and his earpiece sported a yellow and black protuberance that made him look like he was wearing a striped antenna, something that would communicate not just with the people around him but also with Mauna Kea Observatory. Alex paused a moment to hope that Mauna Kea existed in this world.

She approached the counter, wondering if it was possible to conduct this transaction offline. The barista put his hand to his earpiece and nodded at her.

"Ciao," he said.

"Er, ciao," she offered back. "Can I get two skinny mochas with whipped cream? No, make that just one. For now."

"No worries," he said, in an affected Australian accent. Was he running through different dialects and languages in the hope of hitting on the one that applied to her, or was he just a jerk?

"Thanks."

"No problemo."

She cringed. Jerk, then. He turned away from her and started making the coffee. She pulled the bitbox out of her pocket, nervous.

He turned back and slapped the coffee in front of her. It was in a receptacle more suited to an ice cream sundae. It even had a cherry and a teeny little umbrella.

"Thanks," she said. She held the device up, trying to look as if she knew what she was doing.

"Ah, retro. Cool." He nodded at her, his pimples moving up and down.

He delved under the counter to find a device that looked a bit like hers, only larger, and held it up. She moved hers towards it and was rewarded by a satisfying beep.

"The boss'll luurve this," he drawled, switching into West Coast surfer dude mode. "We haven't used it for *years*."

"Glad to be of service," she replied, and picked up her coffee.

She headed for a bench by the window that reminded her of the spot where she'd seen Rik last time she'd tracked him down at McDonald's. Here she could watch Claire's building and see Mike approaching before he came in, if he followed her.

She took a sip at her coffee. It was tooth-achingly sweet, like someone had poured a tub of sugar into a gallon of Kool Aid. She forced herself to drink, hoping that it did actually contain some caffeine. Three sips later, she was rewarded with a sharper version of the familiar kick.

The bitbox was on the counter in front of her. She placed her hand on it, wondering if it would allow her access to the Hive. The barista's response had indicated that people normally paid for their coffee online, and if she'd used this thing to do it, then surely there was a way of connecting the two.

Next to her, a couple was perched on bar stools, wrapped around each other. They wore matching velvet coats which draped around them. Hers was lime green, his electric blue. They seemed oblivious to Alex, but she had to ensure she didn't attract attention. She was relieved Madonna had let her keep the trousers—pairing these with a black t-shirt didn't seem quite as out of place here as an all-black outfit, despite Madonna's insistence.

She took another swig and picked the bitbox up, examining its faces. It was small and wooden, in a shape that reminded her of a cross between a teardrop and a Bucky ball. It had no screen, no buttons, no visible inputs or outputs of any kind. She had no idea how to use it.

Then she had a thought. Mike had described it as a quantum transmitter. Maybe if she looked away from it…

She turned her head towards the bar, trying to find a balance between not being noticed by the other customers and being very definitely noticed by the bitbox. She held still for a moment, feeling its weight in her hand. She let her blind fingers explore it; it was still a smooth, wooden shape. Maybe she should stop touching it; that, after all, was a form of observation.

She cast a quick glance at the velvet-clad couple. They had started chewing each other's faces. This device could be worth a bit and she had no idea what Mike would say if she lost it.

She placed it gently on the counter, not making a sound. She let her hand hover over it, her fingertips not quite making contact, and turned away again.

She felt the object make contact with her fingers. Cursing herself for touching it, she turned back.

She gasped.

She hadn't touched it. She hadn't spoken to it, she hadn't pushed any buttons. She hadn't offered it a treat.

But there, sitting on the table, in the exact spot the bitbox had occupied, was Schrödinger.

She stared at him. He stared back.

"Meow."

She knew that meow.

"Shrew?" she whispered. She looked around the room;

the couple were still locked together, and the barista had his back to her and was humming to himself.

"Meow."

"Shush, boy." She put a tentative hand on the top of his head. He closed his eyes and started to purr. On autopilot, she started scratching between his ears. The purring increased.

"What the haggis are you doing here, Shrew?"

He opened his eyes and cocked his head as if to say *looking for treats, of course.* She fumbled in her pockets then remembered she'd left her jacket, with its pocketful of treats, in the MIU.

"Sorry, boy. No treats today." She held out her hands; empty.

He hissed.

"Whoah. That's not like you."

She eyed him. It looked like her cat; but she was in another universe. And he'd materialized from the bitbox.

"Are you a hologram?"

"Meow."

"No. Sorry. Still no biccies, though."

She reached under his chin and started scratching. He pushed his head forwards, leaning into her hand like he always did.

Then he pulled back. He arranged himself into a neat shape; the shape of a cat ornament, not of a grumpy ginger tom. Paws in front, back arched perfectly, eyes wide.

This wasn't her Shrew.

He opened his mouth.

"Welcome to the Hive," he said. "How can the Hive help you today?"

She fell back in her chair.

"Shrew? What the—?"

Schrödinger blinked. Alex looked around, expecting to

be the recipient of stares. But the barista was swaying with his eyes closed, deep in the Hive. And the couple had left. She looked back at her cat.

"How can the Hive help you today?"

"Shrew, are you some sort of computer?"

"I am a non-immersive Hive access point. How can the Hive help you today?"

Whatever this thing was, it wasn't her grumpy alive-and-dead cat. She leaned towards him and whispered.

"Google 'Alex Strand'."

"I'm sorry, I don't understand that." His voice was sharp, metallic. He sounded like he'd been woken up from a particularly interesting dream about robotic mice.

"Of course you don't, you're a talking cat. Keep your voice down, will you?"

She gathered him into her lap. He let her move him, barely shifting from his tidy position.

She bent to his ear. "Open Google." Maybe taking it one step at a time would help.

"What is Google?"

A world without Google, now that she wasn't expecting.

"Open search," she whispered.

"Certainly. What would you like to search for?"

She felt her heart pick up pace. "Alex Strand."

"I cannot find a 'Alex Strand'."

"That's me, you dummy." She considered. "Try Alexandra Strand."

"I cannot find a 'Alexandra Strand'."

She placed Schrödinger carefully on the table, turning her head away. The barista was standing at the bar with his eyes closed, smiling serenely. Suddenly, he started dancing, not opening his eyes. He made no sound, and no-one noticed him.

Again, she felt pressure on her fingertips. Had it morphed again? She turned to find a sleek black cube on the counter, with a single rotating light on one side. She fought disappointment mixed with relief.

She picked it up and pressed it. It was darker than any black she had ever experienced, like the color she imagined dark matter might be. She turned it ninety degrees and the rotating light followed suit, shifting to the surface which had been on the side, but was now at the top. The light was pale pink and gentle, hypnotic even.

She lifted it up. It was making a sound. She pulled it closer to her ear. Was that purring?

She whispered to it. "What are you?"

"Meow," it replied. She almost dropped it.

"So you're still a cat, of sorts," she whispered. "Makes sense."

"Meow."

"You too."

She put it down again. Even the most intelligent of cat-phone-cube thingies wasn't going to help herself or her mom. She sighed and prepared to turn around again. She had to get it back into its original form before returning it to Mike.

The light switched from spinning gently to flashing wildly. It morphed from being pink, to yellow, to green, to red and back to pink again. Then it switched to red and stayed there. She was now holding a mysterious black box that was flashing bright red.

She heard movement behind her and turned to see that a man had entered the coffee shop. He was looking around, blinking. She plunged the device under her jacket, hoping she could muffle the light.

Instead, she found herself wearing a jacket that flashed red, like E.T.'s chest as he was about to go home. She jumped down from her chair and headed for the door, pausing to grab her coffee.

Damn. She hadn't bought Mike's coffee. She plunged the cube under her shirt, dulling the flashing, and headed back to the counter.

"Another skinny mocha with whipped cream, please."

"Absolutamente. With you in two shakes."

She gritted her teeth while he prepared the coffee, wondering what Mike would be thinking right now. She'd been gone eighteen minutes, which gave them just twenty before they had to leave.

The barista returned with another sundae glass.

"Takeout, please."

"Takeout? What's that?"

"Er, can I have it to go?"

He shrugged.

"OK, can I take this away with me?"

"Of course not. That's a damn fine coffee mug."

"This isn't a coffee mug, it's a… Oh, never mind." She left the coffee and turned for the door.

"You haven't paid," he called after her.

"Sorry!" she replied. "It's a bit difficult right now!"

She pushed out of the coffee shop onto the street outside. It had started to rain, and the street was emptying fast. A few hardy souls were sporting umbrella hats. But Silicon City, unlike her version of San Francisco, was clearly not a place where you ignored bad weather.

The cube was flashing more insistently now and had started to wail. The wailing was less like a siren, more like the noise Schrödinger made when he was accidentally locked out. Or when he woke up from a particularly long period of mortality. She had to get this thing back to Mike. He'd know how to turn it off. She was going to get a roasting from someone, but that was better than everyone here spotting the alien.

She pushed open the doors to the building opposite Claire's and ran through the foyer.

The receptionist stood up from his chair, jerking his eyes open.

"What's going on?" he shouted. The cube was screeching now, like a Parisian rooftop at night.

"Sorry," she called. "Just have to go back upstairs."

"You can't bring that thing in—"

But he was gone. The elevator doors closed and Alex breathed a sigh of relief, glad that they'd worked for her. She waved her hand over the controls Mike had used. What floor had he said? She couldn't remember him saying anything.

The elevator didn't move. She had no idea where she needed to take it. She waved her hand over the control panel again, muttering *shut up* under her breath at the cube. It responded with a loud, angry Meow.

Then she remembered the Morag-inspired Airbnb was directly opposite Claire, who lived on the sixth floor.

"Sixth floor," she snapped, and the elevator rose.

She tried to regain control of her breathing as she headed upwards. She put the cube on the floor, shielding her eyes from the red flashing light with her arm. She turned away from it in the hope it would metamorphose again. But it was no good. She could still see the flashing, still hear the wailing. That counted as a form of observation and would not break the quantum field.

At last the doors slid open and she fell out. She stumbled along the corridor. The poppies followed her, waving in the breeze as if they were moving with her.

She stopped at the door to catch her breath and pounded on it.

"Mike! Let me in!"

The door opened and Mike stared at her. He looked her up and down, his eyes landing first on her sweaty face and hair that was surely no longer sleek, then on the cube in her hand.

"Aw, *hell*," he said.

# 30

# BITBOX

Silicon City
27 March, 11:51am

Mike grabbed Alex's arm and dragged her into the apartment. His face was puce.

"What have you been doing?" he yelled. "You haven't even brought any coffee!"

"They didn't do takeout," she snapped back. "The barista had no idea what I was talking about."

"So what have you been doing? You were gone twenty minutes!"

"I needed caffeine. I drank mine there."

"Oh, great. Thanks. You're swanning around swigging coffee in Hive Earth while I'm stuck up here watching an empty apartment."

"Still no sign of her?"

"No." His face darkened. "But that's not the point. What have you done to my bitbox?"

"Nothing. It just started doing this."

"It just started? When you left me, it was a soft wooden object. Now it's a massive black cube shrieking at us."

"I think it's more of a wail. Have you noticed how—"

"You made it morph twice, for it to be like this."

She blushed. "I don't know what you're talking about."

"What were you trying to do? Break into the Hive, or something? Do you know the consequences if they found one of us in there? Not everyone's like MOO, you know."

Mike snatched the cube from her hand. He turned the object over, bringing it up to his ear and giving it puzzled looks.

"Why did you do it, Alex? I told you we had to go unnoticed."

"I'm sorry."

"Never mind sorry. It's flashing at us, and that means we have to go back."

"What do you mean?"

"It's communicating with us. It's a communications device, you numbnut."

"Oh."

"Or rather, Madge is. She's summoning us."

"Summoning us?"

"Yes."

"Madonna is?"

"No, Madge."

"Your Madge?"

He glared at her. She ignored it. "Cool," she breathed.

"No. It is not cool. It means something's gone wrong."

"Oh."

"Oh," he said, sarcastically. Alex decided now was the time to shut up.

"Come on then," he said. "Let's go."

That she *did* understand. She let him lead her out of the apartment, pausing only to grab his jacket from the back of an armchair, which seemed to be defying gravity just by staying where it was on the floor. He pushed the door open, peered out, then shoved her out and towards the elevator.

The cube was still flashing and yowling. Mike shook it, muttering at it under his breath.

Alex held out a hand. "Maybe if we put it down? Look away from it?"

He glared at her. "The first time you did that, it turned from a beautiful tactile wooden paperweight into something unique to you. What did it choose?"

"My cat."

"Thought so. The next time it morphed into this thing. Do you have any notion what it'll turn into next?"

"No."

"Then quit with the dumb ideas."

They stood at the elevator doors, waiting. Mike waved his hand over the panel next to them three times, shifting from foot to foot.

"I don't think it makes any difference if you keep doing it," Alex offered.

"Don't you tell me what does and doesn't make a difference." He shoved the cube under his jacket. The flashing decreased but the yowling was still there.

"Damn," he muttered, and took his jacket off. He wrapped it around the cube. It helped. A bit. Now instead of sounding like a hundred cats singing, it sounded like just three or four. Maybe twenty.

The elevator still wasn't coming. Mike waved his hand over the panel again then lifted it to hush Alex. He looked down at the bundle in his arms.

"It's not working," he said. "Nothing is. The Hive's detected out-of-world interference. Who can blame it, with this racket?"

He stared at the doors for a moment, not quite ready to give up.

"Shall we use the stairs?" ventured Alex, waiting to be slammed down.

"Good idea."

She allowed herself a satisfied smile. At least she wasn't completely useless.

They sped to the other end of the corridor, where a fire exit sign glowed. *Thank goodness for inter-dimensional health and safety*, thought Alex. She hurled herself at the doors, hoping they would be real doors, not held shut by the Hive.

They fell open under her weight. Mike pushed past her and the door slammed shut behind them—no swish-thunk this time. They clattered downstairs.

After two stories Mike stopped.

"What's that?" he muttered, as Alex barreled into him. They had both come to a standstill, but she could still hear the clatter of footsteps below. Not theirs.

"Let's slow down," said Alex. "Act casual."

"Casual? With a yowling black box wrapped up in my jacket and you looking like you've gone ten rounds with Darth Vader?"

She shrugged. "You have any better ideas?"

He sniffed and started walking, more slowly this time.

The footsteps drew closer. Alex held her breath. They rounded a corner to see the top of a man's head coming the other way.

She grabbed Mike's sleeve and gestured at the man with her head. Mike looked at him, frowning.

"What?" he whispered.

The man looked up as he was about to pass them. He looked startled and flushed, as if he wasn't used to taking the stairs.

"Morning," he said.

"Morning," muttered Alex, trying to overcome her urge to shout his name.

Everything about him was the same; the hair, the voice, the specs, the slim but muscular form. The smell. Even the way he moved upstairs, like a cat. Or a ballet dancer.

The smell.

The man's footsteps receded. Alex and Mike picked up their pace, rattling down the last set of stairs to the first floor. As they tumbled out of the doors to the lobby, Alex turned on Mike.

"Didn't you recognize him?" she gasped.

"Shush."

The receptionist had pulled his earpiece out and was looking at them, his expression teetering between shock and disdain. The cube had loosened itself in Mike's jacket and they were once again blaring out their presence like an ice cream truck on steroids.

Outside, the car had gone.

"Great," Mike said. "It's gone back to base. We're kicked out of the system. As far as Silicon City is concerned, we're a virus now."

"A what?"

"You heard. That summons has put us into shutdown mode. We have to get back to MOO, and fast."

"And how do you propose we do that?"

"We're going to have to run."

"Run? But it's two point two miles."

Mike raised an eyebrow. "That's very exact."

"Yeah, well. I had to do it in our San Francisco. In Rik's car that his second youngest had chucked up in one morning. I was counting down the miles."

Mike chuckled. "This is an improvement, is it?"

"I'll tell you that when we get safely home."

"Come on. We may as well take it at a brisk walk, at the very least."

"Mike, did you not recognize that man, back in the stairwell?"

"Of course I did."

She nodded. "Sean Wolf. Our prime suspect."

# 31

## TELETUBBY

San Francisco
27 March, 2:37pm

"Where the hissing shirtballs were you?"

Monique's face was the color of the Teletubby with the handbag. Her hair kept flopping over her face, waggling as she spoke. She huffed it away, almost screaming every time she did so.

"Long story," whispered Mike, following her lead. "The box went into alert mode. We were kicked out of all Hive systems."

"And by all that is holy, how did that happen? The damn thing's designed to alert you quietly, subtly. It vibrates. It's almost pleasant, for Christ's sake."

"Er, that was my fault," said Alex. "I sort of—I sort of looked away from it."

"You did what?"

"I looked away from it. Put it down. Twice. It was unobserved."

"And what does that have to do with anything?"

"It's a quantum transmitter," said Mike. "It has some—er—some unusual properties."

Monique sighed heavily and looked through the glass into the Homicide department. Inside, twenty-two staring heads immediately turned away.

"You've made me look like a real ass," said Monique. "I had to tell the Captain that we'd lost you for good."

"You *what?*" said Mike. "We were only an hour late."

Monique glared at him. "You know the rules. You know what happens if you break them. Nobody was ever late before." She turned a darker shade of violet. "Not without some sort of disaster."

Mike fell quiet, looking down at his feet. Alex saw that his fists were clenched and his teeth gritted.

"I'm sorry," Alex said. "Really I am. Don't blame Mike. It's my fault. Blame it on the noob. It won't happen again."

Monique looked back at the glass partition. This time, twenty-three heads turned away; Madge had appeared, with the teapot. Monique gritted her teeth.

"Anyway," Monique breathed. "I was about to start the daily briefing. You need to be in it."

"Before you go in," said Alex. "We need to tell you that we saw—"

Monique raised her palm. "Save it. I can't keep them waiting any longer."

Alex and Mike waited as Monique slammed through the doors. The chatter beyond immediately subsided. Alex slipped in and took a spot at the back, Mike following. People kept turning to stare at them. Alex tried waving and smiling but then resorted to staring at the carpet tiles. She thought of the rug in that apartment, and of Auntie Morag's home renovation.

Monique picked up a bottle of water and knocked it

back in one. She sat on a desk at the far end of the room, her nostrils flaring. She thumped the bottle back on the desk, the force crumpling it neatly. She slung it at the wastepaper bin. It missed and landed on the floor with a brittle thud.

"So," she said. "After we were so rudely interrupted."

No one spoke.

"Let's continue with the briefing, shall we?"

A couple of people muttered at the front; Alex couldn't make out what they were saying.

Monique held out a hand and someone slapped a brown envelope into it. She peeled it open and looked through the contents, eventually laying them out on the table behind her. She jumped off it and looked between it and the assembled detectives. Someone at the front coughed.

"OK," Monique half sighed, half yelled. Her voice sounded brittle, as if it would shatter at any moment. Either that or it would rain glass all over them.

"We've had a development. One that affects the investigation. Puts us back at square one, in a way."

Monique held up a photograph, then another, and another. There were five. She pinned them to the board behind her.

Alex edged forward, following the crush in front of her, all moving toward the board to get a better look.

She gasped. It was Sean Wolf. Dead, with half his face blown off. She lifted her hand.

"I thought you'd have learned to keep your mouth shut by now, Alex," said Monique.

"I really need to tell you what we saw in—"

Monique gave her warning look. Alex remembered that only three people in this room knew where she and Mike had been that morning.

Monique frowned and turned her head down to the desk. She lifted a plastic evidence bag containing a piece of paper.

"This is a suicide note," she said. "It seems he couldn't live without his ex-wife. Or so he says. It's possible he couldn't live with the guilt of killing her."

Alex frowned. Three rows ahead, Mike turned and caught her eye.

# 32

# MCFLURRY

Berkeley
27 March, 5:14pm

Rik was sitting in the front window of McDonalds, ploughing through a McFlurry. She skidded to a halt behind his seat.

"Hi," she breathed. "Miss me?"

He wiped his mouth. "Where have you been?"

"They needed me for another day. Expert witness."

"You and I know that's not true. What's really going on?"

"Hang on. I need a coffee."

She went to the counter and brought back a large latte, thinking of the coffee shop in Silicon City.

Rik finished his dessert and wiped his mouth. "You're going back to Scotland, aren't you?"

"Why would you think that?"

"Your dad called."

"He called the department?"

"Mm-hmm. He was trying your cellphone but couldn't reach you." He sighed. "When do you leave, Alex?"

"I'm not leaving. He's coming here. To visit." She lowered her voice. "Don't tell my landlord."

"What does your landlord have to do with it?"

"What did he say it was about?"

Another shrug. "Beats me. He just wants you to call."

"I will."

He stood up.

"You're being weird, Alex. Just tell me what's going on."

"I told you."

He shook his head.

"It won't be for long." She remembered the way Monique had looked at her earlier. "I'll be back at LeConte soon."

Rik didn't look convinced. He stared at her for a moment then shook his head.

"See you around, Alex."

She stared at him. Rik was a good friend, her only real friend here. But staying with him meant staying at Berkeley. Today's trip to Silicon City had given her a glimpse of something so much better.

"Sorry, Rik. It's not what you think."

"Whatever. Here's your research, anyway. I ran it overnight. No idea what it is. But it's yours."

He slapped a manila envelope onto the table between them. She stared at it, suddenly confused. Rik, her family, the MIU. Which came first?

"Thanks Rik. I owe you."

"Whatever."

He turned and left the restaurant without looking back.

**33**

———

# LIMES

Silicon City
27 March, 5:58pm

Claire opened her eyes. She put a hand to her chest; her heart rate was elevated.

She felt something cold on her hand and flinched. She batted it away and was rewarded with a growl.

She looked down.

"Oh, Leo. Sorry, gorgeous."

She bent down to give the dog a cuddle, hoping he would forgive her. He was wearing a new collar, a bright blue one she'd ordered online. The old one, with its new inscription, was hidden in her bedside drawer. She had no idea what to make of it.

After a few moments he pulled away and headed for his bowl. She watched him, thinking over what she'd just done in the Hive.

It was a mistake, she knew. But she'd realized that despite everything, she was lonely. Not lonely enough to leave her apartment, or lonely enough to let the dog walker in. But lonely enough to make human contact in the virtual world of the Hive.

She looked in the mirror over the fireplace. Her cheeks were flushed and there was a sheen of sweat on her forehead.

She looked at Leo, considering telling him about her encounter. But saying it aloud made it real. Even to a dog.

Making a smoothie would calm her down. She headed back to the kitchen. Leo raised his head in greeting then went back to eating.

She placed a steadying hand on the counter. The pale marble was cool; just what she needed.

She fished in the fruit bowl and pulled out two limes. Then she opened the freezer and took out a bag of fruit. She opened a drawer to grab a knife without looking; she knew where everything was in this kitchen.

Her hand hit wood at the bottom of the drawer. She looked down, irritated.

She frowned. She'd put her favorite chef's knife there earlier, after unloading the dishwasher. She was sure of it.

Annoyed with herself, she opened the dishwasher. It was empty.

"Where's my knife, Leo?" she asked. He didn't respond.

She closed the dishwasher door and searched through cupboards and drawers. Claire was an organized woman, who knew where everything was; she wouldn't have put it in the wrong drawer. But then, she had been feeling a little odd lately.

She searched the kitchen twice. It wasn't there.

She looked at Leo. "Have you hidden it, boy?"

He cocked his head and put up a paw. She gave it a shake. She loved Leo. Maybe she should pay him more attention, then she wouldn't need to use the Hive for company.

Her heart rate was up again.

"Where is it, Leo?" she said. He barked once.

Could she have taken it into the living room, cut some limes for a drink last night maybe?

The living area was pristine as ever, the pale cream couch empty except for two perfectly arranged pillows. The coffee table held two books; a business tome and novel. Nothing more.

Then she spotted it. On the carpet in the hallway, lying there like an accusation. Could she have dropped it?

She hurried into the hallway and bent down. She picked up the knife as if it were on fire.

She examined it. She hadn't brought it out here.

So how had it got there?

**34**

---

# DARCY

Berkeley
27 March, 6:28pm

I t felt good to close her front door and kick her shoes off. Schrödinger had even obliged her by choosing this as an alive evening. He meowed loudly as she filled his bowl.

"There you go Shrew. Good day?"

He said nothing, but she could hear him purring.

"Any odd quantum events with you?"

He looked up from his bowl and gave her what looked a lot like a suspicious stare.

"No. Just dying in your box, huh?"

She squatted on the floor and ruffled the fur between his ears. The purring grew in intensity.

"Are you going to parallel universes when you die, Shrew?"

"Meow."

She squinted. "As if you'd tell me."

She needed a beer. She opened the fridge then groaned

to find that all it contained was a half-drunk can of Pepsi and a slice of pizza that was starting to turn green.

She checked her phone; the 7-11 would still be open. Then she remembered her conversation with Rik, her promise to call her dad.

Half past six. It would be two-thirty am at home. It was worth a try.

She dialed his cellphone but hit voicemail.

She hesitated; her dad calling her at work didn't feel like something she could respond to with a voicemail. She put the phone back in her pocket.

Maybe she could try Aunty Morag? But no, she was retired and wouldn't welcome being woken in the wee hours.

She grabbed her jacket and threw it back on. She was about to open the door when someone knocked on it.

She flung it open. Had Rik come to make nice?

"Oh. Hello." She felt herself turn the same Teletubby shade of purple that Monique had earlier. Her heart was thumping in her ears.

"Hey."

"How did you know where I live?"

Sarita smiled. "I know a lot of things."

"Right. Come in."

Sarita peered past her. Alex turned to see Schrödinger on the kitchen table, his back arched.

"Second thoughts," Alex said. "I'll take you to Breselli's."

BRESELLI'S WAS one of the few bars round here whose clientele didn't need fake ID. Alex found a corner table and ordered two beers.

The barman, Joe, gave her wink over Sarita's shoulder. Alex frowned at him.

"So. What brings you here?" she asked, trying to ignore the looks Joe was giving her from the bar.

Sarita smiled again. "Just thought it would be good to make the acquaintance of our newest recruit."

"Don't worry. I don't think I'll be allowed back."

"You're wrong. That's just Monique. She becomes, oh I don't know, worked up, sometimes. Ignore it."

"It felt like more than worked up to me."

Joe arrived with the beers. He gave Sarita an especially wide smile. She smiled back, cocking her head. Alex felt her heart sink.

When Joe was out of earshot, Sarita leaned in. The table was round and dotted with beer rings. She did a good job of keeping her sleeves out of them.

"What's with him? He's not trying to hit on me?"

Alex froze. "I don't think so."

"Good. Not my type."

Alex blushed again. Should she make a move on this woman, who seemed impossibly out of her league? Had Sarita maybe come to see her because the attraction was mutual? Or would it be the biggest professional faux pas since Bill Clinton said *hell yes, let's recruit some interns*?

Sarita swigged her beer then wiped her mouth. Alex stared, shocked and relieved in equal measure. She wasn't perfect. Good.

Sarita put her beer down and rested a hand on the table between them. The skin was smooth and she wore three rings; one on her middle finger and two on her ring finger. Each had a different stone.

"Monique's secretly pleased with what you did today. She likes a bit of initiative. Enjoys ruffling the Hivers' feathers a bit. And I had a word with her."

Alex leaned back. *Don't flirt*, she told herself. *Your career depends on it*. And maybe her half-assed plan to find her mom in Hive Earth.

"We'll be sending you out again tomorrow." Sarita sat back. "Berkeley can spare you for a few days, can't they?"

Alex thought of the manila envelope Rik had given her. It was sitting on the kitchen table, next to Shrew. She still hadn't had time to open it.

"Course they can." She met Sarita's gaze, keeping her face expressionless.

"Good. Glad that's sorted. I need to have a chat with you, Alex."

Alex felt her heart pick up pace. "OK."

"Yeah. Debrief."

"But we did all that with Monique."

"Well, not quite. I didn't get everything I needed."

Sarita leaned over the table, slapping her hands together. She was wearing a yellow leather jacket; it rode up her arms as she reached out. Alex wondered if it was manmade or natural. If Sarita had ever jumped.

Alex sipped at her beer and waited. What would Sarita need to know about the clothes they had worn? Did she need to change the formula? Or maybe this was something to do with the bitbox.

Sarita glanced around the bar. Two guys were sitting at the table nearest them. One of them stared at her, licking his lips. She screwed up her nose and pulled her chair away.

"So," said Sarita. "How was your second jump? Not too sick, I hope."

"I kept it all in this time."

"That's good."

"But I'm not going to be eating chowder again for a

while. In fact, I'm planning to have cauliflower and bread every meal from now on."

"Cauliflower and bread?"

"White food. Stuff I can keep down."

"It probably won't be so bad from now on. You'll be fine."

"I hope so."

"Was it worth it, though? To see another version of San Francisco?"

Alex licked her lips. "Worth it like you wouldn't imagine. You won't believe what the place was like. Like something out of a movie."

"How so?"

Alex frowned; surely Sarita would already know all this? But Alex wanted to talk about her day, and couldn't exactly tell Rik. Or her dad.

"The oddest thing was how quiet it all was."

"The Hive. Plugged in."

"Yes. I get that—some kind of VR via that earpiece. God knows how it works, but it made some kind of sense. But the thing I couldn't get my head round was the dance."

"The dance?"

"Not a dance, more a shuffle. People were plugged in, silent, dead to the world as far as you could tell. And they were moving around, walking. Maybe they were moving around inside the Hive too. But every time they came near to an obstacle, they would avoid it perfectly. Even other people. I felt like Elizabeth Bennet in Pride and Prejudice, watching the ball, listening to that horrible Mr Darcy."

"You didn't like Darcy?"

Alex laughed. "Of course not. Arrogant jerk."

"Even with the wet shirt?"

"Especially with the wet shirt. Not my type." She

blushed, hoping the words *you're more my type* hadn't appeared in big red letters on her forehead.

Sarita seemed oblivious. "I know what you mean." She looked serious again. "So what else was different?"

"Different from what?"

Sarita looked at her for a moment. "From here."

"Oh. Well." She considered. "I had a coffee."

Sarita laughed. "Was that wise?"

"What d'you mean, wise?"

"Think about it, Alex. It's another universe. Your biology is different. How did you know you weren't drinking poison?"

"Oh."

Sarita laughed. It was like the sound of a chandelier in a force nine gale.

"I'm joking. It's just coffee. Mike says it's fine."

Alex's shoulder slumped. "You had me there."

"How did that affect you?"

"The coffee?"

"Yeah. I'm not going to ask you about the bitbox, if that's what you're wondering. Not tonight."

Alex felt herself relax. "Oh. Right. Well, it was actually pretty cool. Once I'd digested the sugar it felt like drinking three shots of espresso in quick succession. I'm surprised the place wasn't full of people crawling on the ceiling."

Sarita laughed. "Here in this world, probably. But there, we get stimulation from the Hive."

"We?"

Sarita's face darkened. "They."

"Have you been there? Do you go on missions?" Alex considered. "I didn't see a Hive version of Sarita."

"No. You wouldn't have."

"OK. So why didn't you go?"

"I don't jump."

"No? You'd love it. You wouldn't have to ask me all these questions."

Sarita narrowed her eyes. "Tell me what else was different. What felt *off.*"

"The cars."

"The Hackneys."

"Yeah. No driver, seats that mold to your butt."

"Seats that do what?"

"I sat down on what felt like this horrible hard white plastic, then suddenly it was the exact right shape for cradling my derriere."

Alex returned Sarita's smile. Her eyes were bright now. *Materials science,* thought Alex. This'll be right up her alley. "Didn't Mike tell you about this?"

"Mike sometimes misses out the details. Tell me about this substance."

Alex told her everything she could remember. Sarita was all but rubbing her hands with glee. "That's new," she muttered.

"So you want to create those here?" Alex asked.

"You never know. What was security like?"

"Security?"

"In the MOO. On the streets."

"I didn't see any. None at all."

"Interesting."

"Is that normal?"

"Hmm?" Sarita was tapping something into her phone now, making notes maybe. "Oh yeah, completely normal."

"And we saw Sean Wolf's doppelganger."

Sarita's head jerked up. "You did what?"

"In the building opposite Claire's. He looked just like him."

"His doppelganger? You told Monique this?"

"Mike did, after the briefing."

"It was definitely his doppelganger?"

"Yeah. Dancer's stride, glasses that make you want to rip your eyes out and forget you ever saw them. Except…"

"Except what?"

Alex considered. She had to be wrong: Sean was dead. He'd died the previous night.

"Except nothing. Can I get you another drink?"

Sarita's bottle was empty; she'd been sucking the last few molecules from it for the last few minutes. "Gin & tonic. Get yourself the same. No more beer."

Alex saluted, "aye, aye," and went to the bar.

# 35

## STITCHES

Berkeley
27 March, 9:57pm

Alex fell into the apartment. Schrödinger was waiting for her, nowhere near his box. Good.

"Hey boy." She ruffled his fur. He purred.

She pulled out her phone. Dad had called hours ago. She hoped nothing was wrong.

It would be almost 6am at home. If Dad was on the night shift, he'd be about to finish.

She stared at her phone. She should wait till the morning, when it would be afternoon at home. When she wasn't drunk. But then, Rik's tone had worried her.

She dialed.

"Hiya, hen." He was whispering.

"Hi Dad. You called me?"

"Och, yes love. Are you sitting down?"

She felt a chill run over her skin. She slumped onto the couch.

"I am now. What is it?"

"Wait a sec."

She heard movement on the other end of the line. It sounded like he was walking. She resisted the urge to shout at him, to tell him to spit it out. Her breathing was shallow. Why had she gone to the bar with Sarita, instead of calling him?

"Are you at work still?" she asked.

"I'm with Aunty Morag."

"She's not been decorating again?"

A pause. "No, hen. We're at the hospital."

"What's Morag doing at your work?"

A pause. "I'm sorry, Alex. She's been attacked."

"Attacked?"

"Someone broke into her house. She's in a bad way."

Alex's mouth fell open. She thought of the night her mom was killed, the botched burglary.

"Is she—is she going to be alright?"

"The doctors say she's responding well. She had to have stitches."

Alex thought of Aunty Morag in her garishly decorated house, alone since Uncle Hamish had died of a heart attack five years ago.

"Why?" she asked. "Have they caught them?"

"Not yet. Probably kids, they reckon. Druggies. Like— you know, like your ma."

The memories flooded in. They'd broken in when Dad was out at work. Alex's mom had woken up and confronted them. They'd hit her around the face with something heavy, something blunt that the police had never identified.

Alex nodded. Tears were dripping off her nose. She and her dad rarely talked about Mom's death. He was a taciturn man, an old-fashioned Scot who didn't believe in showing emotion.

"I'll come home," she said.

"I've still got that ticket. I'll come to you."

"Can you leave her?"

"There's an army of women clucking over her. I'm in the way. Besides, it would do me good to see you."

"Me too," she croaked.

"Good. Anyway, I've a nurse looking daggers at me. Time to go. Call me tomorrow, aye?"

"Yes. Give Aunty Morag my love."

"Will do. Don't worry lass. She's a tough nut, your aunty. She'll pull through."

Alex remembered the night after her mom's attack. They'd said much the same thing, but she was dead within twenty-four hours.

"I'll see you in just a few days," he said. "You be OK without me till then?"

She laughed. "Of course, Dad. I'm a big girl."

"Good. I'll gi' your aunty your love."

"Thanks. I love you Dad."

"Oh, away with you. Don't be talking such nonsense."

She allowed herself a smile and hung up. Schrödinger was in her arms; she hadn't noticed him jumping up to her lap. The fur on his back was damp with her tears.

# 36

## BLOUSE

San Francisco
28 March, 9:13am

"Mike told me what you did. With the object."

Monique was behind her desk, dressed in a heavy green blouse with a large bow at the collar that looked as if it wanted to strangle her.

Alex glared at Mike. The two of them sat opposite Monique. Sarita was behind them, leaning on the glass that separated them from the rest of the Homicide team. She wore a turquoise shirt that caught the light in all the right ways.

"Ms Jones, tell us what you found," Monique said.

Alex shifted to see Sarita giving her a *why didn't you tell me* look.

"Ms Jones?"

Sarita shifted her gaze to Monique. "I ran an overnight download. It's in the bitbox's history. Alex googled herself."

Alex took a breath. "Wouldn't you?"

"Of course not."

Alex considered looking Sarita up next time, seeing if she had an opposite number in Silicon City. Maybe the alternative one wouldn't betray her to her boss.

Her head pounded; gin and tonic didn't agree with her. She could only imagine what entering the Spinner with a hangover would be like.

Sarita sighed. "You're only human, I guess. Only an Old Earther, in thrall to everything Hive Earth has to offer."

Alex looked up. "Not everything. Mike told me a thing or two about—"

"Propaganda. Most of it, at least. They have their own version of Occupy over there. Floor, it's called.

"Floor?'

"They like to sit on the floor. They protest."

"Are you going to let me go back?'"

Sarita narrowed her eyes. "Why should we trust you?'"

Alex needed to go back, to track down the Hive Earth version of her mom. The attack on Auntie Morag had made her more determined. And she had a hunch about Sean, or the version of him she'd seen…

"Think about it," she said. "An airline company that's recently had a crash becomes the safest one to travel on. Same goes for a bank that's been robbed. I'm like that."

"You're an airplane?'"

"I'm a safe bet. I made a dumb mistake and I won't make it again."

"It's irrelevant, anyway," said Monique.

"Why?'" chorused Alex and Sarita.

"Because we don't need you to go back. Mike can take it from here."

Mike didn't look too happy about this idea. "I'm not sure…"

"She's not going back. You said you saw Sean's doppelganger. I need you to check him out. Find out why he was in the building opposite."

"I don't think he was Sean's doppelganger," said Alex.

"No?" Monique gritted her teeth.

"He smelled familiar," Alex said. "At least, he seemed to. I think it was our Sean."

"That's impossible."

"Not for sure. Time isn't straightforward between universes. It sort of *bends*."

"She's got a point," said Sarita. Alex allowed herself a smile.

"You think Sean went to Silicon City? You think he could have gone there after he died here?" Monique's face was pinched.

"No," said Alex. "Before."

"He's dead. He shot himself at 9.37pm the night before last. There's no way you can have seen him yesterday morning. You're talking nonsense." Monique gave Sarita a hard look. Sarita twisted her lips.

"Right," said Alex. "But he had the smell."

"What exactly is this goddamn smell?" asked Monique. She had deep shadows under her eyes and her normally smooth skin was dull and flaky.

Alex considered. "It's sharp. Pungent. It reminds me of something, but I can't place it."

"Well think a bit harder."

"I'm trying. But it's different every time. Sometimes it makes you want to chop your nose off and forget you ever smelled it. Sometimes it's almost... almost addictive."

"Sounds like glue to me," muttered Mike.

"That's it!"

"What? It's just glue?" Mike looked disappointed.

"It's not glue. Not exactly. But that's the closest I can

think of. PVA glue. I smelt it in the lab, and yesterday. On Sean. Or his doppelganger."

"Which means…" began Sarita.

"Which means he's jumped," said Alex.

"That's impossible." Monique looked over Alex's head, at Sarita. "Isn't it?"

"Only *we* have a Spinner."

"Well if he smells like someone who's jumped, maybe there's more than one Spinner," said Mike.

"No way," said Sarita.

"I suggest we go back there and find out." Mike was getting to his feet.

"But if it was our Sean, even with the timey-wimey thing," said Alex, "that's pointless. He's dead now."

"We have to try," said Mike. "Maybe it isn't him who jumped. Maybe he's been with someone who has." He gave Sarita a suspicious look.

"There's only one Spinner," she said. "We'd know."

Alex shifted forward in her chair. "What has CSI said about his suicide?"

"It's clean," said Monique. "Nothing suspicious at all. He used his own gun to shoot himself once, through the back of the head. No one else was in his apartment."

"What about his boyfriend? Philip Gladstone?"

"In New York on a business trip."

"That's very convenient."

"Hold on," said Mike. "Maybe whoever killed Claire killed Sean too. Maybe it's them who jumped."

"That's absurd," said Sarita.

Monique leaned across the desk. The anger had gone from her face and was replaced by a weariness Alex had not seen so far.

"We can't argue with the forensics."

Alex felt her shoulders slump.

"But," said Monique.

Alex perked up. "But?"

"But it doesn't do any harm to check it out."

Mike let out a breathy whistle.

"You're letting us go back?" asked Alex.

"Just Mike. Get back there, and observe. Do not, I repeat not, draw attention to yourself."

"I want Alex with me," said Mike.

"You what?" Monique stood up. "Yesterday you told me she was a liability."

"We don't jump alone. And she can smell this… whatever it is. She can help."

Alex stifled a smile.

"I won't touch anything. I'll stick with Mike, and I'll keep away from Sean if we see him."

"Hmm."

Alex waited. Monique sighed. She looked at Mike, who nodded. "Alright then. But your remit is very, very clear. You're to watch Claire's apartment. You're to see if you can track down Sean, see what he's up to. On no account must either of them know that you're watching them."

Alex and Mike nodded.

"You do nothing to draw attention to yourselves. You don't use that box."

"They can't," said Sarita.

"What?" said Mike.

"It's fritzed. It'll take me a week to fix it."

"But you're a materials genius."

'Very kind of you to say so, Mike," replied Sarita. "But it's Hive tech. It'll take a while to fix."

Monique shook her head. "We have to work with what we have. Get back there. Look for him. Or for anyone who might be from here."

# 37

# EARPIECE

## MOO
### 28 March, 10:50am

"**Y**ou want your own earpiece?"

Alex nodded, hoping Mike and the Prof couldn't hear. They were back at MOO, having jumped about twenty minutes earlier. She'd told Madonna that she had something she needed to discuss with her about her clothing, and that it was of a delicate feminine nature. She'd taken care to compliment Madonna on her hair—piled on top of her head today and resembling a swirl of ice cream. She hoped it was enough.

"Sarita told me you could supply one."

"She didn't tell you about the risks."

"No." She wasn't lying; it was Mike who'd told her about the risks associated with people from their Earth using the earpieces. But she had quizzed Sarita about them before their jump, in the guise of finding out more about the Pearl. It turned out that only those people who had a Hive Earth doppelgänger would suffer. Something to do with the system shorting out when simultaneously confronted with two users having the same genetic code. She, Alex, didn't exist here in Silicon City. Or anywhere on Hive Earth, as far as she was aware.

"People from your Earth tried them before. The results aren't nice."

"Only if you have an opposite number here. I don't."

Madonna frowned. "She shouldn't be telling you that kind of thing."

Alex shrugged. "Look me up."

Madonna considered her suggestion for a moment. Then she put her finger to her ear and closed her eyes, losing herself in the Hive.

After a few moments Madonna opened her eyes again.

"There's no Alex Strand here."

Alex didn't know whether to be relieved or disappointed. She considered asking whether there ever had been an Alex Strand, but then decided she didn't want to know. Not yet, anyway. Besides, having two of her here would just complicate things, once she tracked down her mom.

"Good," she said. "Then you can let me have one?"

"I'm not sure."

"Think of it as research. I'll need a Pearl too."

Madonna twisted her face into a shape that made the beauty spot above her lip disappear into her cheek. "It's a touch irregular," she said. "I'll need to consult with Nemesis."

"Don't!"

"Why not?"

Alex wasn't sure she could talk two people into this. "Sarita said this was top secret. She said you could be trusted. Another woman, you know."

Madonna raised an eyebrow. "Not sure what that has

to do with it, darling." The Prof and Mike were approaching. Mike had a thick, bushy beard. It made him look like he would either serve her a coffee or write her a computer program.

"Please?" said Alex, falling back on her sweetest smile.

Madonna sighed. "Oh, alright. Here."

She slipped a small device into Alex's hand and Alex put it straight into the pocket of her black velvet coat. This one may be Madonna's regulation black, but the velvet felt good, reminding her of that couple in the coffee shop.

"Thanks," she whispered.

"You'll be using a Hackney this time," said the Prof, finally approaching them. "We can't risk the car. I gave Mike my credit card."

"Credit card?"

The Prof laughed at her. "We still have such antediluvian things, my dear. They can come in useful in an emergency. Something I hope we won't be experiencing again."

"No. You won't," said Alex. Without that dumb bitbox to malfunction on them, what could possibly go wrong?

THEY ARRIVED at Claire's in less than three minutes, the Hackney gliding along the shores of the Bay this time instead of taking the roads. Alex was becoming accustomed to the comfort. She wondered if Sarita might be able to replicate whatever technology made these so comfortable. It could be the best invention since the kilt.

Alex glanced at the coffee shop as they alighted and considered offering to fetch a coffee, then remembered the barista's reaction to takeout and decided against it. Besides, Mike would roast her head on a spit if she suggested it again.

They walked into the building in as casual manner as they could, waiting for the receptionist to recognize them and turn them out. But today there was someone different sitting at the desk. Instead of the orange-hued man, there was an elderly woman, like a blue-skinned version of Madge.

Mike showed an ID badge instead of the bitbox this time and the woman waved them through, looking bored. Alex was puzzled by how all this old tech was getting them access. Surely they were past this sort of thing? Or maybe it was like stores still taking cash at home, or using a bus pass.

They headed for the elevator and went up to the sixth floor.

"Shouldn't we take the stairs?" asked Alex. "In case we spot him again."

She thought of the manila envelope Rik had given her, at home on her kitchen table. If she came across Sean again, she knew what she was looking for.

"I doubt we'd get that lucky twice. But maybe we should take a look around the building, see if we can find any sign of him."

"How?" They were on the sixth floor now, making their way along the corridor. The poppies waved at them in an artificial breeze. There was no other movement.

He shrugged. "Let's check out Claire's apartment first."

They entered the apartment from the previous day and Alex squinted, shielding her eyes from the disorientating effect of that gravity-defying furniture. Mike headed for the window and leaned against it, shielding his eyes with his hands. He reached inside his jacket pocket and bought out a tiny pair of binoculars.

"Where did you get those?"

"Nemesis let me have them. He felt bad that we didn't have any tech."

"Cool." So she wasn't the only one persuading members of MOO to furnish her with equipment. Binoculars were nothing on what she had in her pocket, though.

He turned back to the window. "She's there. In her kitchen."

"Good." Alex stood next to him, trying to work out which of the windows opposite belonged to Claire. "What's she doing?"

"Not sure. She's on the floor. Crouching."

"Why would she do that?"

He shrugged.

"Can I take a look?"

Mike handed her the binoculars. Alex stepped away from the window to eliminate glare then raised them to her eyes. They were like no binoculars she'd ever used. Instead of making the view seem bigger, they made it sharp and immediate, as if she was watching Claire on a TV screen. She hesitated. What if Sean was somewhere else in this building, doing the same thing as them? A shiver ran down her back.

"I feel like a peeping Tom," she said.

Mike shrugged. "Comes with the territory. What's she doing?"

"Making a coffee. Drinking it. There's a dog next to her, maybe that's why she was crouching." She pulled the binoculars away and looked at him. "We're never going to get anywhere like this. She doesn't do anything, does she? She's a hermit."

"So what do you suggest?"

Alex thought of the earpiece in her pocket. If she went into the Hive, could she use it to make contact with Claire? Was there a virtual space corresponding to this physical one, in which she could travel down in the elevator, cross the street, and head up to Claire's apartment? In the virtual world, would Claire's door be even better secured than her San Francisco one? Or would she just be able to fly over there and knock on the window, like a cross between Superman and a particularly nosey window cleaner?

She sniffed.

"I need to use the bathroom," she said. "I assume there's one here?"

Mike nodded. "Off the hallway. Don't take too long."

She nodded. Would time in the Hive flow at the same speed as time outside? Would she have time to find Claire and maybe Sean, and then look her own parents up, before they had to get home?

There was only one way to find out.

# 38

# DOLORES

Silicon City
28 March, 12:05pm

The bathroom had orange-tiled walls up to waist height, then wood paneling above which looked like imitation teak. The bathroom suite was a shade of avocado. Alex was relieved that the plumbing in this world looked as if it functioned the same way as in hers.

She closed the door behind her and gathered her thoughts. She didn't have much time; what were her priorities?

After the roasting Monique had given her this morning, the first priority had to be the case. Claire first. Then Sean. Family last.

The toilet flushed almost silently and the lid eased itself closed with a sigh that belied its retro appearance.

Then she sat down on the lid and fished the earpiece from her pocket.

She turned it over in her hand a few times. It was an

odd-looking thing, like a hearing aid had mated with an earbud and grown itself a tail. The tail was thin and looked to be made of organic material. She shuddered; could this thing make direct contact with her brain?

She took a few deep breaths, fighting nausea. Everyone in this world did this. She couldn't chicken out now.

She lifted it to her ear and closed her eyes. Slowly, she fed the tail into her ear. She felt it move inside her, as if it was seeking something out. It tickled. Then she pushed it in deeper and the sensation turned to pain, like having your ears syringed when you hadn't bothered to soften the wax first. She hesitated. Should she pull it out? Was she supposed to feel pain, or was it a warning? She'd never seen anyone in this city insert an earpiece; they'd always just activated one that was already in place. Maybe they were designed to be inserted once and then never removed. If that was the case, would she ever be able to extract this thing? And what would happen when she jumped back home? This was certainly man-made, and she had no idea how it would react to the Spinner.

*Breathe*, she told herself. She squeezed her eyes shut and held the earpiece still, letting it send its tendrils deep into her ear. She swallowed. There was a dull metallic taste at the back of her throat. *Don't be sick, don't be sick*, she thought.

Finally the earpiece settled down and became still. She patted her ear; it seemed to be firmly inserted, the visible part snug inside her ear. She took a few breaths.

She tried to picture the people she had seen operating these things. What was it they did?

She heard Mike's voice outside.

"Are you going to be long in there?"

"Sorry. The jump has caught up with me. Delayed reaction."

If he thought she was bringing up her banana and porridge breakfast, he wouldn't venture in here.

"Eww. Be as quick as you can."

"OK."

It was now or never. She closed her eyes and put her finger on the earpiece. She let her body slacken, waiting for the Hive to envelop her, to plunge her into a virtual world.

Nothing. She heard the flush finish. Outside, Mike was moving around.

She tried to loosen her eyelids, removing the tension in her face. It wasn't easy. She took one deep breath, then another, pursing her lips and focusing on the air passing through them. Maybe she should've gone on the Mindfulness course back at Berkeley.

She twisted her finger on the earpiece. Maybe there was a special move. And then, all of a sudden, the world turned purple.

She resisted the temptation to open her eyes. Was she in the Hive, or had Mike just turned on some lights? She held her breath, waiting. Nothing happened for a few moments, and then a trail of pink bubbles floated upwards in front of her closed eyes. They were followed by more: pinks, yellows, reds. It was beautiful.

Should she open her eyes?

*Let's try it*, she thought. She eased them open, waiting for the bathroom to reappear.

It wasn't there. She stood in a long thin room with a window at one end. She looked up and down the space. Where was she?

She walked to the window. The carpet beneath her feet turned to grass as she passed over it. Long, yellowing grass interspersed with poppies. She reached down and brushed them with her fingertips. Then she looked back and saw that the floor behind her had turned back into a pale pink carpet. It was thick and luxurious, but it wasn't a poppy field.

She pulled in a deep breath. The air was clean and fresh. She looked up to see a blue sky above her head. Was she outside?

Ahead of her, where the carpet became pink, the walls were definitely there. They were purple, with orange and yellow bubbles passing up them.

She high-fived the empty air. She didn't expect this. No wonder people in Silicon City spent their whole lives in here.

At the far end of the corridor was that window. She hurried towards it, hoping it would tell her where she was. She leaned against it and looked out.

She was in the same building, across the street from Claire's. Opposite her, formless shapes moved in the windows. She couldn't remember which apartment was Claire's. She searched her mind for a memory of where she'd looked before, through those binoculars. Sixth floor, on the front corner, but the windows reflected the sun and she couldn't see inside. She blinked a few times. Suddenly the reflections cleared and her gaze focused in on them, like the binoculars but clearer. Claire was sitting on her bed, sipping coffee. Alex watched as she put her mug on the bedside table and walked to the window. She pulled the drapes closed.

Alex squinted. Would this technology allow her to look inside?

A voice sounded inside her head. *Warning. Privacy law violation risk.*

She laughed. Even in this virtual world, there were rules. Of course there would be. And the system prevented transgressions. Now she knew why she'd seen no evidence of a police force.

So she knew where Claire was. Tick one. Now for Sean.

She tried to cast her mind around the building she was in, exploring behind doors and into unoccupied rooms. She could gain access to most of the apartments on the floor she was on. But they were all empty. She tried to travel through a third door, but came up against that warning again. So she couldn't go into a room if it had someone inside. Or at least not someone who hadn't invited her in. She was a virtual vampire.

If Sean was here, he would be behind one of those doors. How was she to find him?

Then it occurred to her. She retreated along the corridor and stood in front of the elevator. There was no sign of a panel. She reached into her mind; was there a way to summon it mentally?

No sooner had she asked herself the question, than the doors swish-thunked their way open. The sound was even more pleasing than in the real version of Silicon City. She laughed again and gave the wall a gentle punch as she stepped into the elevator.

*Warning. Potential property damage violation.*

Oops. "Sorry."

This system was like having the world's most boring teacher looking over your shoulder all the time.

She willed the elevator to hurry and it did, speeding downstairs at a pace that made her worry about the impact at the bottom. When it reached the first floor it slowed and came to a gentle rest. She looked at the doors and they opened.

The receptionist was nowhere to be seen. The lobby area had metamorphosed from a featureless, blank space to something resembling the bridge of the Starship Enterprise, Captain Picard version.

"Make it so," she muttered to herself. She ran to one of the displays, running her fingers over it. But it was just decorative.

She needed to get on with her job. She pushed through the doors and out into the street. It was deserted. She felt something brush her hair and looked up. Above her, its trunk skimming her head, a purple elephant floated past. Two more followed it.

She darted across the street and entered the building opposite. Again, the foyer was empty. She paused, expecting another replica of the Starship Enterprise. But this was the Tardis, Matt Smith version.

"I love this place!" she shouted, her voice echoing off of the central console.

The elevator doors were, of course, blue. She looked at them a moment and then raised her hand. She clicked her fingers. They opened.

Inside the elevator, she thought about the sixth floor.

*Sixth floor. Coming right up.* Was that the voice of Amy Pond?

The elevator doors swished open. If she was lucky, the apartment corresponding to Mike's would be empty. She ran along the corridor, feeling the space around her turn into a mountain range as she moved. She put her hand on the final door and it opened. *Yes.*

The apartment was devoid of furniture; nothing to attack her eyes, trip her over or make her doubt the anatomy of her own body. She rushed to the window and leaned against it.

She quieted, her gaze traveling over the building opposite. A purple elephant, larger than the one she'd seen before, passed in front of her, blocking her vision. She scowled and it metamorphosed into a replica of

Schrödinger which would be one hundred per cent accurate if it weren't ten feet long. And flying.

"Not you again."

He turned to her, waved a paw languorously then blinked out of existence.

She could see into the windows of the building opposite now. There he was. Mike, standing in the window, peering out through binoculars. He looked as if he was in a gray bubble, a little pouch of the real world surrounded by virtual lunacy.

She let her gaze travel along the windows of his floor, searching.

Then she stopped.

Standing in the window four along from Mike, staring straight at her, was Sean Wolf.

She threw her arms out, almost losing her balance in the shock of his intense stare. She pulled back. Had he seen her? Of course he had; he was in the Hive too. Did he know who she was, why she had come here? Did he remember her from the day before?

This window had sheer drapes on either side. They seemed to be made of a fine yellow gossamer that reminded her of butterfly wings. She pulled them closed, hoping this would hide her. He was still there. Four windows along from Mike. He held a pair of binoculars that looked like a bright blue version of the ones Mike held, with pink tassels hanging from them.

She backed away and sat down. So Sean was here. And those binoculars could only mean one thing; he was watching Claire.

She had to get back to Mike, tell him what she'd seen. How she'd do that without revealing that she'd gone inside the Hive, she had no idea. She'd expected an entire virtual world, something completely removed from reality. What she was experiencing was more like augmented reality, a rendering of the world with an added sheen of gloss and whimsy. Now she knew how all those Hivers avoided crashing into each other.

But she had one more objective. Did she have time for a quick poke around in virtual space, before going back and warning Mike?

"Hive," she said, feeling silly.

"Call me Malcolm," it replied in a British accent.

"Seriously? Malcolm?"

"Or you can use one of the twenty-three alternative names available, if you prefer."

"What have you got?"

It started listing names, in the tones of a well-spoken man from the English home counties. Was that Benedict Cumberbatch's voice?

She found a name she liked.

"Doris, please set an alarm."

"Doris? What kinda name is that?" the AI asked her in a Southern drawl.

"It's one of the options you gave me."

"Urrgh. It's ghastly. Call me Dolores, if you must."

"Dolores. Please set an alarm."

"Why certainly. For when would you like me to set the alarm?" it said in a voice that sounded a lot like Blanche from *Golden Girls*.

What was it about AIs?

"Five minutes."

"Five minutes what?"

"Er, five minutes from now?"

"The word you're looking for, honeybunch, is please."

"Five minutes, *please*."

"Certainly, sweet pea. Would you like me to bring you back to this room at that time?"

"Yes. Please." She hesitated. "No, hang on a moment."

"And what exactly would you like me to hang on to?"

She rolled her eyes. "Can you send me back to the room I was in when I entered the Hive? The bathroom?"

"I sure can."

"Thank you. Dolores."

"That's my pleasure, sweetie."

Alex took a deep breath and prepared to dive deep into the Hive.

# 39

# MORSE

Silicon City
28 March, 12:51pm

Mike wasn't in the mood for surveillance. It would be so easy to just leave a camera in here and let that do the grunt work.

But Monique liked the human touch. And besides, any video evidence he did manage to bring back would be destroyed in the jump.

None of this was made any easier by having a partner who went running off to the bathroom every five minutes.

He took a last look over at the building opposite then went to the bathroom door. He gave a gentle knock.

There was no reply.

"Alex?" he called.

No answer.

"We need to get moving soon."

Again, no response.

They didn't have long. She'd have to save her

upchucking for the journey back. He was sure there'd be more of it then.

He knocked again, more forcefully this time.

"C'mon Alex, I need you out here. We have a job to do."

Nothing.

This was getting out of hand. First they'd given him a partner who looked like an extra in an episode of *Outlander*. Then she turned out to have a stomach that was about as resilient as a kitten in a tornado.

"I'm coming in."

He leaned into the door.

"Last warning. Make sure you're presentable."

He waited. How long would that take her?

He counted to sixty. That should do it.

"OK. Open the door now, Alex, or I'm coming in."

He pulled back and then slammed into the door with all his weight. It didn't budge. He tried again, feeling it shift a little this time. On the second attempt it fell open.

"Alex?"

She was slumped on the toilet, her eyes closed. In her ear was an earpiece. Hive technology.

"No!" he cried.

He considered trying to rouse her. But that might cause permanent brain damage.

He grabbed the mobile phone Madonna had given him. Old tech, but it still worked in some places.

He dialed the only number in its memory.

"Mike? What's up?"

"Sarita?" That was unexpected.

"Yes. Be quick. Tell me the problem."

"It's Alex. You asked me to tell you if she did anything odd."

"Can't this wait until she's back here?"

"No. She's gone in."

"Gone in where?"

"In the Hive."

"She's *what*? How did she get an earpiece? Where is she?"

"She's in the bathroom. She pretended she was sick. She's slumped on the pan, out of it."

"Don't disturb her."

"You sure? I shouldn't pull her out?"

"We have no idea how that would affect her. Just leave her be. She isn't to know that you saw her. Or that you've spoken to me."

"I disagree. She needs to be pulled out. And I'm not lying to her."

"Mike." Sarita's voice was harsh. "Do as I say. It's important. And watch her. Find out why she did it."

# 40

# HIVE

The Hive
28 March, 12:51pm

Alex waited, looking at the drapes. They'd started shimmering now, bright swathes of color drifting across their surface. These would look great in her bedroom.

Then it happened. She blinked, and all of a sudden she was outside, miles away. Two-point-two miles away, to be precise.

In front of her was the Hall of Justice. Not the low, mercury-like building in Silicon City, but the real one, the one in San Francisco. Had the Hive sent her home?

No. It was just picking images from her head.

She headed toward the revolving doors. People were coming out, talking amongst themselves. None of them wore earpieces. A man crashed into her.

"Sorry," he said, and continued on his way. He didn't register anything unusual about her.

She pushed at the door. It didn't budge. She pushed

again. Nothing. She leaned her weight into it, puzzled. Still no movement.

A group approached from inside. She stepped back, waiting to hop into the doors as they started moving. But when she tried, she couldn't. It was as if an invisible force field was preventing her from going inside.

"Dolores, why can't I get in?" she said.

"Can't get in where, honey?"

"Can't get in this building. The Hall of Justice."

"You mean you are unable to enter the building, not *can't get in*. Tut. And this is not a building. It's a figment of your imagination."

*Tell me something I don't know*, she thought. "OK. But why can't I get inside?"

"Inside what, my dear?"

"Inside the Hall of Justice. Why can't I *enter it*?"

"Oh, that. You can't enter a building you created in your head, because it don't exist."

"It does. I went there."

"Not in Silicon City, you have not."

Alex wrinkled her nose, wishing there was some physical manifestation of the AI that she could give a good slap.

Then a woman materialized next to her. She looked just like Blanche from *Golden Girls* except she had a large ginger cat cradled in her arms, and wore an apron of shimmering satin over a pink and blue silk dress.

"Schrödinger?" Alex said.

"Meow."

"Rather a handsome fellow, ain't he?" said Dolores.

Alex put a proprietorial hand on Schrödinger's back. He purred. "Is he real?"

"As real as anything, honey. You wanted me?"

Alex stared at her. She looked too kindly to slap. "Sorry. No."

There was a kind of puff, like the sound Alex's phone made when it sent an email. Dolores/Blanche disappeared. So did Schrödinger.

"Maybe you're looking in the wrong place," came her disembodied voice.

Alex stepped away from the doors. "How long do I have?"

"I'm sorry, I don't understand."

"How long till my alarm?"

"You have no alarms set."

"Yes, I do. I asked you to set an alarm for five minutes. I said please."

"You would like me to set an alarm for five minutes?"

"No! I already did. How long until you're scheduled to pull me out of the Hive?"

"Oh, that. Three and a half minutes. Give or take thirteen seconds or so."

"Thank you," Alex said through gritted teeth. She didn't have long.

She turned away from the building, surveying the street. This was the familiar sight of Bryant Street from her own world. Bail bond agencies flanked the opposite corners and a cop stood outside, leaning on his motorcycle and squinting at her.

Along the street was a phone booth. Probably out of use, most likely vandalized. But it might give her access to records. Virtually speaking.

She hurried along the street, shimmying through the crowds. It felt good to be back in her own city.

She bundled herself into the booth. There was a shelf, covered in graffiti. And on top of it, something she'd never seen before. Or at least it looked like…

"Dolores, what is this?"

"It's a telephone directory, sweet pea."

She started rifling through it. It was thick already, but as she flicked through, it seemed to morph around her hands, the sections she had leafed through dematerializing and being replaced with more that she hadn't looked at yet. Was this an infinite phone book?

"Dolores, please tell me what geographical area this phone book covers."

"The entirety of Planet Earth."

"Which version?"

"I'm sorry, honey. I don't understand you."

"Hive Earth, or Old Earth, as you call it?"

"I don't call it anything, darlin'."

Alex sighed. "Does this phone book correspond to the virtual world in which I'm standing right now, or the real world outside the Hive?"

"Oh. I do know that. The phone book corresponds to the real world. Does that answer your question?"

"Not quite. Which real world?"

"Why, this one, of course."

"Thank you."

"Glad to be of service."

"Thank you."

"Meow."

"Shrew? Do you still have him?"

"As I said, he's a very handsome young man."

"Be nice to him."

"Would you expect different of me?"

Alex opened her mouth to speak and then thought better of it; a conversation with Dolores could last a lifetime. Instead, she pictured her own name in her mind, the letters spelled out in the kind of blocky serif font you'd find in a phone book. The book's pages started shifting beneath her fingers as it rifled through itself. Eventually it came to a halt with the back cover facing upwards and the book closed in front in her.

She pictured her name again, substituting *Alexandra* for *Alex* this time. The book flicked through itself again, working from back to front this time. After a few seconds, it stopped, with the front cover on top and the book closed again.

She closed her eyes again, picturing her mom's name. *Heather Strand*. The same result. Then she tried her mom's maiden name; *Heather MacDonald*. Still no result. Feeling at a low ebb, she tried it with her dad's name. Again, nothing.

"You might want to try a previous version of the phone directory," said the disembodied voice of Dolores.

"I'm sorry?"

"The book you are searching through corresponds to the Earth of this exact second. Try working backwards."

She stared at the book. That would take too long. "Dolores, can you speed this up?"

"I thought you'd never ask."

She smiled. "Good. Please can you find me the most recent phone record for Alex, or Alexandra Strand, and for Heather and Duncan Strand."

"Of course. There is no record of an Alex or Alexandra Strand. Nor an Alexandria, an Alexandre, a Xander, an Alexa, Alexis, Alejandra, Alastrina, Aleka—"

"OK, OK. I get the idea. I don't exist here. I never have. What about my parents?"

"The most recent record of their names is in 1997. In Gretna, Scotland, United Kingdom."

She felt her heart lighten. So her parents did exist after all! But why no record of them after that? Not even her dad?"

"Dolores, how long do I have now?"

"Based on your current heart rate, muscle tone and the

kind of food you eat, I estimate that you have approximately forty-eight years and four months. And a day."

"I didn't want to know how long I have left to live." Was her diet really that unhealthy? "How long before you're due to pull me out of the Hive?"

"Oh, that. Two seconds."

"Two seconds?"

"One second."

"One?"

"Zero seconds. Sorry, honey."

Alex felt a rush of air. The street around her went hazy and the phone booth began to shimmer. She put a hand out to steady herself. It rested on something cold and smooth. She opened her eyes to see an avocado bathtub. She leaned over and threw up into it, feeling the earpiece fall from her ear.

"You OK in there?" It was Mike, outside the bathroom in the apartment opposite Claire's. So Dolores had done exactly as she'd asked. That was the biggest surprise so far.

She raised her arm and stuck her thumb up, then realized he wouldn't see. She shifted her weight to bend over the toilet and hurled noisily into it. Going into the Hive did have a physical effect on her after all.

She took a deep breath and pushed herself up, closing her eyes. She grabbed the earpiece from the floor and pushed the door open. Mike was standing outside, looking like he'd just swallowed the kind of wasp that could go five rounds in a wrestling ring. That made a change from him looking annoyed.

"You look like hell," he said.

"Thanks. Can I get a glass of water?"

He went to the kitchen and returned with a tall blue glass filled with water. She drank it in one.

"Thanks. Get me another one, will you? Just in case."

"Here." He already had a second glass in his other hand. She smiled her thanks.

"What were you doing in there?" he asked.

"How long was I gone?"

"About an hour."

"I've got something to tell you."

He raised an eyebrow.

"Let's sit down, near the window," she said. "I need to look at the horizon."

He led her to the windows, pausing occasionally to look over his shoulder and wait for her to catch up. At last they reached the cool glass and she leaned against it. She eased herself to the floor. The cold surface on her cheek felt good.

She took a deep breath, hoping her enfeebled state would prevent him from losing it when she told him what she was really doing.

"I went into the Hive," she said.

He cocked his head.

She pulled the earpiece out of her pocket. "I got one of these. I went in."

"What did you do that for?"

She closed her eyes, trying to ignore her stomach. "I wanted to find Sean."

"You could've died."

"I checked first."

"What is there to check?"

"If you don't exist here. If you don't have an opposite number. It means you can use the Hive. It doesn't like duplicates, or something."

"So does that mean they lied to us? MOO?"

She shook her head, then regretted it. "I think they're trying to protect us. I had to persuade Madonna to give me this. I told her to look me up."

Mike paled. Alex could hear his breathing, short and sharp.

"Did she look *me* up?" he asked, in a small voice.

"If she did, she didn't tell me."

"Right. So what was it like?"

"What?"

"The Hive, of course. Is it as bizarre as everything else around here?"

She allowed herself a chuckle. "It's like augmented reality. You're traveling in the same physical space, but with a virtual layer added on top. And you can make things happen just by thinking about them."

"What did you make happen?"

She looked at the building opposite. "I went over there. I found the apartment opposite this one. I saw you, watching Claire from over there."

"I didn't see you."

"I'm not sure I was really there."

"Oh."

"I saw Sean too."

"Sean?"

"Her ex."

"I know who he is, dummy. Where did you see him?"

She swallowed. Her throat felt as if it might spontaneously combust. "He's four windows along, behind me."

Mike's eyes widened. "In this building?"

"Yes. He's watching her too."

"We have to get back to base. God knows what Monique will make of this."

"No, Mike. We have to find him."

"We have our orders. Don't interfere."

"But he's watching her. She's in danger, you already said. We can't just up and go."

"It's not as simple as that."

"Why ever not?"

"I've handled too many cases like this. Too many cases where someone has died in one version of San Francisco and is perfectly fine in the other."

"But there's too much coincidence going on here."

"Wait," interrupted Mike. "But then, maybe with a delay of a few days, they mirror each other."

"What d'you mean?"

"Events repeat themselves in the other world. Someone who dies here also dies there, and vice versa. It's happened too many times, Alex. Claire may be alive here now, but she's at risk. If we get this right, we can prevent both their deaths. We have to tell Monique."

**41**

---

## GLUONS

San Francisco
28 March, 3:46pm

Monique was under stress, and it was showing.

Her hair looked like it hadn't been washed or brushed since yesterday, and her skin had a blank dullness that came from wearing foundation but no other makeup.

She sat behind a mountain of files on her desk, stifling a yawn as Mike brought her up to speed.

"It was definitely Sean?" she asked, steepling her fingers in front of her face and resting her nose on them.

"Yes," said Alex. "He was watching Claire's building. In Silicon City."

Monique sighed. She'd lost the fire that Alex had noticed in her, and looked like someone who'd be happier curling up for a nap under her desk than sitting in this meeting.

"I know it doesn't make sense," said Alex.

Monique dropped her face into her hands. "Nothing

about this case is making sense right now. I think we have to discount what you've seen in Silicon City. I think this is that rare case where there's no relationship between what's going on in the two worlds."

Alex cleared her throat. "I disagree."

Monique looked up, a flash of the old fire crossing her face. "I beg your pardon?"

"She's right," said Mike. He turned to Alex. "You smelled it, didn't you?"

She nodded.

"Where?" asked Monique.

"The stairwell in Claire's building. It was full of it. Someone there had jumped."

Alex's eyes widened. "I know what it is," she said. "And Sean was covered in it."

"Yup," said Mike, not looking all that sure he knew what Alex was talking about. His credibility wasn't helped by the fact that his beard had turned white and bushy. It was as if Santa Claus had come down from the North Pole to solve the crime.

"I asked my lab partner to run some tests," said Alex. "The smell. It's the same thing we get with our research. The same thing my cat smells of."

Monique stood up. "Your cat?"

"I know what it is now. Rik got a pal in the Chemistry department to analyze it."

"You mean you've been telling your Berkeley buddies about the MIU."

"No, absolutely not. I told them it was for something else. That you've hired me as an expert witness."

"Hmm. So tell me, what it this substance?"

"It's gluons."

"Gluons?"

"They're subatomic particles," said Mike. Alex grinned at him; he'd been paying attention.

"What are subatomic particles?" asked Monique.

"Errr…" said Mike. He looked at Alex.

"They're really really tiny things," said Alex, "way smaller than a molecule, or an atom. Hence subatomic. They're the building blocks of the universe."

"I wish I hadn't asked."

"Look," she said. "Rik and I are doing this experiment—well, we aren't really doing it, Professor Katz does most of the good stuff—but we're analyzing it. It's called the Cheshire Cat experiment. We use something called an interferometer."

Monique sighed. "Maybe you should go back to your day job."

"That's what I'm saying. The interferometer, it produced the same smell. The night Claire died. I got my lab partner to run the data."

"Your lab partner?"

"I didn't tell him what it was for. It's gluons. And that's what I smelled on Sean."

"Our Sean, or Silicon City Sean?"

"Both. It's the same guy."

"How can it be the same guy, when our version is dead?"

"Mike told me."

Monique looked from Alex to Mike and shrugged.

"The temporal delay," he said. "Nemesis told me it's something to do with general relativity."

"Jeez." Monique pulled a hand through her tangled hair. "More oddball physics."

"But it messes with time when you jump," said Alex. "It's the gravitational field in the Spinner. That's why there's a delay between crimes in the two worlds."

"Wait a sec." Monique stood up. "You're telling me that the version of Sean in that world is an earlier one than in this world?"

"Yes. And in that world he's going to die too."

"But Claire's still alive over there."

"She was. We don't know if she still is."

"How can Claire be behind us over there but Sean be ahead?"

"It's to do with whether someone has jumped. I believe Sean has."

Mike stood to face Monique. "She's right," he said. "She has it. The Sean we saw over there isn't our Sean's doppelgänger. He's the same guy."

# 42

# RAMIFICATIONS

San Francisco
28 March, 3:52pm

Alex's heart was pounding. Monique looked between her and Mike. She didn't seem convinced.

"I think we should go back," Alex said. "See if we can make contact with either of them."

"Don't be absurd," replied Monique. "The first rule of the MIU is you never make contact with someone in Silicon City who's part of a case here."

Alex said nothing.

"Understood?" asked Monique.

"Understood."

"Good. How did you get into Claire's building, anyway? That's how you're saying you saw him watching?"

Alex felt her skin run cold. She waited for Mike to tell Monique what she'd done. She racked her brains for a convincing lie but nothing came.

"Alex discovered that the entry code worked for both buildings," said Mike. "The code we had for the apartment I hired worked for its opposite number in the other building."

Alex wanted to hug him.

Monique raised an eyebrow. "Really? That seems a little lax."

Mike shrugged. "Most people over there move between buildings inside the Hive. I guess security works differently."

Monique scratched her nose. "Maybe so. Well done, Alex. Nice work. Sorry it's no use to us."

Monique folded her arms. "Now get lost, the both of you. I need to think."

Mike stood up. "So we can jump?" he asked.

Monique frowned. She tapped her desk with her fingernails. Alex winced.

"Not yet. I need to consider the ramifications. I need to get someone to talk to Sean's next of kin."

Alex hesitated. "But what if—"

Monique glared at her. "Didn't you hear me?"

Alex nodded. She followed Mike toward the door.

"Thanks," she whispered. He shrugged.

Sarita was approaching beyond the glass. Alex stiffened; what now?

Mike opened the door. Sarita pushed past him, glaring at Alex.

"Is it true?" she hissed at Alex. She glanced at Monique, who was opening up her laptop.

"Is what true?" asked Alex.

"You talked Madonna into giving you an earpiece. You went into the Hive."

Alex looked back at Monique, then shook her head at Sarita; *not here*.

Sarita licked her lips then looked from Alex to Monique and back again. Her face was damp with sweat and her hair, normally piled impressively on top of her head, was slipping to one side. Had she sprinted up here?

She grabbed Alex's arm and pulled her outside.

"Do you know how risky that was?" she muttered. "You might have died. Or worse."

"What's worse than dying?"

Sarita gave her a look. "Not just *you* dying. Who's to say if it could have affected Mike, or the MOO guys, or any of us?"

"I checked it out," replied Alex, trying to keep calm. "I asked Madonna to check that there isn't another me over there."

"So?"

Alex frowned. "Surely you know that it's only people with a Hive doppelgänger who can't go in? Something about confusing the system with duplicates."

Sarita glared at her. "You're a fool, Alex. I should tell Monique."

"Er, guys," muttered Mike.

Alex spun round.

"Tell Monique what?"

Alex felt her muscles slacken. Monique was standing in the doorway to her office, watching.

"Hi," said Alex, trying to sound nonchalant. "How long have you been standing there?"

"Long enough. What the hell did I recruit you for, Strand?"

"I got results. I found Sean. I used my initiative. A few minutes ago, you were pleased with me."

"A few minutes ago, I didn't know you'd broken the first rule of MIU."

'I thought you said the first rule of MIU was to—"

Monique held up her hand. "Stop. Right now, before you dig a hole so big you'll come out in Madagascar."

Alex bit her tongue. She tasted metal. Now, on top of everything, she felt like she was going to puke again. This was turning into an occupational hazard.

"Sorry."

Monique tapped her foot. "It's not good enough."

"I'm *really* sorry?"

"Don't push it. I'm taking you off the case."

"What? But we were just—"

"You were just nothing. You've broken the three biggest rules of MIU."

"I thought it was just t—"

"Are you dumb as well as stupid, Alex?"

Alex decided not to inform Monique that the two words meant the same thing. "No. Sorry."

"I'm sending you back to Berkeley. We'll have to find someone else."

Alex swallowed. "Can I pick up my stuff from downstairs, first?"

Monique raised an eyebrow. "Mike will escort you."

"Right."

<br>

ALEX SIDLED BACK to the MIU, her tail so firmly between her legs she could be mistaken for a dog. Not a cat, of course; a cat would never appear contrite.

She thought of Schrödinger in the Hive; had it been him, or a figment of her imagination? Had the sneaky ginger so-and-so found a way to travel between universes? Was that the key to the Cheshire Cat experiment?

Nemesis was hunched over a console, muttering something about bacon sandwiches. Alex peered around, hoping to see Madge. If she could talk Madonna into giving her an earpiece, maybe she could do something similar with her alter ego.

"Bye, Nemesis," she called. He waved a hand in dismissal. Had Sarita told him?

She turned for the doors to the parking lot. Mike hovered next to her.

"Sorry," he muttered. "I thought we were onto something."

"Yeah." An awkward pause. "I hope you solve the case. Keep Claire safe over there, yeah?"

"Yeah."

He shook her hand and closed the doors. She walked away, blinking back tears. She thought of her desk at Berkeley, the numbers waiting for her. Maybe she should just go back to Scotland and find another job. She could teach Science to snotty school kids.

Outside, she hesitated. She couldn't face the BART, not yet. She checked her watch; it was gone four, too late to get back to work anyway.

She needed to catch her breath.

She walked for a few blocks then slid into a diner. She could smell bacon frying. Bacon, pancakes and maple syrup. That would help, at least.

She sat down and browsed the menu. She wasn't hungry.

"Is this seat taken?"

Alex looked up to see Sarita sliding onto the bench opposite. "How did you find me?"

"You left the building as I was on my way back down. I followed you."

Alex blushed. "Oh."

"Is it good here?" Sarita picked up a menu.

"No idea."

They stared at their menus in silence. The waitress arrived and poured coffees. She waited for them to order but when she got nothing she walked away with a huff.

"Sarita, can I ask you something?"

"You can ask. You may not get an answer."

"Do you report to Monique?"

Sarita scoffed. "Of course not."

"Nemesis or Madge, then?"

Sarita laughed. "No!"

"Well, who?"

Sarita waved her menu. "Are you eating, then? That waitress is giving us dirty looks."

Alex leaned back, knowing better than to push Sarita. If there was one thing that working in the MIU had taught her, it was to wait until people were ready to divulge information.

"No. Not hungry."

Sarita raised an eyebrow. "Seriously? I heard about your appetite. It's legendary."

"Is it?" Alex blushed. Sure, she liked her food. Especially if it had no nutritional value whatever. But she didn't consider her appetite legendary. She scowled. "I didn't know my reputation preceded me."

"Sorry. I haven't gone easy on you, have I?"

Alex shrugged.

"I like your outfit by the way."

Alex looked down to see that she was still dressed in her Hive clothes. In all the anger and recriminations, no one had noticed.

"How can I make it up to you?" Sarita said.

Alex met her gaze. "It's OK. Don't bother."

"No. I mean it. I want to fix things between us. I didn't

mean for Monique to overhear this afternoon, and I'm sorry you were taken off the case."

Alex slumped down, staring at her menu. Her eyes had glazed over and the words danced in front of her, bacon mixing with blueberry pie in her mind. She fought a wave of nausea. At least there would be no more of that.

"So how can I help?" Sarita asked.

Alex looked up. "Really. It's OK. I don't want to get you into trouble."

Sarita stood up and downed her coffee. Alex sniffed. The BART wasn't far from here. A snuggle with Shrew on the couch and a few episodes of *The Good Place* were what she needed.

"Come on." Sarita put a hand on her shoulder. Alex shrugged it off.

"I already told you. It's OK. I just need to stew."

"No you don't. You need to go back."

Alex perked up. "Sorry?"

"You need to go back."

"I can't. I've been taken off the case. Nemesis isn't speaking to me, so I can't exactly march back into the MIU and ask them to stick me in the Spinner."

"You said you thought Sean had jumped. He doesn't have a Spinner, you know."

"How are you so sure?"

"I would know. Trust me. So if you think he jumped, how?"

"Huh?"

"How did he jump? Is there another way to travel between universes? You're the physicist."

Alex felt her jaw drop.

"What? Something I said?"

"You're right."

Sarita smiled, waiting for her to continue.

"There is another way. At least I think there is."
"And you're going to try it?"
"I am. I might need help though."
"Count me in."
"How good are you at building fortresses?"

43
___

## FORTRESS

Berkeley
28 March, 5:58pm

Schrödinger pretended not to watch Alex and Sarita as they built the structure in the center of Alex's living room.

They'd pushed the couch and assorted piles of physics books and pizza boxes to one side to make the most space they could in the cramped apartment. Alex wondered if there'd be more room at Sarita's place but didn't dare ask. She had no idea where Sarita lived anyway.

They'd stopped off at the 7-11 and Alex had begged the guy behind the counter for the biggest cardboard boxes he could lay his hands on. At first he'd been reluctant, thinking it was some kind of prank, but Sarita had flirted with him, giving him looks Alex wished she was on the receiving end of. It worked; they'd emerged with five of the biggest cardboard boxes Alex had ever seen. One had been from the guy's flat upstairs; it had held a TV. And another was for the computer monitor in the back-room office. The manager had been keeping it just in case, but their new ally was convinced he wouldn't notice it missing. It was at least ten years old; the monitor was CRT.

They'd spent the last half hour arranging the boxes, trying to keep them as intact as possible while combining them into a structure that would hold a human being.

"Why aren't you coming?" Alex asked Sarita as she sealed a joint with duck tape.

"Too risky. I may have a doppelganger."

"May? You'd know, surely."

"I'd rather not."

Alex considered telling Sarita about her quest to find her family, then thought better of it. Sarita had agreed to help her because they were working on the case.

"Should we fetch Mike?" Alex asked.

"He'd have to tell Monique. Chain of command, and all that. This is just you."

Alex pushed down a cardboard flap that had bashed her in the face.

"You OK doing this?" Sarita asked. "It's a big risk."

"If Shrew can do it, so can I." She eyed her cat, who stretched his front paw and yawned.

She grabbed him and held him to her chest. "I'm taking you with me, boy. I think you know more about this than I do."

"Is that a good idea?' asked Sarita. "A cat on a murder investigation?"

"He's not just any old cat. And he's been to Silicon City before. I wouldn't be doing this if I didn't believe that."

Sarita tugged at a join in the cardboard. "I think it's ready."

Alex swallowed. "You sure?"

"Alex, we've been taping up these joins for five minutes. They aren't going to get any more secure than this."

"OK." *Here goes.*

Schrödinger lay in her arms, purring as she scratched under his chin. She held him tight as she lifted one leg and then the other to climb into the cardboard fortress.

It was a structure worthy of any self-respecting five-year-old. It would even be at home in an episode of *Community*.

She stared at Sarita, who was looking back at her. Sarita's gaze traveled from Alex's face, to the fortress, to Schrödinger, and back again.

"It's not working," said Alex.

"No."

Alex looked at Schrödinger's favorite box, sitting on the kitchen counter. "I need to get fully inside. Can you close the lid?"

"You sure?"

Alex nodded, her heart pounding. How would this compare to the Spinner?

She shuffled down into the cardboard structure, taking care to hold on to her cat.

"Meow."

"Sorry boy. How do you do this, anyway?"

He yawned in response.

"You're always asleep when you do it, aren't you?"

"You have to go to sleep?" asked Sarita. "How are you going to do that?"

"Turn the lights off. The switch is over there. And close the lid. Maybe play my Cheeky Girls playlist."

"Cheeky Girls?"

"It works."

Alex curled up at the bottom of the woman-sized cardboard box. She wrapped herself around her cat, whose breathing was already slowing. She had to follow him into sleep, fast.

She closed her eyes as the dulcet tones of *Hooray, Hooray, It's a Cheeky Holiday* started on her speakers. She smiled.

She opened her eyes. "What will you do, while I'm gone?"

"Not much, I imagine."

"I mean, will you wait here, or at the MIU?"

"Let's just see what happens, huh?"

Alex swallowed the lump in her throat. Her skin felt cold. Schrödinger was fast asleep.

She closed her eyes and followed him.

**44**

———

**STIR-FRY**

Silicon City

28 March, 8:36pm

Claire had finished work for the day. She was looking forward to a cuddle with Leo followed by a home-made stir fry and a movie.

She extracted her earpiece and laid it on her desk. She rubbed her temples. She didn't like doing business inside the Hive; it felt too much like personal interaction. But she had the authority to insist on no face-to-face contact. It was all done via virtual telephone. She liked telephones, the anonymity of them. Hers, in the Hive, was an old-fashioned Bakelite number, the kind her grandparents might have had. It made a pleasing ding when she hung up.

There were problems in one of the Chinese factories that manufactured the Pearl. A labor dispute. The factory manager didn't want to meet the workers' demands; she knew it was good business to listen to them. She'd found a compromise that kept all parties happy. Production would be up and running within the hour.

"Leo?" she called. "Mommy's home."

She pushed open the door to her study, braced for the impact of him hurling himself at her. He hated it when she went into the Hive and would sulk in his basket until she re-emerged.

She stood at the door to the hallway, puzzled. If Leo was awake, he would already be on top of her, attempting to push her to the ground and lick her face. She sniffed the air; he smelled different when he was asleep. Her well-trained, confined nose could sense him rousing. Then she gagged.

The smell was new; sharp, heavy and metallic.

She swallowed; heavy, thick bile. She held still for a moment and considered hiding in the bedroom until the air filtration system had cleaned it up. But there was her beloved dog to think about.

The hallway was in darkness and there was no sign of movement. No Leo.

A movement caught her eye. The drapes in the bedroom to her right were swaying. She placed her hand over her heart, willing herself to stay upright. Had someone been in here?

# 45

# CARDBOARD

Silicon City
28 March, 8:37pm

Alex felt something wet and rough pushing at her face. She pushed it away, muttering.

Then she remembered. She opened her eyes. Above her was the familiar cardboard box. And in her arms, struggling to escape her grasp, was Schrödinger.

She kissed the top of his head. "You came with me."

"Meow."

He pulled out of her arms and disappeared through a gap in the cardboard.

She sat up and threw the cardboard to one side. "Shrew! Come back!"

But he'd gone.

She rubbed her eyes and allowed them to adjust. She wasn't in her apartment. She could smell the Bay, hear the faint hum of the electric shields she'd run into with Mike. She was in Silicon City.

She allowed herself a muttered *yes*.

Berkeley was a distance from Pacific Heights. She had to get moving.

She climbed out of the box and pushed the flaps down carefully. She'd need this for the return journey.

She was in a dark space, dim light in one direction at the end of what seemed like a tunnel. She tried to remember which way the box had been facing, back in her apartment.

"Shrew? Where are you, you stupid cat?"

Could she make it back without him? Looked like she was going to find out. But in the meantime…

"So how do I get across the bridge in Silicon City?" she asked herself.

"Hello, honey."

She stumbled backwards, almost flattening the cardboard box. "Dolores?"

"That is my name."

"The same Dolores I was talking to earlier? The one obsessed with manners?"

"Uh-uh. I'm Dolores Mark three-point-zero. Pleased to make your acquaintance."

"How can you exist outside the Hive?"

"I told you. I'm not that other one. She can only exist inside the Hive. And a damn good job, too."

Alex hadn't considered that AIs could have personality clashes.

"I must say that's a very impressive edifice you came here in."

"Oh. Thank you."

"My pleasure."

"Dolores, did you see a large ginger cat?"

"Oh, yes. He went south, through the tunnel."

"The tunnel."

"The Bay Tunnel, dear."

"But I'm nowhere near the Bay."

"Yes you are. You're right beneath it. In the Bay tunnel."

The Bay went further south in Silicon City than it did at home. Maybe it went further north, too.

"You mean, there's a pedestrian tunnel under the Bay?"

"There sure is. And we're standing in it."

Dolores materialized beside her. She was wearing a floaty sky-blue coat and a deerstalker hat. She winked at Alex. This time she looked like Lily Tomlin. "Much nicer when you're in the Hive though."

"Can you help me with that? Get me into the Hive?"

"Oh no, dear. I really don't think that would be wise."

Of course not. "So I need to walk south to get to Pacific Heights."

"The tunnel comes out very close to where you're heading, you'll be pleased to know."

"Good." She started walking, glad of the faint light emanating from the hologram at her side.

After a few minutes, there was still no sign of light up ahead.

"Dolores, how far is this tunnel?"

"Nine point two seven three miles. You landed zero point three four miles in, and have travelled zero point five six miles so far, which means you have—"

"Eight point three miles. I know."

"Eight point three seven three miles. Eight point two miles now. Listen to me, bamboozling you with numbers. I'm so sorry."

Alex ignored the insinuation that she wasn't good with Math. "That'll take hours."

"At our current speed, two hours and forty-three and a half minutes."

"I don't have that long."

"Would you like me to talk to you while you walk? It can make the time pass more quickly. Or at least, it can make it seem so."

"No. I need you to help me get there faster."

"I'm sorry dear. I'm afraid I can't do that."

Alex sighed. "Alright then. Give me progress reports."

"Progress reports."

"Every ten minutes. Tell me how far we have to go, how long it's going to take. I need to speed up."

"Very well."

Alex picked up the pace. "And talk to me."

"What shall I talk to you about?"

"Tell me something about Silicon City."

"Very well. Silicon City was founded in seventeen hundred and twenty-seven, by a group of colonists from Spain."

"That's earlier than in my world."

Dolores said nothing. The tunnel was very quiet. Alex shivered. "Go on."

"You don't plan to interrupt?"

"I wasn't interrupting."

"I was telling you about the history of Silicon City, just as you asked, Then you—"

"I'm sorry. Alright? Just carry on talking."

"Thank you. It was originally a part of the Mexican territories of the Western Americas, and became part of the USA in—"

"'Ello 'ello, what's this then?"

Alex stopped walking. "Dolores, was that you?"

"It most certainly was not." Dolores dimmed a little in irritation.

"Shush."

The air around her was cold. She smelled stale urine, cigarette smoke, human sweat.

She looked towards Dolores, who had dematerialized.

"Dolores?" she whispered.

Nothing.

She crashed into something. Something soft, and large, that smelt of rotten fish that had eaten yet more rotten fish.

"Who the sweet Jesus are you?" it asked.

**46**

---

## ZIPPO

Silicon City

28 March, 8:41pm

A flame flicked on in front of Alex. She drew back. Beyond it was a face, its lip curled. It belonged to what she imagined was a man, although she couldn't see much of him through the dirt that ringed his mouth and eyes. His forehead was wrinkled, but his eyes looked young.

She swallowed. "I'm just passing through," she said. "I don't want any trouble."

"This is my tunnel," the man told her. "You can't just come waltzing through like you own the place."

She took a deep breath. She thought of the Tai Kwon Do class she'd enrolled for at Berkeley. A shame she hadn't actually turned up.

"Just let me pass and I'll be out of your way," she told him. "No harm done."

He laughed, hot rank breath gusting at her. "No harm

done?" he said. "I was asleep. You woke me. I don't like being woken."

"I'm very sorry," she said. "If you let me pass, then you can sleep again."

"Sleep? Who said anything about sleep?"

"You just told me I woke you."

"No I didn't."

"Yes. You did."

This was hopeless. She felt as if she was talking to Dolores, not to some thug who wanted to mug her. Then she realized she didn't have anything to steal. That probably wasn't a good thing.

She started backing away. The man was short, not much taller than her, and judging by his hollowed-out cheekbones he was skinny too. Not so much of a threat as he thought he was. Maybe she could push past…

"What's going on, Carrot?" Another voice, older this time.

"It's alright, Grandad. I'm just telling this woman she woke me up."

Alex squinted at him.

"Why does he call you Carrot?" she asked, hoping to distract them.

"Because of his goddamn hair," said the older, invisible, voice. "Not very bright, is she?"

Her eyes had become accustomed to the gloom now and she could make out the first man's entire head in the light cast by the flame. He was clearly bald.

"But you don't have any hair."

"Yes I do," he replied. "It's a lot like yours." He reached a hand out and stroked her hair.

"The time is eight forty-seven. You have eight point one three miles to go."

"Dolores?" Alex felt herself breathe again.

"Wha?" asked Carrot. "Where'm I going?"

"Dolores, *shush*," Alex hissed.

"Do you need me to cancel the reminders?"

"Yes."

"Say please."

"Sorry?"

"Politeness costs nothing. Say please."

"Please."

"Very well."

"Thank you, dear."

Carrot's hand was still in her hair. He watched her, his forehead creased. She wondered who had the fewest marbles of the two of them.

He took a ginger strand and twisted it around his finger. It glimmered in the light of the flame, which he brought closer.

"I think you can make an exception to your rule," she said.

"What rule?" The owner of the other voice stepped forwards. He had a long purple scar running down his cheek and the remains of a black eye. He opened his mouth to flash her a grin, showing just three teeth.

"Your rule about not letting people come through here. Not letting people wake you up. I'm a ginger, like him."

This would only work if he really believed he *had* hair, and that it was red.

The younger man laughed. "You really are stoopid, foreign lady! I'm not gon' let you through here just 'cos you're a ginge. You passed the first test is all."

"The first test?"

She wondered which would take longer; humoring him, or going back and taking the long way round. Maybe she could flag down a Hackney. But there could be more like him behind her.

"Yeah," the old man said. "Carrot likes 'is tests. "E 'as a second one, an' all."

"Go on then," she said. "Try me."

"Ooh Grandad, we got us a real good 'un 'ere! She likes a challenge."

Alex licked her lips then regretted it; she could taste the stench of these two on the air. She gritted her teeth and clamped her mouth shut.

Suddenly it went dark.

"Aww *hell*!" the old man cried. "What you done with Percy?"

She wondered who *Percy* was; surely he didn't name his lighter. Then the light came on again. Carrot gripped it unsteadily in his left hand, licking the fingers on his right. He leaned in towards her.

"Ready for the second test?"

She nodded, not wanting to open her mouth for fear of passing out.

"Good. Tell me where you're from."

"Where I'm from?"

"Yeah. You don't have one of them dongles on your ear. Which makes you an outsider. Where you from?"

"That's it? That's your test?"

"Yeah. We collect foreigners, me and Albert 'ere. Last week we 'ad two Frenchmen and an Italian. British is the best, though. Meaty."

Alex felt the hairs at the back of her neck bristle. Were these men eating foreign tourists? *British* tourists?

She had an idea. "So which are the worst?" she asked.

"Huh?"

"The worst. The worst nationality. The ones you don't like." She closed her eyes. "Not meaty."

"Tha's easy. Scottish."

She felt a warm glow run through her. For once she

was glad to face someone who didn't know that Scottish people *were* British. "Scottish?" she replied, letting the soft vowels of her birth come out in her speech. No hiding the accent tonight.

"Yeah. Why?"

"Och aye, laddie," she said, hating herself. "I'm a wee Scot myself. Haggis. Nessie. Toss the caber. Och aye the noo." She hesitated. "Not your type at all."

Carrot shuddered. "Eww. Too much blurkin' haggis for me. Go on then."

"Sorry?"

"You be on your way. Wishin' you a good evenin'."

She stared at him for a moment, then realized what he was saying. She started to push past him. He pulled back, letting her through. There was no sign of his elderly friend.

As she walked, keeping her pace brisk but avoiding a run, she heard their voices again.

"What you do with her?" asked Albert.

"I let 'er go. She's Scottish. Blarrghh!"

"You stupid little eejit."

"What? What did I do wrong?"

"She was lying to ya, daft little runt. Come on, let's get 'er before she disappears."

Alex dropped the nonchalance and started to run. It was dark ahead; she had over eight miles to go.

"Dolores! Help!"

Dolores shimmered to life in front of her. Alex glanced at the AI then kept running.

"Stop them, Dolores!"

"Stop them?"

"Yes!"

"Are you authorizing me to use force?"

"Just stop them!"

"Very well."

Alex heard an electrical sound, followed by two cries. She stopped running and turned to see Dolores standing over two inert forms. She had a halo of red light round her, like the Ready Brek kid.

"What did you do?"

"You authorized me to use force."

"Not…" Alex approached the two men. She prodded one of them with her foot. "Not deadly force."

"You should have been more precise. They are no longer a threat."

"No." Alex stared down at them, glowing red in Dolores's light. It was fading now to the faint blue she was used to.

How would she report their deaths? Would the authorities in Silicon City even care?

She would tell Madonna, at least. If she ever saw her again. Could she be arrested for a crime committed by her AI?

She clenched her fists. "Just get me to Pacific Heights, Dolores. We need to hurry."

**47**

---

## LAMB

Silicon City
28 March, 8:39pm

Claire tiptoed into the living room, sniffed again, and almost fainted. The smell was stronger in here. It was coming from the kitchen. Maybe Leo had gotten into the fridge, broken the packaging for tonight's dinner.

She took a series of sharp breaths.

"Malcolm, please tell me if the front door has been opened."

"The front door was installed on September 19, 2014. It has precisely eight locks and a ZenSec camera trained on it."

"That's not what I asked. When was it last opened?"

"It was last opened by Tammy, the dog lady, at seven forty-five am."

She felt her chest relax. There was no one here.

She turned back to the bedroom. The drapes were still; it was just a breeze, from the change in temperature when she opened the study door.

But she should check, just in case.

She edged her way to the window and reached her hand out, expecting the glass to push back. Instead, she found herself almost falling through a gap where the sliding door had been left open.

She grabbed the drapes and pulled herself upright, her mind racing. No one could get through her passcode security, and no one could get up to the sixth floor. How had the door opened?

The drape had ripped where she'd grabbed it, leaving a ragged shard of fabric in front of her eyes. She looked past it at the world outside.

Out there, in the huge, smelly, terrifying world, people were moving around.

Hackneys glided above the rooftops, taking advantage of the restricted fast lane that only they could use. In the apartments opposite, lights glinted in the darkness. Below her she could make out the faint yellow haze of the electricity barrier that kept Hivers out of the Bay.

The balcony outside the glass showed no sign of occupation.

She turned back into the room.

"Malcolm, has anyone come though this door?"

"The window was exited at eight thirty-eight pm by Claire Pope."

"No, has anyone gone through it before me?"

"Thank you for asking. Yes, I can change the day of your grocery order."

"No, Malcolm."

"I'm sorry. Please can you repeat your order?"

She sighed.

"It's alright, Malcolm."

"That's very kind of you to say so."

"Malcolm, *stop*."

The AI went quiet. That smell was stronger now. Did she have the courage to investigate it, or would she have to call the police?

Police would mean people with dirty boots tramping through here, barking into their Hive connections and drinking her best coffee. She shuddered.

She crept through to the hallway. She stepped into the living space.

She grunted. The smell was huge now, filling the space with its heat and depth.

"Please tell me what you would like me to order for you."

"Malcolm, shut up!" she grabbed a wooden ornament from the hall table and hurled it at his wall unit.

"Please don't damage the wall unit," he said. She screeched at it then turned back to the kitchen. All this noise should have woken Leo.

"Leo?" she called. "Leo, you lazy boy, are you awake?"

She thought of the dinner ingredients in the fridge.

"Mommy has some nice lamb for you."

A sound. A cross between a growl and a whimper.

She rounded the wall between the living space and the kitchen, her eyes flicking to the spot under the kitchen island where Leo's dog bed was.

She screamed.

She ran to it, tripping over her robe and slamming onto the floor with a painful thud.

The dog whimpered at her.

She put out a hand and felt the fur on his back. It was wet. It was red.

# 48

# MICROFICHE

Silicon City
28 March, 9:03pm

Alex's run soon slowed to a brisk walk.

"How are we doing, Dolores?" she asked through clenched teeth. "How far?"

"Congratulations, you now have seven point eight three miles to go. You are making good progress."

"Congratulations? You just killed two people, and you're congratulating me?"

"It seemed appropriate."

*Appropriate.* This was why AIs were dangerous.

"OK. While we walk, you can make yourself useful."

"With pleasure, my dear."

"And stop talking like that."

"Like what, my dear?"

"Like that. All the over-the-top politeness. The 'my dear'ing. Call me Alex."

"Certainly Alex."

Alex bit down her anger.

"How would you like me to make myself useful, Alex?"

"Can you help me with something?"

"Try me."

"Can you find me records for my parents?"

"Aren't you here to save the damsel in distress?"

"Yes, but we have almost eight miles to walk. We may as well fill the time."

"You have to solve her murder. Save the day, win the girl. Blah, blah."

"Dolores, what movies have you been watching?"

"I can consume a standard Hollywood movie in the space of two point six nanoseconds."

"That doesn't answer my question."

"Apologies. All of them."

"What?"

"The answer to your question is all of them."

"You've watched every movie ever made?"

"Every movie. Every TV show. Every book."

"Even *The Apprentice*? Even *Fifty Shades of Grey*?"

"Some things aren't suitable for the delicate sensibility of a respectable AI like me."

"Go on then, Dolores. Get me those records."

"You do realize you need to be back here by midnight?"

"I'm Cinderella. I don't believe it."

"There's a limit to how long an Old Earther can stay here without becoming, let's say, trapped."

"Trapped?"

"Well, not trapped. Not really. But that's the closest word you have for it."

"So how long have I got? Before midnight."

"You have one hundred and sixty-nine minutes and ten seconds."

"Till midnight? But it's only about half past six."

"Not here, dear."

"Oh. Why's that?"

"The gravitational pull of the jump. It messes with time."

"Not a word I'm sure Einstein would have used."

"Who is Einstein?"

Alex sighed. "Never mind. Give me a reminder every fifteen minutes, starting at nine fifteen."

"Alarm set at fifteen-minute intervals starting at nine fifteen p.m."

"Thanks. And get me those records."

"Are you sure that's wise?"

"Get them, please. And hurry."

A desk materialized in front of Alex, moving with her as they walked.

"What's this, Dolores?"

"It's a projection. A hologram. Tell me what records you want to bring up. And make it snappy. Please."

"I want the most recent records of my parents. Heather and Duncan Strand."

"Very well."

On the top of the desk, a screen appeared. It looked a lot like a microfiche reader.

"The time is nine fifteen p.m. You have one hundred and sixty-five minutes exactly before you need to jump."

"Thank you, Dolores." Alex looked at the microfiche reader. "Is this the best you can do? Isn't it a little low tech?"

"Stop grumbling."

Alex peered at the microfiche screen. In its center, magnified perfectly, was a newspaper article.

Alex read it. She stopped walking. The reader stopped with her.

She read it again.

"Your body temperature has fallen by two degrees," said Dolores. "Do you need medical attention?"

Alex turned to her. "We're in the middle of this stupid tunnel and you've killed a man. And now you say you can call 911?"

"I'm concerned about you, dear. Are you alright?"

Alex squinted at the microfiche. This changed everything. "No, Dolores. No, I'm not alright."

# 49

## BAKELITE

Silicon City
28 March, 9:17pm

Claire cradled the dog in her arms, rocking him back and forth.

He'd been stabbed twice in the shoulder. One of the cuts was shallow, like a trial run. The other deep.

She closed her eyes and took a deep breath. She placed her fingers on the cuts. They were small, created by a fine, sharp instrument.

Not her chef's knife, then.

Her earpiece was in the study. That was the only way of calling for help. She couldn't leave her dog.

He whimpered in her arms.

"Shush, honey. It's OK. Mommy's here."

She had to do something. She reached towards the sink and grabbed a tea towel from the hook. She balled it up and pushed it against the wound. Red bloomed on it, making her gag again.

She pulled him gently onto his side, so his weight

would keep the pressure on the towel. She couldn't just stay here.

She watched his face as she moved him. His eyes were dull and he stared straight ahead. She felt a lump form in her throat.

"Sorry, Leo. I'll be right back."

She pushed up and sprinted to the hallway. She stared at the door. Could she go out there? Did she have the strength to call for help, not knowing who would come?

Her throat was dry, her palms wet.

No. She couldn't face it. Besides, her hands were shaking so much she never would have pulled all eight of the bolts.

She ran into her study. Her earpiece was lying on her desk, right where she had left it. She grabbed it and plunged it into her ear.

It hurt. Inserting an earpiece was a delicate operation, something that shouldn't be done in a hurry. She'd probably injured her ear. She didn't care.

She kept her eyes open, staying in the upper levels of the Hive so she could still see her apartment. She stood up.

She heard movement, in the kitchen. Leo?

She froze, her senses alive. She could hear every sound in the apartment, like the building was breathing.

The building wasn't breathing. Over the deep sound of Leo's panting she could hear shallow breathing, fainter than her own.

There was someone here.

She squeezed her eyes shut and dove into the Hive. Her Bakelite phone was waiting for her, on a plain white table in an otherwise empty apace. She'd spent weeks perfecting the art of creating this space, of hiding her real whereabouts. She grabbed the handset.

She dialed.

"I need you to come over here. Now."

He materialized in front of her, smiling. She squinted; behind him, his offline location shimmered like a film set. He looked like he was in an apartment very similar to hers. It even had the same color walls. Was that where he lived, in real life? Or—?

When he saw the fear in her eyes his smile fell. "What's wrong? What is it?"

He took a step towards her. She shrank back. Could she trust him?

"No. Not in the Hive," she said. "I need you to come to my apartment."

# 50

# OLD-FASHIONED

Silicon City

28 March, 9:23pm

Alex's eyes were tiring and her feet were aching.

"What's that noise?"

She'd heard a rumble beyond the wall of the tunnel.

"That'll be the cable car, dear. I mean *Alex*."

"It goes under the Bay?"

"It most certainly does."

"Can we ride on it?"

"Only from a station."

"And they're only on land."

"Oh no, Alex. There's one just ahead."

Alex felt her heart lift. "Why didn't you tell me?"

"You didn't ask."

Alex ran ahead, listening to the faint rumble beyond the grey concrete. Up ahead was a dim light; she'd thought it was the distant shoreline, but now she knew better.

The tunnel spat her out into a dimly lit space with a single track running along it.

"Be careful," warned Dolores. "It's fast. You don't want to stand on that track."

Alex stepped back, just as a bulky object whizzed past, nearly taking her nose off. "That's the cable car?"

"It is."

"It's fast."

"It needs to be. You wanna stop it?"

Alex nodded and Dolores brought her forefinger and thumb to her holographic lips. She let out a piercing whistle. Up ahead, the car shuddered to a halt.

Alex ran towards it and swung herself onto the backplate. Dolores dematerialized.

Alex fell into a seat as the car lurched into motion. The conductor approached. He was in his seventies, and didn't seem to be wearing an earpiece. His skin was blue.

"Where does this go?" asked Alex.

"All the way to Vallejo Street," he replied.

"The time is nine thirty. You have one hundred and fifty minutes before you need to jump."

"Who's that?" he asked. "No AIs on the trolley, Miss."

"Sorry. Will we go past Lafayette Park?"

"Lafayette Park? Ain't no such thing, I'm afeared."

"No. Of course. Gough Street?'

"Oh no, Miss. I can get you as far as Washington and Hyde. Then you'll need to foot it."

"Right. How far is it from there?"

"I reckon it's about five blocks, Miss. Maybe six. May I see your ticket please?"

She padded her jacket, wondering if Dolores would have deposited something in a pocket. Then an object flashed in her hand. She held it out. It was a paper ticket.

"Thank you, Miss. We like to do things the old-fashioned way on the cable car."

"Yes. Thanks."

The car sped up and the conductor moved away into the darkness. A man and woman sat ahead of Alex, both plugged into the Hive. There was a moment of confusion when the conductor asked for a physical ticket. Then the woman put a steadying hand on the man's shoulder and reached into her ear. She withdrew two small paper tickets. The conductor smiled and clipped them, whistling as he headed towards the front of the car.

Alex felt movement beside her. Dolores shimmered into life, giving her a wink. She'd lost the blue coat and was wearing a purple kaftan with a long chain of seashells around her neck.

"You again. He mustn't see you. Stop the reminders," Alex whispered.

"Just trying to help."

"Help me with this. Sean Wolf. Who is he, in this world? Where does he live?"

"Give me a sec."

Dolores opened her eyes again. "He's a retired ballet dancer. Forced out of the profession by a calf injury five years ago. Now manager of the San Francisco Ballet."

"Manager? Not Philip Gladstone?"

Dolores's eyes closed again. "I can't find a Philip Gladstone."

"Philip Gladstone. He's the manager. Or maybe he's a dancer, if Sean is the manager."

"No one by that name anywhere in the Bay Area. Sorry."

Alex felt air hit her face as they left the tunnel. The trolley didn't slow down, instead taking turns and running red lights as if it had a red light on its roof.

"Right," she said. "And where does Sean live?"

"In Vista Del Mar, my dear. Alex. He has a rather grand apartment with an ocean view. Six separate AIs. That's just greedy."

"Here we are, Miss."

The conductor was gesturing towards the window. Washington and Hyde. Alex thanked him and jumped down.

She had to get to Claire's apartment, and fast.

51

## BEER

Berkeley
28 March, 9:49pm

Mike knocked on Alex's door. He didn't like doing this, but he equally didn't like the way Monique had spoken to his would-be partner.

She was an idiot. She'd been a liability in Silicon City, too impulsive and naïve. But she'd cracked the gluons thing. She'd even explained it to him in a way he could understand.

Monique wouldn't let her back on the case: that was about as likely as a year without fog over the Bay. But she had that file still; maybe he'd be able to make sense of it. Maybe he could ask her to help him.

The door opened. "Mike?

"Sarita?"

"Mike."

"Er, I'm sorry. I didn't realize you two were…"

She grabbed his arm and bundled him inside. "Don't be stupid. We're working together, is all."

He looked around the apartment. No sign of Alex, or that cat of hers. "Where is she?"

"She went to get beers."

He eyed Sarita. "Beers?"

"I was thirsty, OK?"

He looked around the space. A bottle of beer sat on the kitchen counter, condensation dripping down its sides. It was almost full.

"Going for a heavy night, are we?" He gestured towards it.

Sarita shook her head. "I think you should leave. We can talk in the morning."

"Why is the world's biggest cardboard box in the center of the floor?"

"Alex had a delivery."

"Of a kangaroo?"

"Physics stuff. She'll be back soon, and she won't be happy to see you."

He frowned. The status of Sarita and Alex's relationship was no business of his; clearly they'd taken advantage of Alex being hauled off the case.

"Right," he said. He wondered if he had time to stop off for a beer on his way home.

As he grabbed the door handle, there was buzzing behind him. He turned to see Sarita's hip glowing purple.

He approached her. "What's that?"

"My phone. You were leaving, weren't you?"

"Whose phone glows purple and is…" She withdrew it from her pocket. It was a solid white cube, shrieking and glowing alternately purple and orange. "…that's a bitbox," he said. "Why did you take a bitbox out of the MIU?"

He lunged for it but she was too fast. She threw an arm out and placed her fist on his chest. She was surprisingly strong.

With her other hand, she twisted the bitbox and it stopped yelling at them. "This isn't good."

"Why not? None of us is over there right now. Unless it's Claire?"

Sarita looked up. Her eyes were dark and her jaw set. "It's Claire. And Alex."

"Alex?"

"She jumped."

"I just came from the MIU. She left."

"She used alternative technology."

"Like what?"

Sarita gestured behind her. "Don't ask. Look, Mike. We don't have much time. Alex is in trouble."

# 52

## GIGABITS

Silicon City
28 March, 9:47pm

Claire's building was only a few blocks away. Alex ran, occasionally stopping to dance around a passer-by who was inside the Hive.

The street was busier than it had been earlier, brightly colored figures passing through, doing that familiar dance around each other as they came closer. A family passed her: mom, dad and a little girl. She wore an earpiece with a brightly colored Pearl adorned with tiny parrots.

Alex rounded the building opposite Claire's and stopped. She leaned against it and bent over to put her balled fists on her thighs. Riding the trolley car, talking to Dolores about Sean, had taken her mind off what she'd learned in the tunnel, from that nonexistent microfiche. But now the panic was over, the terror gone. She was back in familiar territory. Her mind cleared and created space for the shock to take a run at her.

Her parents were in that Hive Earth phone directory

for a reason. They'd lived in the same house her dad lived in now, in Gretna. Prior to the rise of the Hive and the obsolescence of any other communications technology, they'd had a telephone. In her world, it sat on the table at home, still there like a museum piece despite her dad reluctantly switching to a cell phone a couple of years back. She'd taken him out to their closest branch of Carphone Warehouse to buy it; he wasn't going to be coaxed as far into the twenty-first century as to order it online. There he'd engaged the salesman in a bizarre conversation about bandwidth, gigabits and data. She'd been impressed until she'd spotted the dawning look of incomprehension on the salesman's face. Her dad had read about phones in the *Reader's Digest*, hadn't he? And none of it made the first bit of sense to anyone who actually understood them.

In the version of Scotland almost five thousand miles east of where she stood now, that phone would never ring. Its owners had been killed in a car accident in 1992, six months before she should have been conceived.

She tried to convince herself that it didn't matter, that this was a parallel universe and had no bearing on her real life. But ever since Mike had told her about the technology, she'd had two goals. To solve the case and bag herself a job at the MIU; and to find her mom. To see her face and breathe in her familiar, warm scent again.

And now it would never happen. Not only was her mom not here, but nor was her dad.

She wanted to go home.

She leaned back against the smooth pink building. The walls of all the buildings around here sloped at an oblique angle, which made a perfect spot to rest. She wondered why no one else did it.

"Dolores," she whispered. "What time is it?"

"Nine fifty-three- and twenty-four seconds p.m.,"

Dolores replied in a whisper. "You have one hundred and twenty-six minutes and thirty-six seconds."

Alex sniffed and wiped her face with the back of her hand. Her mascara was all over the place.

Then she saw him.

Sean Wolf, letting himself into a building to her right.

She stood up, suddenly alert. She must have had it wrong; there was another building between her and the one she and Mike had entered, and she was leaning against it.

As the door swish-thunked closed behind Sean, she stretched out her sore neck. She headed after him, taking care to avoid the growing swarm of Hivers.

She was between the two buildings now. She looked back at the one she'd leant against. On this wall there was a coffee shop identical to yesterday's. The Bumble Bee. This one was The Wasp. She peered inside. There was that barista, standing behind the counter and staring into space. She frowned. It was one thing having two yellow-and-black insect-themed coffee shops, but quite another having two identical baristas.

She looked back at the building opposite, the door Sean had disappeared through. Then it hit her. He had gone into Claire's building. He was on his way to kill her.

# 53

# BALCONY

Silicon City
28 March, 9:51pm

Alex ran into the building. There was no sign of Sean in the deserted lobby.

"Dolores, how long now?" she whispered.

"You cancelled the reminders."

"I know, but how long do I have now?"

"Do you need me to start reminding you at fifteen-minute intervals again?"

"No. Yes. Oh, I don't know."

"I'm sorry, I don't understand."

"Nor do I. Give me the reminders. Please."

"Thank you for asking nicely."

She hurried to the elevator. After a few moments' wait, the door glided open and she stepped inside.

The elevator was playing some sort of Star Wars simulation. As the doors closed, the walls went black and became dotted with stars. A TIE fighter zoomed past, making Alex jump. It was followed by an X-wing. Then, even more dramatic than in *The Empire Strikes Back*, the second version of the Death Star, complete with an unconstructed section, rose from the floor beneath her feet and settled into place on the wall beside her. She put out a hand to touch the wall, but was disappointed to find it smooth and unresponsive.

The elevator stopped and the simulation blinked off, replaced with dull pink walls washed with light from above. She pushed her disappointment to one side and stepped out into an empty corridor.

Maybe she was imagining things; maybe Sean hadn't been here at all. Surely Claire wouldn't have let him into her apartment? She was a recluse, and he was her ex. But maybe he had access to somewhere else here, to the apartment she'd visited herself when in the Hive.

She made her way along the corridor as quietly as she could. The walls here were similar to those in the building opposite, except instead of walking through a poppy field, she was walking through a hay meadow. The ground crunched under her feet.

The door to Claire's apartment was blank and featureless. She scanned the walls around it and spotted a tiny camera, directed at her.

She gave a sheepish wave and knocked on the door. She stepped back to stand away from the camera, which followed her. She tried to ignore it and focus on the door. It didn't open.

She stepped forwards and tried again. No response. She frowned and checked her watch. She was running out of time, but something in her gut told her she had to get in there.

She looked towards the end of the corridor, just one door away. There was a fire exit.

She hurried towards it and thundered through the

door, teetering on a shallow fire escape as she burst out into the cool night. Through the gaps in the pink-hued metal, the street was six stories below, people passing beneath as dim shadows.

She pulled back and leaned against the door, breathing heavily. To her left, the Bay gleamed in the moonlight. A Hackney glided above it, making a low-pitched whirring sound.

She stepped forwards again. There was a balcony along the wall from her, about three feet away. Could she make it?

Of course she could. She gripped the fire escape and leaned out into the night, reaching out for the balcony rail. Closing her eyes so as not to see what was below, she let her weight shift forwards and stepped across to stand at the edge of the balcony. She swung a leg over and was astride the rail before she'd had the chance to stop herself.

She opened her eyes again, her heart clattering in her ears. Behind her, the empty air between this and the other building gaped ominously. She heaved her other leg up and brought herself onto the balcony, sliding to the floor.

Light spilled out from the nearest window, which was wide and full-height like those in Claire's apartment. She edged towards the window frame to see inside. She was looking at a dining room with orange walls and a blobby yellow sideboard. In the center was a circular blue table with green leather chairs surrounding it. In two of these chairs sat a couple, looking down at the table. Each of them had a plate piled high with a gray gelatinous substance that made Alex want to heave. Each had their eyes closed and was wearing an earpiece. Surely they would unplug to do something as visceral as eat?

She watched as the woman, seated nearest to her, pushed her fork through the mound on her plate, bringing the quivering jelly up to her lips. She ate it and smiled, wiping her lips with a spotted red napkin. Alex felt her nose wrinkle. But inside the Hive, they were probably experiencing this food as something else. Something delicious. A joint of meat, a bowl of caviar, or that grilled cheese Alex had made last week and never managed to replicate.

She watched them eating. If they were sufficiently engrossed, they wouldn't spot her on their balcony. But the Hive was augmented reality, and who knew what kind of security they had.

It was too late to turn back. She dropped to her stomach and wriggled across the balcony, keeping close to the window. Every now and then she would freeze, just in case they were looking. At the other side she pulled herself up against the balcony rail, relieved that there was a sliver of space past the window. The next balcony along belonged to Claire.

She put her hand over her mouth, willing herself not to look down. Again there was a gap of about three feet. Without the fire escape behind her, it felt further.

*Do it*, she told herself. She placed one foot on the railing and brought the other one up. Then quickly, relying on her own momentum, she stepped across. She pushed her weight forwards and tumbled onto Claire's balcony.

She flattened herself against the floor and paused to get her breath. The window closest to her was Claire's bedroom. She had a visual memory of it, its drapes closed. She looked to the building opposite, seeking out the window she and Mike had stood behind, just yesterday. She tried to remember which window she'd seen Sean watching from, but in the darkness they all seemed to melt into each other.

She looked at Claire's window. Heaven help her if she ended up having to go back the same way.

She started to pull herself upright, then heard a sound. She froze.

The bedroom doors were sliding open.

She stared at them. Was she about to find herself face to face with Claire? She remembered all Monique's instructions, her threats. Don't make contact with the subject of the investigation.

Claire didn't emerge. Instead, Sean slipped out, tangling himself in the drapes as he pushed through. Alex felt her forehead break out in sweat. Sean stepped onto the balcony and headed away from Alex, towards the view of the Bay. He leaned against the railing, looking out over the expanse of night.

Alex watched as he pulled an earpiece out of his back pocket and brought it up to his ear. Her breath was shallow and blood rushed in her ears. She waited for him to move. Did she dare slip inside?

"It's ten p.m. Sixty minutes until—"

"Dolores, *stop*."

Sean span round.

Alex stared back at him, each of them waiting for the other to say something; to react, to explain what they were doing on Claire's balcony. She opened her mouth. Could she arrest him?

She was interrupted by a scream from within.

He dropped the earpiece. It disappeared behind him, falling to the ground below. He turned back and looked down, grasping at the air.

Then there was another scream. Sean came out of the trance and ran into the bedroom.

# 54

# BLOOD

Silicon City
28 March, 10:02pm

Alex ran after him.

The bedroom was empty, fabric billowing out behind the open doors. She ran through into the hallway and then the kitchen. Under the island in the center of the kitchen was a hunched figure which looked like the body of a woman with the head of a large Labrador.

Next to it, leaning over, was Sean.

Claire blinked, trying to make sense of the scene. Even the Hive hadn't prepared her for this. She took a step sideways and realized that she was looking at a woman hunched over a dog. After a couple of blinks the two figures became clear, like an optical illusion resolving itself into a young woman wearing a fancy hat when just moments earlier it refused to be anything other than an old crone.

She realized that, apart from the dog, this was the same

scene she'd seen in those photos from the crime scene in San Francisco. Claire bundled up on her apartment floor, blood pouring from her side. The dog was next to her, bleeding too.

Alex dashed towards Claire, yanking off her own jacket and balling it up. She held it against the wound, pushing as hard as she could to stem the bleeding. Next to her, Sean was wailing.

She looked at him sidelong. *That won't work on me*, she thought. She pulled Claire towards her and wrapped her arms around her, using the strength of her grip to secure her jacket against the wound.

Alex felt the blood seeping through her jacket and onto her clenched fist. It was covering her hand now, heavy and red.

She swallowed and blew a stray hair out of her eyes. She looked back down at Claire. She couldn't step away from her, not without letting the bleeding get worse. But she couldn't stay here forever.

"Will you help me," she asked Sean, more of a statement than a question.

"Of course." His face was pale, his purple-dyed hair disheveled. "Tell me what to do."

She narrowed her eyes at him. This was the oddest murderer she'd ever met. A murderer who comes running when he hears his victim scream, and then tries to help save her life.

She had no choice. "Can you contact the emergency services."

"Of course. I just need my… *damn*."

"What?" She pulled back from him, wary. Claire's limp body dragged with her.

"My earpiece," he said. "I dropped it. Outside."

He dragged his hands through his hair and stared

towards the window. Alex had seen it fall out of his hand, spinning toward the ground below. Could an earpiece survive that drop?

"Don't you keep a spare?" she asked.

"No one does."

Of course not. She looked around the kitchen, trying to find some sort of communications device, something she could use to call for help. Surely Claire had an earpiece herself.

She turned Claire over carefully. The woman was muttering under her breath. Her skin was like porcelain.

In her opposite ear, the one that had been on the floor, was an earpiece. Claire was in no state to use it. Alex would have to extract it.

She looked at Sean, then back to Claire. Pulling that thing out of her ear might finish her off.

She pulled Claire back towards her, twisting her jacket into the wound. The blood flow was slowing, but so was Claire's breathing.

"Go," she told Sean. "Run. To the next-door apartment." She remembered those people, eating their gray blancmange. "There's people there. Hammer their door down. Get them to call an ambulance. Anything."

He nodded and stood up. "Is she going to be OK?"

She frowned at him. "Course she's not going to be OK. Why do you suddenly care?"

"She's my wife."

"Your wife?"

He nodded.

"She's your ex-wife. Isn't she?"

They both turned at the sound of the bedroom door closing. A man stood in the entrance to the kitchen, a metal object in his hand.

"He was lying to us all along. They never divorced."

# 55

# PIROUETTE

Silicon City
28 March, 10:11pm

It was the oddest fight Alex had ever had. Instead of lunging for her, or pulling her away from Claire as Alex had expected him to, the man did what could only be described as a pirouette across the floor towards them. It was a damn fast pirouette, though, and he was on them before Alex had even registered what was going on.

Sean stood up, his face pale.

"Philip?" he gasped.

But the man ignored him, instead dipping his torso down towards Alex, his leg going up behind him for balance. He was wearing trainers, but Alex was sure he had his toes pointed.

Philip sent his arms out wide and span them round, the back of his hand slamming into her face. He was still bent over, dipping towards her in a way that made her think of yoga classes. She stumbled backwards, feeling Claire fall away from her.

She yelped and fumbled for Claire, grabbing at her clothes and trying to find her balled-up jacket. It had gone, sent away by her attacker's other hand as it came round to follow its twin.

She draped herself over Claire, hoping she could use the weight of her own body to stop the bleeding. But then she felt herself being pulled upwards. Two hands gripped her waist, arranged evenly, symmetrically. As if he was about to—

She screamed. He ducked and then rose, pushing her up to the ceiling. Was he giving her a ballet lift?

She sent her arms out wide, brushing the lampshade over the kitchen island and feeling like a kid playing at airplanes. She tried to struggle out of his grip, but his fingers were strong. After a moment's inertia at the top of the arc, he brought her back down again. Instead of dipping over her and bringing her body beneath his in a dance move, he slammed her into the floor. She cried out, looking around for Sean and trying to work out where Claire was.

She expected him to let go, to leave her bruised and battered on the floor, but instead he brought his hand round behind her shoulder and pulled her upright. He leaned around her and twisted his body, hauling her over his back. Suddenly she was flying through the air again, her back to his and her eyes towards the ceiling, skimming over him as he drew her over his body. She felt herself come down again on the other side.

Again, instead of pulling her into some sort of dance pose, he shoved her into the floor. Her back hit the oak boards with a crunch. She tried to yell but all that came out was air.

At last he let go, leaving her twisted on the floor. Claire

was next to her and Alex could feel her hair tangled in her own fingertips.

Sean was running for the door. "I'll get help!" he cried. Alex could do nothing more than blink. She stared up at the ceiling, feeling cold. Had he broken her back? Would she be forever paralyzed? How would she jump home?

"The time is ten fifteen. You have one hundred and five minutes— Oh."

"Dolores. Get help. Now."

"Very well."

The man—Philip—looked up, searching for an AI that had never appeared.

"What was that?"

"Dolores," she croaked.

"Dolores?"

"You'll see."

She blinked up at him. His face was thin and dark, marked with a day's worth of stubble. He brought his fists up above her and she closed her eyes, waiting for them to make contact with her face. Why oh why had she disobeyed Monique?

Suddenly Sean was backing into the room, staring ahead of him towards the door. Alex tried to lift her neck. But there was something cold beneath it, something damp. Her own spinal fluid?

"Go," she croaked. "Go, now."

He turned to stare at her, shaking his head. "Er, I think help has found us."

She looked past him. Barreling through the door, in a tangle of limbs, raised voices and facial hair, was the world's most bizarre rescue party.

# 56

## WYATT EARP

Silicon City
28 March, 10:20pm

Alex blinked up at them. At the front of the group, looking like someone had taken a large tomato and put an Einstein wig on it, was the Prof. Behind him, gray with nausea and wearing her yellow leather jacket above a red skirt and orange and blue striped tights, was Sarita. And bringing up the rear was Mike, sporting a handlebar mustache worthy of Wyatt Earp.

Alex stared at them.

"What the—?" she breathed.

Sarita bent to her, putting a hand to her forehead. "Don't move. You're going to be fine."

"Don't worry about me. Don't let him get away."

"It's OK. I've got him." Mike was standing behind Sarita, holding Alex's attacker in something that looked like a pair of electric handcuffs.

Alex tried to smile. "What are those?"

The Prof stepped forwards. "Mine." He blushed even

more deeply, turning from a gray-haired tomato to a gray-haired plum, and took a step backwards.

"Where's Sean?" Alex asked. "Claire? Where's Claire? Oh bum, is she OK?"

Mike tossed Philip onto a chair and bent down next to Sarita to examine Claire. He grabbed Alex's ruined jacket and balled it up at Claire's side.

"Sean has called an ambulance," he said. "She'll be OK. Thanks to you."

"You have to be joking. I banjaxed it up big time, guys." She squeezed her eyes shut, not wanting to cry in front of Sarita. "Don't tell Monique about this, will you?"

Mike looked away from Claire and towards Alex. "You're kidding me, right? You'll get a commendation."

"Yeah, right."

"No, seriously. You got him."

"I think he got me."

Mike shrugged and turned back to Claire. She was muttering something again. He put his ear to her mouth.

"She says he was watching her. Stalking her."

"But that was Sean."

"No," said Sean. "I was protecting her."

"Why?" asked Alex.

"Why do you think?" Philip was slumped against the kitchen island, the handcuffs fizzing at his wrists. "Sean was going to go back to her. I couldn't let him."

"How? You don't exist here."

A shrug. "I followed a cat here. Via a box room in the theater. Found another version of Sean, and Claire. A year ago."

"A year ago?" said Sean. "But that was when we…"

"When we met. I know. I couldn't believe my luck when I found out there was another one of you. But it turned out you both wanted to leave me."

"Both of me?"

"It's complicated."

"But how did you get into Claire's apartment?" Sean asked. "She's the most security-conscious person I know."

"One of the locks was bust."

"She has eight of them. They all work just fine."

"One of them is broken in my world. Old Earth, people call it. It gave me a way in, after I jumped."

"I don't know what you're talking about."

"We'll explain later, Sean," said Alex. "But you're going to have to make a statement to…" She looked at Mike. "Who does he talk to? Us or SCPD?"

"Neither. MOO will deal with Sean, we'll be taking Philip back with us. He's one of ours."

"I had to keep them apart," Philip said. "It wasn't fair."

"The smell," said Alex. "It's you. You jumped. And Sean had been with you."

She turned her head towards him but all she could see was the dog.

"You killed her dog."

"There's a vet on the way," said Sarita. "He missed the major arteries; the dog will be fine. It's you we need to worry about."

Alex blinked. "I think he's broken my back. There's spinal fluid all over the floor beneath me."

Sarita put her hand behind Alex's back, easing her fingers in gently. Then she pulled it away and held it in front of Alex's face. Clear, gloopy liquid dripped onto her face. Alex grimaced, horrified.

Sarita eyed the liquid then sniffed it. She held it away from her face, shrugged and licked some off her finger.

"Sarita!" cracked Alex." "That's disgusting."

"Yeah. Pretty yucky." Sarita brushed it off her hands.

"What did you feel, when you hit the floor? What did you hear?"

"There was a crunch. Then I felt splintering beneath me."

Sarita looked up. "Listen to this, everyone. Alex fell onto a box of eggs, and she thought it was her spine exploding."

"Shut up," replied Alex, glaring at Sarita. "Anyway, why are you here? I thought you don't jump. What if you bump into your opposite number?"

"Shush now. You've had a serious spinal injury. You need surgery."

"What?"

Alex felt her limbs slacken. Behind her, the fluid was still seeping, making her back cold.

Sarita was snorting.

"It's not funny."

"It is."

Sarita reached out a hand and fumbled at Alex's side. She drew an object up between them.

A box of eggs. Smashed.

"You were lying on this. Get up, you lazy ginger."

Sarita hauled Alex up as two orange-clad paramedics rushed in. They slid a stretcher underneath Claire and sped off with her. Sean followed, the dog whimpering in his arms. He nodded towards Alex as he left.

"She'll be fine," said the Prof. "As long as you're alive when they get you, you'll always be good as new."

Alex marveled once again at this version of her city. Could she steal some of this tech, take it back with her?

"I know what you're thinking," said the Prof. "You're allowed to steal one idea. Just one. If you can convince the Luddites in your world to use it, then good luck to you. But nothing physical. The Spinner would never forgive you."

"Have you stolen any ideas from *us?*" Alex asked. She put her hand behind her back and grimaced. Her back was indeed covered with broken eggshells.

"Ouch," she breathed. She may not have broken her back, but being slammed into the floor like that meant she wouldn't be running a marathon anytime soon.

Sarita stood behind Alex and started moving her fingers across her back, testing the muscles. Alex closed her eyes and leaned into it.

"Ow," she muttered as Sarita hit a painful spot. Sarita stopped moving her fingers and started massaging that spot, dipping her fingers into Alex's flesh through her shirt. Alex reminded herself to hurt her back more often.

"The time is ten-thirty p.m. You have thirty minutes before you must jump."

"Thanks Dolores," said Alex.

"Dolores?" asked the Prof.

Alex shrugged. "Suits her." She turned to Sarita. "How did you find me?"

"Madonna was tracking you. We knew you'd found him. And then Dolores—as you call her—raised the alarm."

"Madonna?"

"Yup."

"But how? I didn't come through the MOO."

"Our Mads knows more than she lets on," said the Prof.

"Oh," replied Alex. "If anyone was tracking me, I thought it might have been you."

"Me?" said Sarita and the Prof in unison.

Alex laughed, then winced. Sarita shifted her fingers a little and continued kneading.

"Both of you, I suppose," Alex said.

"Didn't you realize?" asked Sarita. "Madonna's a genius."

"Well I never thought I'd hear those words all together in one sentence."

"She is. She developed the Hive. She created the Spinner. She's Betsy Woznik."

"She's the recluse who built the Hive?"

Sarita pushed a muscle with her finger, making Alex gasp. She wasn't sure whether it was a gasp of pain or enjoyment. "The woman's a genius."

"I just thought she was a geek. A geek looking like a 1980s pop star."

Sarita laughed. "No. She's a nerd. A proper, full blown nerd. Not a geek like you."

"What's the difference?"

Sarita's hands stopped moving. "Nerds aren't sexy." She pulled her hands away and brushed them together as if shaking off dirt. "Come on, you'll be fine after a couple of beers."

Alex felt heat travel up her back. "Yeah. I think I will."

Mike gave a theatrical sigh. "Will you two just get a room?"

"Do you need extra workspace?" asked the Prof. "I'm sure we can furnish you with an office at the MOO."

Alex felt her chest tighten. She ignored what Mike had said and avoided Sarita's eye.

"Come on then." Mike twirled his mustache with his free hand and looked at the Prof. "Let's get this sucker back to the MOO."

**57**

---

**KISS**

MOO

28 March, 10:51pm

Madonna was waiting for them at the MOO. She led them to the stairs ("the elevator doesn't work at this time of night") and up to the roof.

The circular structure that housed the Spinner was there waiting for them. Alex blinked at it, glad that this time she wasn't alone. It helped to have your friends working with you. It meant someone could hold your hair while you threw up at the other end.

The Prof stepped forward. His face had lost its fruity quality and was back to its normal Einstein-resembling self, his hair more disheveled than ever. Alex gave it a friendly tug, expecting it to come away in her hand.

"What are you doing?" he asked, sounding affronted.

"I'm so sorry. Oh God, I really am. I thought it was a wig."

He patted it. "Don't be ridiculous."

Sarita gave her a conspiratorial look. Alex looked away, blushing. Mike strode towards the Spinner, pulling Philip Gladstone with him. What shape would his facial hair take on, when they jumped? And how long would he have to put up with it until their next jump? If Alex was ever allowed to jump again.

Alex stopped in her tracks. "I need to find Shrew."

"Shrew?" asked the Prof.

"Schrödinger. My cat. He ran off."

Madonna smiled. "He's back at your condo. He's fine. Gorgeous boy. You need to feed him a bit less, though. And get him neutered."

"Right. Thanks." Alex stepped towards Madonna and held out her hand. Madonna held out her own limply. Alex tried to shake it but then gave up and brought it to her lips instead. Madonna gave a squeal of delight that reminded Alex of the sound effects in *Like A Virgin*. She resisted the urge to tell Madonna what she was thinking.

Instead, she opted for sincere and mature. "Thank you," she said. "I heard you were looking out for me."

Madonna shrugged. "It was fun."

"Fun?"

"We don't get a lot of people like you round here. The way you talked your way past that bald kid was priceless." She pursed her lips, her beauty spot moving up and down. "But you need to be going. You're already later than my former husband."

Alex nodded, trying not to think about the ramifications of that last sentence. She looked across the roof toward the Bay. Had there really been a virtual microfiche underneath it less than two hours ago? Had she talked to Dolores, or was it Madonna all along? She hoped she'd get the chance to come back and find out.

She turned to Sarita. "Come on. Time to jump."

Sarita looked pale. "Oh, hell."

"Is that why you don't jump? It makes you sick."

"Kinda."

Alex sighed. "I'll help you. We both will."

Mike had the door open to the Spinner. Alex steered Sarita inside then followed. She gave Madonna and the Prof a quick wave. Sarita had turned a shade that reminded Alex of an elephant crossed with a jellyfish. She took her hand. "It'll be OK," she said.

She screwed up her eyes and waited for the world to start spinning.

THEY STUMBLED out and into the MIU, relieved to find Nemesis waiting at the other end.

"Where's Madge?" asked Alex.

"Ohh, I don't feel so well," said Sarita.

Alex turned to her. "Take deep breaths. Don't think about cauliflower."

"Cauliflower?"

"It doesn't matter. Here, this'll take your mind off it."

She leaned in and gave Sarita a quick but gentle kiss. Then, suddenly aware of Nemesis watching, she pulled back, stuttering.

"Oh, *bum.*"

Sarita started to laugh. "Yeah. Don't do that again."

"I'm sorry. It was the relief. Of getting back in one piece."

"I'm sure it was."

"I cured you of your sickness though, didn't I?"

"Yes. You're going to make a good colleague."

"Colleague."

"Yes, colleague."

Alex turned toward the Spinner. Philip lay on the floor, groaning. His face was half-buried in a pile of vomit.

She frowned. "Where's Mike?"

Sarita pushed her to one side. "What?"

"He's not there." Alex turned to Nemesis. "Has Mike already come back?"

"No. He was with you."

"He was when we were at the MOO. He was in the Spinner with us." She felt her heart pick up pace. "Where is he now?"

Sarita put a hand on her arm. "He's probably back at the MOO. Leave it with me and Nemesis. You go brief Monique and we'll get him."

"Are you sure? Shouldn't I—"

"It wouldn't be wise for you to go back again after spending so long there. Let us handle it."

Alex slid to the ground.

"I can't just abandon him. Not after he came to get me."

Mike had been rude and dismissive when they'd first met but he'd come to rescue her, regardless of the consequences to his facial hair. He was her partner.

Sarita's hand was still on Alex's arm. "We'll get him. Alex. Now go."

**58**

---

**MIKE**

The Spinner
28 March, 10:53pm

Mike slumped against the wall of the Spinner as it slowed. When it came to a halt he felt his chin as always.

It was bare. That made a change.

He withdrew his hand, not wanting the others to see him checking his beard. It was something he preferred not to mention. Something that embarrassed him.

He looked up.

The Spinner was empty. There was no one with him.

"Sarita? Alex?"

He stood up and looked around. The Spinner was quiet, its gray walls giving nothing away. Had they already left?

He turned, expecting to see the open doorway behind him. The wall was a blank nothingness.

He put his hand to it. It was smooth, and cold.

"Nemesis?" he called. "That's enough. Let me out."

No reply.

"Madge!" he hollered. "You're playing a trick on me, aren't you?"

He waited for a reply.

"Very funny. Now just let me out."

He leaned against the wall, hoping it would open under his touch.

He moved around its circle, shifting his hand up and down the smooth material. Nothing changed; no indentation, no change in temperature.

He swallowed.

"Come on now, guys. I had a long day, I just saved Alex's hide and I want to be let out."

He had no idea which part of the wall the door would be in, but he had to start somewhere. He hurled himself at it, letting his shoulder barrel into the surface.

It didn't give. His shoulder hurt.

"Ow."

He slid to the floor. Nothing for it but to wait.

"Please don't damage the walls," came a voice.

'Nemesis! I'm sorry. Let me out now, OK?"

"Who's Nemesis?"

Mike felt his chest constrict.

"Very funny."

"If you think this is a joke, that's fine. It isn't."

The Spinner started to shift. He leaned against the wall, feeling the familiar motion.

"Stop!" he cried. "Let me out!"

There was no response. The Spinner picked up speed.

**59**

---

# PIZZA

San Francisco
31 March, 8:03pm

"Rik, this is my dad. Duncan. Dad, this is Rik Patel, my lab partner."

Alex's dad put out his hand. "Pleased to meet you."

Rik waved the pizza box he was carrying by way of apology. As he placed it on the table, Alex slipped him a couple of twenties; the promise of free pizza had broken his bad mood.

Rik wiped his hand on his jeans then shook Duncan's hand. "Just landed?"

"Alex picked me up from SFO a couple of hours ago. I met her cat. He's an odd 'un."

Rik nodded and opened the box. Alex grabbed a slice. She was glad to see her dad, but hadn't lost the sensation that a panic attack might overtake her at any time. It had started when Mike disappeared.

She eyed her dad. She couldn't tell him anything about the MIU. Nor Rik.

"How's Morag?" she asked.

"On the mend. Slowly. She sends her love."

"Good. You sure she's OK with you being here?"

"There are twenty-three women on rotation by her bedside. They look at me funny whenever I turn up."

"Well, it's good to see you. I've had an odd couple of weeks."

Rik looked up. Cheese dripped down his chin. "Alex was an expert witness in a murder case."

Duncan's eyes lit up. "You're working with the cops? Do they give you a gun?"

"Don't be daft, Dad. I'm only a witness. I had to appear in court, that's all."

"Oh. Just as long as you're keeping out of mischief."

"Of course," she replied.

Her phone rang: Sarita.

"Give me a minute, will you? Don't eat it all."

She slipped outside. The night was cool, the remains of a fog dissipating.

"Sarita. Did you find him?"

"No."

"Isn't he in Silicon City?"

"The Prof and Madonna haven't seen him. They did a check of the Hive and there's no sign of him."

Alex leaned against the wall. She felt wobbly. "I feel responsible."

"Don't."

"He jumped to help me. You did too. I know you aren't supposed to jump. Maybe it caused a problem, some kind of anomaly?"

"We don't know. But we do need to find him."

"Right."

"Monique wants you back."

Alex felt a smile spread across her face. She quickly banished it.

"Me?"

"Yeah. You up for a new mission?"

She looked into the apartment. Her dad was standing in front of Rik, telling him some kind of story. Lots of hand gestures and marching. She rolled her eyes.

"I've got my dad here. My aunt was attacked."

"I know."

"How?"

"I just do. Look, will you help, or not?"

She looked at her dad again. He was laughing with Rik, bending over her lab partner with his hand on his shoulder. It looked like they'd known each other for years.

Then she thought of the look on Mike's face when he'd burst in on her and Philip Gladstone. The relief she'd felt.

"Yes," she said. "Yes. I'm in."

⁂

WHERE IS MIKE? Can Alex find him?

Find out in Lost in the Multiverse, a FREE short story. Download now at multiverse-investigations.com/lost.

# READ ABOUT SCHRÖDINGER'S EXPLOITS - FREE AND EXCLUSIVE

Schrödinger is a very special cat. When he gets in his box, you never know if he'll be alive or dead. He's worked out how to do quantum tunnelling by slamming into walls. And he has a stomach that's so capacious he believes it has a portal to a belly in another universe.

Find out how Schrödinger spends his year by reading DIARY OF A QUANTUM CAT.

Only at multiverse-investigations.com/diary.